QUOTIENTS

QUOTIENTS

TRACY O'NEILL

My President (My President Is Black (Remix)) Words and Music by Justin Henderson, Christopher Whitacre, Jay Jenkins and Nasir Jones Copyright © 2008 Songs of Universal, Inc., Nappypub Music, Henderworks Publishing Co., Universal Music Corp., Nappy Boy Publishing, West Coast Livin' Publishing, Universal Music - Z Songs, Sun Shining, Inc., Emi Blackwood Music Inc. and Young Jeezy Music Inc. All rights for Nappypub Music and Henderworks Publishing Co. Administered by Songs of Universal, Inc. All rights for Nappy Boy Publishing and West Coast Livin' Publishing administered by Universal Music Corp. All rights for Sun Shining, Inc, administered by Universal Music - Z Songs. All rights for EMI Blackwood Music Inc. and Young Jeezy Music Inc. administered by Sony/ATV Music Publishing LLC, 424 Church Street, Suite 1200, Nashville, TN 37219. All rights reserved used by permission reprinted by permission of Hal Leonard LLC.

Published by Soho Press, Inc.
227 W 17th Street
New York, NY 10011

Library of Congress Cataloging-in-Publication Data
O'Neill, Tracy, author.
Quotients / Tracy O'Neill.
New York, NY : Soho, [2020]

ISBN 978-1-64129-111-8
eISBN 978-1-64129-112-5

1. Life change events—Fiction. 2. Secrets—Fiction.
3. Man-woman relationship—Fiction. 4. Mystery fiction.
PS3615.N465 Q68 2020 | DDC 813/.6—dc23

Interior design by Janine Agro, Soho Press, Inc.

Printed in the United States of America

10 9 8 7 6 5 4 3 2 1

For those who enlarge closeness

TABLE OF CONTENTS

PROLOGUE

He'd found a small way to resolve the future. The year he believed that, though in fact the belief would not last the year, was 2005. It was a various year, one he trusted those who euphemistically might be called his cohort and then didn't, where he quit assuming a fake résumé and an ardor for details could occlude misfortune's gaze. He decided to keep stories to the rooms where they'd happened, but he also aspired to sensible collations of evidence, although—or in particular because—it was a time of perfect aberration. It was when he met Alexandra Chen.

In his mind, there was a procedure to calm successions. It began with the call center. There, you could rely on emergencies. And so, the night before the year torqued, Jeremy Jordan turned on his headset. A red light in a grid lit. He asked how could he help, not in the manner of hopelessness.

My life's action is gravity, callers said their own ways. Help me catch what's falling; what's falling is me.

His training was follow the slope of a suffering mind before it inflicts itself on the body, but listen too for what fills the air one cannot see. A source quivers energy off it, persuades the air around it to shake. Sound huddles waves into intimacy. That is the way of a voice or explosion, telephones. He could hear that somewhere in London a woman lay silverware in drawers, knives slapping knives, matching.

Signals: they were everywhere if you knew how to heed them.

There was some static, a rustle, the woman there and yet closer, in his ear at the center and her house, kilometers reduced as she recalled her husband slamming a door hard enough a mirror shattered. He slammed it so hard, she said, the image of his departure rained down in shards. From the caller's unseen room, he heard reflections, noise returning. The word—it's thrown and it strikes off the surface, arrives in homecoming a little different. Sometimes the waves ripple out. Other times, they die. It is water where the word travels clear. No-man's-land.

Sometimes, she said, she wished it were too late for her.

He dispatched a mobile crisis unit. He aspired to totem comfort. He told her, "You are not alone," meaning only any more than anyone else.

Jeremy's head was heavy with the hour of night, and still to come was his putative real job at the fund, but he would remain on the line until the team arrived for her. And though his voice was reasonable, though his collar was crisp, this was talisman in action, superstitious math: offer safety so what life exacted from him would not be Alexandra.

He listened to the stranger survive. He said, "Stay with me."

PART ONE: DIVIDEND

It is dark one inch ahead of you.—*Japanese proverb*

CHAPTER 1

Alexandra Chen saw that they looked at her in search. That unplaceable face. All her life people had wanted to fix her features on a map, and they couldn't. It made people clamp down on her with their eyes. They would coast a room in gaze, then halt. They were trying to figure her out.

She had on a flat gray suit and spoke in her client voice, contained and reassuring. The front of a room did not come naturally to her, but she'd practiced how to land her eyes on a small audience and let her voice settle. She had practiced how to sell a country on her selling their country.

She'd done it in Uganda and Sweden, had successes enunciating small former Soviet states still in spinout from the Cold War. Her clients wanted investors from abroad or tourists, to unravage images, firm up legitimacy. Proper trade deals. That's where they'd arrived in history. There's the Lisbon Strategy on one hand, and then globalization means chunks of cartography are left behind. They did not want to be left behind.

The board room had no windows. There was the woman at the head of the table who had called the firm first. There was a man with pink hands like overstuffed sandwiches. These were individuals with government posts, commercial interests, ties to the embassy. They had clean-cropped haircuts and trim shirts, professionally empty faces. But her brother had taught her poker, had taught her, "In bets, you find out who the dreamers are at the table." And she was in the business of dreamers. She was in the business of casting bets on national narratives, then waiting for them to gain ballast.

"And can it all happen by the game?" someone leaning over the oblong of the conference table said.

She was at the whim of FIFA.

When she'd practiced her pitch with Jeremy, he'd said he'd trust her with a country. He'd trust her with anything. But her firm, Orbet, had been called late to Germany. There was only a year until the World Cup, a blip of a lead-up. Already the business security firm Orbet often worked with, Tyle, had dug up evidence of meetings between Blair's and Schröder's people beyond the public-private partnerships.

"Germany does not have the problem of an Estonia," she said. "Vast demographics couldn't picture Estonia. They couldn't point to it on the map. Germany has an image, and German culture *can* be globally competitive. Yet, there is delicacy to it. What is a German brand of soft power, one that travels, invites? Rather than a German nationalism."

"You're referring to the Anschluss and the Sudetenland," the man said bitterly.

"Or emotion."

She was a student of the image. The way at a certain angle a nation caught light. She believed in second chances, third, and so on. You pieced together the tropes, then turned them. Yet she did not yet know how to tell Jeremy that the account would mean a year away.

"In public opinion polling, what we see is the intellectual history, the art is submerged beneath an identity of engineering and Volkswagen, beer gardens, efficiency. It's ridiculous, of course. But it's an issue of foregrounding. This is the country of Goethe and Einstein. Herzog."

"Miss Chen," someone making a show of his watch said. "We know whose country this is."

They were untucking their phones from the insides of their jackets. Typing. Slapping them shut. Someone's whisper cut into her riff. The woman at the head of the table cleared her throat. "I'm sorry, Miss Chen," she said, already standing. "But we'll need to end this meeting. There is a matter at the Foreign Ministry."

Alexandra collected her things. She folded the computer and turned off the projector. She'd never persisted with a man, and still, if the Germans offered a contract, she thought she and Jeremy could once a month have weekends together in the aura of Alsatian Riesling and something like holiday, that perhaps it would defend them from the ordinary rhythm of fracture. She shook the hand of the woman from the Foreign Ministry.

"Please," the woman said, extending an arm toward the door, walking her to the exit faster.

Alexandra moved into the hallway, and out the window there was a weather that could be described as early. It wasn't rain or shine, just a sense of open time beating down.

By the elevator, she looked at her phone.

As fast as news, she forgot how to walk. Her legs could only stand in the manner of sprinting. There was a door registered only after the rush through, stairs above and behind and below and ahead. Something cold untied in her stomach. Bombs were exploding across London.

CHAPTER 2

Jeremy could not move, speak. Happenings were happening too fast, and his mind switched from simple sentences. There was no subject, object, predicate, meaning predicated on simple words one after the other. He was stuck on four syllables: Alexandra.

Alexandra held hostage, Alexandra beneath a crush of rubble. Four syllables with life pulled out from under her. He thought of how he'd never told her he wanted them to die very old, him first, of course, and holding her hand. He had not even told Alexandra he wanted to choose paper towels with her.

Assimilate to the moment: in the offices of Strategic Hedge International, the volume of the television normally tuned to Bloomberg was turned high. Coffers stood erect before the men. It was tragic, the explosion, explosions, he told them, and the lesson from oh-one was it was time to execute the list. They must, he said, offload. Sell before the fall. Banks and hotels, British Airways. Buy up pharma. It is the responsibility owed their investors.

Gavin Thomas's hands already maneuvered over his desk.

Try again: once, twice. Fingers clumsy on his mobile. At his ear: this is the sound of not reaching Alexandra.

Soon the internet servers failed, and at some point after it had been confirmed phone lines had gone down, Jeremy heard talking torsos declare normal programming had ceded to breaking news. One dead. King's Cross and Russell Square. Old Street. Moorgate. One turned to twenty. *Twenty dead.*

"More information is worse news now," someone said.

And it was true, Jeremy knew. Jeremy knew breaking news became broken history, knew news early in an emergency was a broadcast of provisional facts. Later, they'd shed authority, permute, redetermine. Information would redouble. He listened for names. Hers. From the flatscreen, the police commissioner announced it wasn't coincidence on the Underground; it was terror. Jeremy did not need to be told.

Around the room, the men of Strategic turned to each other. Speculation shaped their lips. Proximity to the US Embassy at Grosvenor and a dense shopping strip meant that another attack could take them too, or else, maybe that was optimistic. Maybe everywhere meant open to the end.

"In a city of eight million people," Thomas was saying, "consider stat's twenty in eight million. Fact is, good fraction. Good odds."

But Jeremy could not weigh probabilities. He could only think of the impossible. He once had had the other phone, the one his people had given him, not these numbers to nowhere, buttons that wouldn't reach. He could only think of the impossible, though even if he did have the old phone, even if she were alive to call, she'd be on the regular service, the felled one. Alexandra couldn't answer on the secure line. She, after all, had never been a spy.

CHAPTER 3

In the nights after the Underground bombings, they clutched, and they were alive, fortunately, wonderfully alive. Alexandra told him he was too far when they were next to each other.

In the mornings, because she'd admitted what she was too impatient to enjoy, Jeremy removed pomegranate seeds from the husk, and because she did not want him to first think to discard the imperfect thing, she fussed a small screwdriver to repair his watch, though always it was breaking. When they watched a movie, he asked after if the gladiator would live, and no matter the quality, she declared the warrior's future thrive. She began to pay attention to men's shirts in shop windows, cuff links.

They had met in May and now it was July, and as days ticked off, the calendar grew suggestive. "I've seen you more than the inside of my own refrigerator this week, you know that?" Alexandra said.

"A dry goods woman, are you?"

"Just north," Alexandra said. "Freezer."

"That's the one shaped like a boot."

"It's an intemperate country, but you'd be surprised at the

idyll," she said. "Food never spoils, and there is no fever, war, or taxation."

Her foot was in his hand. "I will levy no impost," he said. "But I cannot speak for the food."

That afternoon, he noticed that she paperclipped magazine pages to keep her place. He remarked on it. Later, when she removed an issue from her overnight bag, she found a note clasped where she'd left off reading. *Have a drink with me. Or have a museum with me. Have tea.*

Am I allowed only one? she wrote on the blank side of a receipt. And when after a week he did not find her small letter, she did not tell him its contents, but she did invite him to meet her best friend.

At the bar, over glasses of whiskey and ice furnished with regular fleet, Jeremy removed and layered clothing, muttering too warm, too cold. He reiterated what she'd told him of Genevieve Bailey in the form of questions. Did Genevieve still prefer for different foods not to touch, and was it true that she preferred to write in pencil?

"It is true," Genevieve told him.

"I like him," Genevieve told her.

Once, Alexandra would have on the occasion of bringing him flowers said she was bringing his house flowers. Less to lose then. Less frightening. Now, she asked, "Can we be trusted to raise a houseplant?"

He brought home two kittens.

The Abyssinian they named Jill. The all black, So-So. The shell-pink felt of the pads on their paws shocked the sequester of her where careful language stacked, modular, ready-made. They lay on the carpet, jouncing shoelaces, and she made fool noises.

CHAPTER 4

Jeremy was in the habit of walking. Sometimes, he would wake up on a weekend and just walk from Islington, passing the Columbia Road Flower Market with its stalls of tight bouquets clumped by the dozen, get lost in the tessellations of petals gathered in crystalline cellophane and white paper, continuing all the way down to Canary Wharf. These were not errands. It was only the quiet power of observing the world stayed where you left it, accommodating your passage, homes and trees and automobiles made tractable in a sense. In the panic of too much, you could lose your surroundings. This was legacy wisdom. His mother had never believed in psychotherapy, but she believed in walking.

Just walk it off, she said.

It had not always worked, the walking cure. It had not worked of late. It was why he was going to Wright's.

Because now, Alexandra's very presence incurred a sense of deprivation, what it would be for her to be disappeared. It happened quickly. Someone familiar could do it. Someone decided and then never again. Never again when lying in the dark would they whisper for no reason other than the way it sanctified information, passed sentences. Never again would she say, "Put the geniuses on for bed?" The violins would not rise. Cellos would not come in through a song that lived across borders, proseless and mysterious in meaning. Never again would the appearance of her hair, thick as a paintbrush on the pillow, disrupt his vascular system.

The day of the bombings, July seventh, Seven-Seven, a day of doubles, Gavin Thomas, the fund researcher, had been unharried. Gavin Thomas, Jeremy supposed, would have known that they would profit marvelously because it was Gavin Thomas who had advised that they purchase credit default protection against transport just a week before. Gavin Thomas would have known that the value of the CDP would gallop uphill as quickly as trust in the Tube shot down; to the detriment of civilized society, Strategic would take in a load. The question was how he had known the value would swing, how Thomas had predicted catastrophe.

Thomas was too connected. Jeremy was sure of it. Charisma was multiplying in secret cells around the globe, men offering ideas to organize lives. Men offering ideas to organize deaths. To orchestrate terror was to tell young men what to do with tomorrow, an irresistible charm. You are part of a recipe for disaster. I can give your rage an occupation. He did not know how the system worked or what it meant. He did not know where the sides cut, who Thomas's people were. Yet it was enough to suspect that Thomas had people at all, that someone had known when to bet against the safety of the city. It was enough to thicken the distance.

London had grown warmer in recent days. Jeremy could feel the heat on his neck as he walked. He looked at the horizon, something longer than truncated autobiographies. Wide blue.

He had a way of gentling the air around him, fading into it. Outside Wright's, a two-floor flat that he kept to only half of, Jeremy made the call. He was not conspicuous on the stoop. The door opened without a word. A slip inside from view.

Toward the back of a dark, dusty room, Jeremy sat on the couch by an end table topped with a typewriter. Wright poured a glass of something and nudged it over. He crossed his legs, and Jeremy sipped, then waited for the ice to go soundless in the glass again, settle. For Wright to.

"The official stories are insulting. Were they that insulting when it was us keeping them?" he said finally.

"Everyone has secrets," Jeremy said, "especially a country."

"But the world was more spread out then," Wright said.

At the end of when Wright and Jordan were Wilmington and Allsworth, they had flamed out of the army's Intelligence Corps the way that either you decided was part of the job or that made you ask for a new name. When he'd first been recruited to Operation Banner, the Intelligence Corps mission in Northern Ireland, Jeremy had known only the outlines, that the Provisional Irish Republican Army had taken up terror in the name of a united Ireland, and loyalist paramilitary groups like the Ulster Defence Association and the Ulster Volunteer Force responded in kind, and neither the police in the Royal Ulster Constabulary nor the British Army had been able to stop the violence. At the end, he did not know much more. People with access to high grades of classified materials manufactured credentials and rerouted them to other professions. Now Wright taught courses on the philosophy of the mind and the philosophy of language at King's College London, where probably there were other men who needed aliases, but all the while into the rest of their lives after Northern Ireland, it was Jeremy and Wright who on occasion met. They found shadows slanted across corners. They whispered, something centripetal leaning them toward each other, spinning, circling on snippets, rumors.

Wright's assumption: there were current intel guys tracking him. His former employer would want to make sure secrets stayed. And so together was the only place they allowed the rage to express on their bodies since duty. The world was deadly, and they were pretending to be gentle men.

"I remember once One Rock telling me about when he was a young handler." Jeremy leaned back into a chair. "He was telling me the problem was the route to Mecca. Arab nationalists in Aden. The National Liberation Front blew up a party at the home of a Foreign Office official. It had seemed so quaint. So far away and ancient."

"MI5 wants to distinguish geometry now," Wright said. "Self-starting rumors they stopped trailing Khan and Tanweer because the two were merely 'on the periphery' of another operation."

"When there is no periphery to terror."

"It promises death anywhere."

Jeremy watched Wright pour another drink. Drink it. Pour another. He could sense the risky nostalgia in the room, in Wright musing that there would have been a trail of transmissions to follow, A to B, B to C, C to D, D for direction. Intercept the signals of the Underground Attackers, he was saying. *Semper vigiles.* Someone had told someone: it's time. Time to make the most private thing a person could ever do, dying, a public event. And MI5 had permitted it to happen.

"We have to realize what's not ours anymore," said Jeremy. "We did what we could."

Wright stood. "Don't treat me like one of your call center sobbers. If it were over, you wouldn't be here." He crossed his arms. "Bastards waited for the G8 Summit."

"Because Blair would be away at Gleneagles."

"Because drop panic in the center," Wright continued. "Watch the ripples. All the eight go home unadjourned by terror. Might've been UK news. But now it's worldwide. They've scaled down the globe with perfect timing."

"At Gleneagles they were meant to pool terrorist data," Jeremy said.

Wright wrung his lips into a tight coil. "These bombers have mastered their irony."

Mastery. Irony. The drink organized Jeremy's hands in the shape of the glass. Steady. "Thomas shouldn't have known," he said. "Why credit default right then?"

Usually, it was he counseling Wright against big picture theories, what the opposition was doing, who was the object of extinction. Wright collected news clippings. He was certain the story wasn't the story when it was official. He did not know the ops, but he knew there were leaks. Wright obsessed over who had circulated dossiers when they were handlers. Over splinter groups. Over elections. Jeremy would say you could go crazy worrying about strangers in Belfast, Sudan, the Balkans. There were too many people you didn't know. So you recognized your finitude. You did not clarify the codes. You went on eating breakfast, popping sleeping pills. You could suffer more for the remote suffering, or you could realize your business wasn't the public good anymore. It was one day, yours, at a time. He would say those things before Alexandra.

"Thomas, he's just part of a trend. They believe all those triple-A CDOs can collect interest free of loss, that the CDP will earn out eventually. Simple as go bullish, go bearish, go to the country home."

"I know how it works," Jeremy said. "I'm the one hedging."

And yet.

During the anthrax panic, Strategic had maneuvered the long and short game on Bayer and a handful of generic drug companies. Though the patent had expired in nearly every country, Bayer still held the patent for Cipro, a drug used to treat anthrax, in America. In the midst of an ally emergency, Strategic made an inconceivable dump of capital.

"I'm quitting."

"And just say you're right," Wright said.

"I *am* right."

"Just say you are. What is the use of the walk away?"

"The away," Jeremy said. "It is a good quality to be in the circumstances."

"Can't get away from what's inside you."

"What's inside?"

"The listening, the half-breath."

But for now, the strategy: Continue the image, especially to her. Continue the regular fictions of the person he was supposed to be. He was supposed to be someone nonchalant in love and lies, someone who quipped and would never tell Alexandra he preferred her to food and water. "Three weeks earlier, I'd have said nothing."

"But it wasn't three weeks earlier."

"It was right before the bombs," Jeremy said.

An angle of the chin. A tunneling with the eyes. It was not pity exactly, Jeremy knew, but the look dropped down a shaft of silence between them, a punctuation mark in the face. Wright recrossed his arms, a reversal of right and left. He worked his tongue over his upper teeth, and finally he spoke.

"Ring the prepaid if you want to talk," Wright said.

Then he stood up and walked, and Jeremy followed. The lines of the hallway seemed almost to choreograph his exit. They did not shake hands. It was simpler, the gesture. Not even a sigh, and Wright opened the door out into the London fog for Jeremy to fade back to the theater of his new life.

CHAPTER 5

Alexandra wanted to be wry and knowing, like the women in New York who somehow had it all, calm and casual in their thin cashmere sweaters, buttering bread for their children at brunch on the weekend and stepping crisply to hail a cab from work at five, and all of it, their happiness, ignored like a given. There was an unfeathered romance to these women, how normalized the abundant life was to them. But it was abashing a little, the big weather of feeling for him. At night Jeremy Jordan astonished her body, his much stronger than the drawn face and lean legs would suggest, a thin man but sprawling, with all that warmth rising off him. He was capable of reminding her how wide his shoulders were as they blotted out the cool cast of the moon in the window. The rage of his rising and falling matched her own; they knew each other then as they couldn't in words.

In his apartment in Islington, they lay looking at each other side by side with the tips of their fingers just touching on one side of a breath, pulling apart on the other, a sort of stretching come from their lungs. The voice of someone famous reached from another room. A newsperson.

"But you love your job," Alexandra said. "You obsess over it."

"I am preoccupied by it," he said.

"I think the word for it is occupied," she said. "You are occupied. That's what an occupation does."

"I want to do something valuable," he said, "instead of lucrative."

"You could do both," she teased, "be a regular George Soros."

"And break the Bank of England?"

"A humble man would allow that perhaps in his hypothetical second career he would only cause the market to tank occasionally, but you, you must be the architect of national economic crisis."

"In my hypothetical second career, I will not settle for less than disaster," he said. "I will know my worth."

She could see he did not want to think for a while. He moved his hands into her hair, and then her shirt, pants. She spread out on the bed. When he collected the bone of her pelvis in his hands, she closed her eyes and there was depth in the darkness. "Look at me," he said, and she watched his eyes grow closer to something like alarm. What it is: tiny tilts, shifts, but the objects, views, fell off, and then she heard something her own, plaintive and undemanding, an unresigned sigh, and there were no qualifications between them.

Or else, there was only one irking detail, one marring absence. But that could change. She believed that. Change, after all, was what she had done with herself. She had not wanted to be a persuaded woman, so she entered a field where she could prevail upon. And when that didn't work, there was standing in proximity to the best people she could find, the ones who would not make a fool of her suggestibility. Genevieve Bailey. Lyle Michaels. Jeremy.

And perhaps, after all, soon she'd hear from Ray Gutierrez.

Ray Gutierrez was supposed to be a man with an affinity for minutiae. Ray Gutierrez was supposed to be a man whose expertise was searching—better: a man whose expertise was finding. Ray Gutierrez's secretary had said he would know how to locate loopholes in the vastness of the planet to find her man.

There was still a flush in her body. She moved a box of roses from the bedside table so that it rested between them, ripped a petal off and rubbed it against her cheek. "Poor Gavin will be inconsolable when he hears you've left Strategic, you know."

"Gavin?"

"Thomas," she said. "Gavin Thomas. Called me yesterday with a referral. It seems he's got some developer friends with skin in the game for a Belfast makeover."

Jeremy's voice was sharp, right-angled and boxy. "And what would Gavin want with Belfast?"

CHAPTER 6

Alexandra thought of telling Jeremy, so she did not tell Jeremy when Ray Gutierrez called to accept her case. She knew it was only the urge to deposit some of the unseemly, febrile nerve knocked through her. The irony, of course, was she would have told Shel if what she had to tell wasn't that she was seeking him.

Because Shel was a person who had shared whispers with her. They had whispered to hold out the loud pronouncements: who they were, what was wrong. They had known what people said about them and their church bin clothes, what people said about their mother. But in whispers they had had a secret from their mother and from everyone else, and it was that they were better people than they looked, that when one day they left that place, and they would, they would, they would be even better, alchemized.

There was combustion to his talk, punk rock. He burned up with shunting past idols. But, too, sometimes she would, when they were young, see her brother across a way asking the direction to a store or if he could sit down, and though he was the older, an awful tenderness colonized her in the tectonics of his face altering, surprised to be the recipient of kindness, decency. It was never something she could have mentioned, but she wanted to be someone in his life who made him less surprised by the absence of malice.

It was this thought, this hope, that had made her a little short of breath on the call. Alexandra's cheeks—she had felt the pink on them. "Remind me how long since he disappeared?" Ray Gutierrez had asked.

"He didn't disappear," Alexandra said. "He is simply appearing where I don't expect."

And so she had continued. She had more to tell, and Ray Gutierrez listening nearly forgave something of the past, made it sit differently. She was involved in the process of finding. Ray Gutierrez was. And as a result she would not need to think every time news broke, a shooting, a terrorist attack, that if Shel had been there, she'd never know. She could imagine a family again, and she could remember that Shel had once told her bad luck did not run in sprees.

CHAPTER 7

Jeremy had selected the time and place, and now, across from the restaurant, at the settled hour, his view telescoped toward Lawrence, formerly of 12 Intelligence Company. Lawrence was seated at a circular table with embroidered flowers falling down its sides, a heavy tumbler to his right, and a menu beneath his forearm, and even at a distance, Jeremy could see that in the twelve years since they'd last seen each other, Lawrence had become a composed man. He ordered a pint, wore a smart tan suit, and he didn't lean over the table. The one remaining tic was a triple-blink every so often.

He had been the one person left Jeremy could think to call.

Casual gait—an aspiration for his entrance.

When Lawrence stood for Jeremy, they shook hands. Firm grip, dry. Left hands grabbing shoulders. It was all very brisk, and they exclaimed over lengths, over how long it had been. "My girlfriend speaks very highly of the firm," Jeremy said. "She's with Orbet."

"A good account," Lawrence said, unrolling cutlery from a cloth napkin.

They sat across from each other with their menus opened

in angles. Jeremy had already decided what he would order but moved his eyes down the lunch selections anyway, did not glance up a few beats before saying, "So you're properly private now."

"There is money there. Executives want to know if such and such Russian oligarch is only a local gangster or ambitiously criminal before the handshake. And you?"

"I'm weighing my options."

A man came to their table to take their orders. Lunch salads. Clean. Light. And of course, in preparation, Jeremy had already eaten.

"You were always good with computers," he said when the waiter left. "We didn't realize the applications then."

"You mean *you* didn't," Lawrence pipped. "*I* always knew. I was saying, what are these researchers up to?"

"You were prescient."

"No," Lawrence said. "I was paying attention to what was happening right then in the present."

"And you're married now?"

"Lydia," Lawrence said. "She's a nurse, so she says she doesn't need children. Every adult is a child in the hospital."

"Does that suit you?" Jeremy asked.

"I have clients. Every adult is a child in business."

For a while, they spoke of the Olympic construction through the city, and they spoke of Lydia, of Alexandra, places to holiday. Their salads came, and Lawrence requested another beer. There was a song leaking through the restaurant.

"Was surprised to hear from you," Lawrence said. "Most people come to Tyle *before* a hire, not after."

Jeremy shifted his weight in his seat, moved his arms to resettle the shoulders of his jacket. "I was curious."

"But you're not in craft anymore."

"I'm not in craft. I have a life worth keeping as it is."

"And this has nothing to do," Lawrence ventured.

Jeremy furrowed his brow. He shook his head. Control the flow of knowledge. Quarantine. Distribute. He had missed the signs at Strategic. Now there was cordoning off signs of his own.

"Because some of us," Lawrence said.

"Not me," Jeremy said.

For a while in the barracks of Lisburn, just beyond Belfast, he had been pleased to notice something choral was happening to him. When it had begun he didn't know. One day it was simply that he noticed himself thinking, and all of what he thought had once been directives delivered to him, thoughts that meant he could sense himself spin backward, reporting from the future his adherence to command. Telling his commanding officer, One Rock. Telling Wilmington. Actions tailored to the telling. Objective: live up to the correct story. He couldn't distinguish instructions from his own watery mind, and he had thought it made him stronger. His feet planted and the advice became him, sank deep into his guts like it had always been a part of his makeup, so that when he looked in the mirror, he did not see the occasional stammerer, pink-faced and apologetic, but a man who handled, a man who was not afraid.

He had been wrong to not be afraid.

And so now, he looked at his plate as it was set down, the long fingers of rocket snarled around each other, green and dressed in lemon. The tuna was clumped on top of slim stalks of asparagus, and there were hard-boiled eggs split open, the yolk audacious and staring. He cleared his throat. "You know, once One Rock told me something."

"There's a classy man. Never coughed on a cigar. Never coughed period. And of course, always in his whiskey just one rock, at the barracks pub."

"Clockwork."

"He was decent, and he was dignified. I never knew anything about him."

"No one did," Jeremy said.

Lawrence's eyelids flapped, quick as insect wings. "So One Rock," he said.

"It was early in my tour," Jeremy began. "I didn't know what he wanted to tell me. If I was in trouble, if I was to be promoted. I went in, and I'll never forget it. He told me, 'Sometimes what we see, the psychologists call it countertransference. The analyst projects wishes, hopes, desires on the patient. Handlers and informants, analysts and patients. Seeking love, seeking truth, maybe, but often, most often, what we see is a desire for closure. Neat plots.'"

Lawrence worried a mole at the edge of his chin with one finger, head tilted. This feature was one Jeremy had never before noticed.

"He asked how I knew what I got was everything from my informant, how I knew I'd seen the edge of disclosure and not an appeasing fraction of the picture. I'd the sense that to know was different than to be able to evidence, but I said I'd wager my life." He paused. "One Rock told me I was wagering abundantly more than mine."

"Go on," Lawrence said.

"I thought he was after proof my informant's pledge was in good faith," Jeremy continued. "But he thought the Irish were different, more Mediterranean in temperament, that their women were dictators and that they looked like but weren't us. So he told me, 'Operation Banner is a contest of exhaustion. Northern Ireland unfolds and unfolds. Who retires upstairs first, Allsworth? That is the only question.'"

"Sounds like him."

"Because he said it," Jeremy said, more sharply than he'd intended.

"I believe you."

"I promised him that my informant wanted to succeed, and he saw right through me. He said, 'So do you, Allsworth.'"

"So you're saying."

"There's no permanent success to intel. I'm happy without it. I do not have the stamina for getting mixed up in another plot spinning through perpetuity."

There were damp orbs growing in his armpits. He kept his elbows tight to him. Back erect. He sliced a length of asparagus. He could hear someone drop a glass. Apologies.

"Thomas came up clean," Lawrence said after a moment, sliding a file across the table. "You'll see for yourself in the report."

Jeremy secured a pink brick of tuna on the prongs of a fork. He had learned to wipe himself out of his face. The face can be taught to no longer answer, bland as a boiled potato. The trick is clamp onto language. Don't let it penetrate the dermis. He did not touch the folder. He knew Lawrence was waiting for him to react, but even now, all these years out of HUMINT, it seemed foolish to show relief.

"You're certain."

Lawrence signaled for the dessert menu. "I'm certain," he said, "that I wasn't able to find anything."

CHAPTER 8

Northern Ireland had asked her back repeatedly for meetings. Northern Ireland had not decided repeatedly if she added value to their long-term objectives. And so, Alexandra had stayed late at the office to review her final pitch: nations were seeping out, losing borders to companies spread across continents, transnational legal frameworks, global telecom. The internet disperses culture; therefore, the nation needs a way to hold the noise together. It was this or continue watching capital jump across borders. What she gave, it was a gathering device. There was a social science to it. Two hundred and thirty metrics. But in layman's terms, all that data compressed is a story, a brand: this is the birthplace of Thin Lizzie.

Outside the office, it was raining. She tied the belt at her waist tighter and raised an elbow, drawing open her bag. She looked for an umbrella in the papers and devices, waterless soap. A shadow slid, and there was a cold feeling in her stomach that meant the touch of someone she didn't know. Man's hand: size of a paperback novel.

It had happened to every woman she knew. There were plenty of theories. Scream, or in silence do what you are told. Find the solar plexus, soft spots. Use a key. Do not give reason for a weapon. Something white and hard as bone stilled her limbs. He had her wrist, and there was weather coming down onto them. The smell was damp smoke.

"I know you," he said.

CHAPTER 9

Jeremy tried her mobile as he looked at a print on the wall, *Leviathan*. His financial advisor had told him it was a non-volatile asset, but it was horrifying, an enormous, smiling sea thing beneath a small boy's fishing canoe, miles of ocean with no other human in sight.

Seven digits to four syllables. Alexandra.

For too long he had not trusted luck.

Until Alexandra, his life had been mostly noise, a few false signals, and even now, he did not know who had recommended him into secrecy. He had not at the time asked questions. It was simply one phone call and he'd adhered to another agency after the Wall fell. The Intelligence Corps recruiter had been calm, meditative almost, musing, or maybe mirthlessly amused: "Executive power is limited to reaction politically, and reacting is a little late when we're past insurgency into car bombs, Armalites, cordite sunup to -set. Corpses don't react, if you see what I'm saying." Jeremy had not quite seen what he was saying, had seen only someone telling him, remarkably, he was needed.

He was supposed only to get answers.

He had not always gotten the right ones.

And so that day, *the* day, the day he met Alexandra, he had wanted to hear nothing for a few hours once more. He'd taken the aisles of the library slowly. Numbers on spines announced boundaries. The subject is not that, they said, delineation in digits. Probably, he had appeared lost because he was searching, and this woman, then a stranger, offered to help him find what he needed. Jeremy removed his gaze from the codes. She came into his eyes sudden and permanent as a photograph. It was an accidental smile, his. He had forgotten happy accidents.

He would trust happy accidents, he decided now.

"You've reached Alexandra," the recording said when she did not respond to his call.

CHAPTER 10

He peered behind books on the shelf. He looked in the corner where a diploma hung. He ran a hand over the top of a filing cabinet. The smell of cleaning chemicals clung to Alexandra's office. Bleachy. Sharp. She took in the shape of the skull, hairline. So many times she'd tried to picture and failed.

"I didn't know if you'd want to see me," he said.

"You stole a bike for me."

"Allegedly."

"Pointedly," Alexandra said. "Where have you been?"

"Turn your phone off," Shel said. "Not just sound. Not vibrate. All the way off."

It was instantaneous, the flip back into the old roles. Little sister. Big brother. She did as she was told. He folded at the waist and unplugged every appliance from the power strip.

"Point's you're here," she said. And then, because it was strange, that is, wonderful, worth corroborating, she said again, "You're here."

There was a water bubbler in the corner. She watched the orbs rise up and break, let the cool slide to the back of her throat. She did not know how to ask what he'd been doing more than half his life. She didn't even know where to look on him. Time had grown Shel's shoulders, made his hair mellow. All that difference expressed.

"You should get out of this business, Lex," he said finally. "There won't be much left of it soon for those like us."

She gazed into the howling mouth on his shirt. "Like us?"

"Humans," he said.

Alexandra laughed. He walked to the window, opening it with a flatulent little groan and lighting a joint. His pupils were fat as dimes.

"Don't be blind," he said. "You won't be equivocating states forever. It's been a good run for you. But Kasparov was beat by Deep Blue a decade ago." Smoke drifted out the window. "Minds are slow and life is short. That is not true of computers. You think you want them to pick up the slack, but the slack cuts in, ends the dance. Computers will *be* the global conscience, Lex. You can kiss the commandments goodbye. Juries. This is who lives. This is who dies. Send the drones. It will happen. It does."

She took a tissue from her pocket. The overhead lights latched onto the edges of his face, dimmed, brightened, so that he appeared to waver before her. Something in her belly contracted, flipped. He was saying forget the man who'd called her to Northern Ireland. He was saying something about the man's troubles. He was saying avoid an outcome, then avoid better.

"Can we talk about something else?" she said.

"Else."

"Because I'm uncomfortable."

"All of America is uncomfortable when it's convenient.

Discomfort is your red, white, and blue standard-issue panic button. Everybody keeps their front-load washers in America. All the blankies in all the world and the Second Amendment to sleep at night. Every patriot loves his fabric softener."

"I don't know what you're talking about."

"Western civilization with its neurotic skin. Hives. Allergies. Every American is worried about niceties, little Tommy's peanut problem."

Her voice shot high, broke. "*You're* American."

From across the room, she saw his teeth. "I always told you, never give the tells you're a dreamer, and here you are with the moon in your eyes, a grown woman wringing her hands around a tissue."

She put the tissue in her pocket. She remembered her image, its fragility, but she did not know what shape would keep him here. The bleach scent was doing something to her head.

"Maybe I'm not trying to win," she said.

"It's the only thing you know how to do, Alex And *Dra*. Isn't that what this entire getup is meant to convey? That you, in your pantsuit and sensible bob cut, don't take no for an answer? I'm telling you the truth."

On the ground, plugs splayed. Caring made air of her, turned her transparent. The aphorisms and bland, expensive garments fell away. For a moment she was thirteen again, watching her mother throw garbage bags of her brother's clothes out the door onto the dying lawn, thirteen again, telling him she couldn't change anyone's mind. She had remained in the threshold until evening, long after Shel had gone down the street with a bag and a skateboard, while her mother smoked cigarettes and sighed, cried over a can of soup and declared she had not known she had a stupid daughter.

"I'm sorry," Alexandra said. "I was only a kid."

"And what was I?"

They didn't look at each other. The tissue was in her hand again. It seemed ever since he'd come, objects had begun to appear without any sign of eventhood.

"You won't tell her I was here," Shel said finally.

"Whatever you want," she said.

"Or anyone, Lex. You could put me in a position."

"What kind of position?"

"Corner kind. Kind you don't come back from, those corners."

The danger of asking questions was being permitted no more questions. She was quiet as from his jacket, he removed a lighter.

"It's simple. If we're going to have a relationship, the promises have got to be Hippocratic. First, do no harm and all that. So, I'm not here."

"Of course you aren't," she said.

Just to make the moment hold.

He nodded, his eyes indicating that his mind had wandered outside the room. "Okay," he said, to himself perhaps. "Okay." He fidgeted a lighter with his thumb, making a flame hop, and the noise of it scratched the air, scratched the air, scratched the air. "You remember that movie *Fatal Attraction*?" She nodded. "That's good," he said. "That's good. It was a warning for all men. Once you enter the Forrest, you can never leave."

There were years between them. There was a loop in her stomach from trying to fit him with the image she'd carried so long. He returned the lighter to his pocket. "I'm glad I saw you."

Alexandra grasped to make sense of his standing. There was a lag, and he was at the door by the time she perceived feet moving. She was still thinking of who he might have been at seventeen, eighteen, where he'd been the day he first thought himself a man.

"Is that it?" she said. "You're leaving?"

"I'm only leaving because I came, Lex. There's a seat over the Atlantic waiting for me. You'll remember me, won't you?"

"When will I see you again?"

"I can find you."

"I don't even know where you live."

"I can only tell you a big hunk of the map. I can tell you the American Northeast."

Her face was turning colors. Swallow and she'd blank her face out again. That unplaceable face. She swallowed. She held her own hands.

"You can't tell anyone, Lex."

"I won't."

He took the doorknob with the bottom of his T-shirt. "Get out while you can."

PART TWO: OBELUS

As the pain that can be told is but half a pain,

so the pity that questions has little healing in its touch.

—*Edith Wharton,* The House of Mirth

CHAPTER 1

Jeremy had told her as a boy, he was called by his mother Jam, since his face turned red as jam. Later, he had learned to be less embarrassed. Less pensive. He remantled himself, had even changed his surname, and when he told her, Alexandra thought she recognized something of herself, a sense of destiny's fungibility.

Jeremy had told her too that when he was growing up there was nowhere much to go in Edwinstowe. That the nothing made it ripe for stories. It was a picture-book place outsiders knew as the Robin Hood village. Steal from the rich, give to the poor. Their childish hearts were tense bows, tongues rolling happily ever after, and the men they knew were fathers and uncles who tunneled into the earth, rose with blossoms of coal. Only as teenagers had they learned that the enemy was Thatcher, and then only later, for some, had it become apparent that their fathers and uncles did not rise. They stooped in soot and glazed out over beers to the FC playing. They were men who knew their days down below were numbered and still carried on, though the strikes had failed.

To Jeremy, it seemed bleak, but still, what he had told her, or rather because he was who had told her, it rang ascendant to Alexandra. And so when he invited Alexandra to his parents' house in Northern England for dinner, her lips spread and her hands went moist in her pockets, the invitation plump with anagrams of regular fairy tales.

That afternoon in Edwinstowe, Alexandra knew she wanted Mrs. Allsworth to like her when Mrs. Allsworth talked about her in the third person. "Carl, we've got *company*," she said, gesturing to Alexandra. "Turn off the telly." Later, it was about the silverware. "Carl, we've got *company*. The good silver, if you will." The house was small and warm like a toaster oven. For a while, Mrs. Allsworth fussed around the kitchen roughly with thick, efficient arms as Mr. Allsworth, Carl, looked at Alexandra shyly. Anyone could tell he wasn't used to shaking hands with women. He moved a chair for her to sit down and then paced when he didn't know what to do with himself.

Round sheaths of pink ham on their plates, they drank whole milk, talking over a bouquet of wildflowers. There was an assumption fat amongst them, she thought, a lengthy romantic habit suggested in turns. "I don't follow politics anymore because I want peace," Mrs. Allsworth said, "but Carl follows politics because he wants peace too. That's everything you need to know about marriage."

"That's everything you need to know about *their* marriage," said Jeremy.

"He's the polite child, if you can believe that," Mrs. Allsworth said.

"Shane was the bad one," Jeremy said.

Mrs. Allsworth dropped more green beans on his plate. "*A bad one.*"

"Don't listen to a word she says," Jeremy said. "She's very sly."

The afternoon glided on, frictionless, as Alexandra teased Jeremy with questions directed at Mrs. Allsworth and Carl. She could see that they came to like her too when she asked them about their boy. Speaking of him in the third person linked them beyond Jeremy. She looked at them, wondered aloud if, as she suspected, he'd always been best in class, copping extravagant paranoia, good-natured chicanery. The Nottingham Forest spread nearby, ancient and mythic and real, but it was inside where Alexandra wanted to remember everything. Dish of butter. Brown bread. Lace on Mrs. Allsworth's dress. She had never sat at a table with a family that she wanted to photograph.

CHAPTER 2

The kittens had become cats. They had become *regal*, Alexandra said. They took the laundry baskets as their duchies, were spoiled with breakfast kippers. Sometimes, she called him from the office. She asked what So-So and Jill were thinking about.

"They want to know why we haven't got them mobiles yet," Jeremy told her, "conveniently forgetting they've not washed the dishes in ever."

"This generation," she said.

"A whole other species, you'd think."

For a while, she'd talk about her work. He liked to listen to her take a whole place and make it fit in the grip of her hand, tell it in a sentence. Lately, she was researching a new internet scrapbook of sorts, Cathexis, and though it was still only for individuals, she said just he wait. She said just wait and nations would declare themselves in online patchwork, any brand would, and he was a little drunk with her clarity, her faith that there was clarity. We are past the Iraq fallout, the agrarian deal. We see consistent positives on innovation. You see Spain's strategy in '82, '92. When there's the thought to fall to one knee, it will be beneath the Galata Tower at sunset.

He'd had the thought.

And in time, he thought he was clearer too. He was clearer because he knew she ate meat but did not like to see the raw slop. He was clearer because he came to know she did not watch sports except horseback riding. She did not wear perfume. She wore scented lotion. He'd look at the nightstand and see her bottle. Together, they were becoming the routine of his longing.

So it was that in the routinization, he became fluent. The New One was whomever Genevieve Bailey was dating. Lyle Michaels was the journalist. So-So Jordan was So-So when she'd done something naughty with her claws. Jeremy understood the implication when Alexandra relayed that she was sure the wife must know her boss was playing snooker with the secretary.

"Come closer," Alexandra said. And that translated too.

On weekends, he spent hours in the consult of texts. He made lists. He loved to walk to the store with his list and see below his her handwriting—crème fraiche, strawberry cake. He went to the butcher. He'd salt. Tenderize. While she read in the other room, he followed the procedures step-by-step. And when there were specks of herb on his forehead, she took to leaning in the doorway, one hand over her eyes, asking, so hopeful, so apple-bright, "Still gruesome in there?" until dinner was ready. After, they played poker, and she did not let him win unless she'd had a wretched week at work. She rarely had a wretched week at work. In this way, he managed to give her many chocolates.

One day, he tucked a note for her in a magazine: *What does it feel like to make someone happy?*

Don't play stupid, she wrote in a cookbook. *You know.*

CHAPTER 3

Alexandra Chen had once told Lyle Michaels anyone fortunate enough to have an irritating father was fortunate enough to have a father. It was just the sort of tautological thing she'd say. Besides, after the CUNY journalism panel, he was not ready for Frank.

He was hanging around a municipal trash can, smoking cigarettes. Bri Freeman had just arrived, and he was narrating the blow-by-blow. The editor of the *Trib* had looked right at him as he said "blogs" profited on repackaging real journalists' original reporting. Looked right at him as he said Lyle's employer, Noze, acted as a platform for unverified information—and what happens when you become an open microphone for the craziest thing a crazy person will do or say? What happens to our politics? He was telling Bri Freeman all that when he saw his father approach but didn't let on until it was precisely necessary, not until Frank raised his arms, here I am, a lumbering rectangle in plaid.

"Hello," Frank said. "*Come stai*, baby?" Frank said.

Lyle exhaled. "Dad, this is Bri Freeman."

Hand out, half bow. "And you're a website writer too?"

"From the program, Dad," he said. "Which is to say, contrary to popular belief in the Michaels household, other people also choose to spend a lot of time at half-filled seminar tables."

"Which is to say listen to this one announce his intellectual affiliations. Naturally, even Lyle's affiliations were disaffiliations. He criticized the consensus view no matter what the consensus view was."

Frank squinted. "You drop out like my son too?"

They had not spoken since his father told him he didn't know a single person with a baby on the way out of an annulled marriage, not one who wouldn't try to make it work with someone one in a million like Ingrid. Lyle did not know why Frank had come, but here he was acting the status quo. Lyle grabbed the strap of a bag from Bri's shoulder, arcing it over his head so that it rested diagonally across his own torso.

"Oh no, Bri abandoned me," he said. "For Los Angeles and the tenure track."

"It wasn't me," Bri said. "It was al-Qaeda. The departments have money for the Middle East suddenly. I can't complain."

"Just teach the future military advisors. Make the neoliberal case for the humanities."

"I missed you too, Ly," she said.

Lyle raised his eyebrows at Frank. "Missed me so much she missed the whole damn panel."

Her fingernail polish was chipped, and there was an ugly watch on her wrist, and it suited her. That way she had of drawing one shoulder to her chin, nonplussed, untouchable. He hadn't seen her in over a year. "My flight was delayed."

"I think Lyle beat him," Frank said.

"It wasn't a debate, Dad. Nobody wins."

"But you still beat him," Frank said.

"All right, Dad." Lyle pinched the skin between his eyebrows.

By stance, Lyle knew into his father's mind. He could see his father shifting feet, the way he did when he refused to take painkillers for his back. For years, his mother had been hectoring Frank that the hours had to stop, and Frank, insisting on referring to the family not as the Michaelses but as the Micellis, told her the Micellis had always worked. Lyle had given up on that argument years ago. He turned back to Bri again.

"So what I was saying was, I told him at Noze we are not buying Walter Lippmann–style snobbery. I said the implicit value is citizen report. I said our ethos is it is as much news as all the print journalism dispelled by the Iraq War, by Judith Miller and her imaginary WMDs."

"Very Arendt," Bri said. "'If everybody always lies to you, the consequence is not that you believe the lies, but rather that nobody believes anything any longer.'"

"'And with such a people,'" Lyle continued, "'you can then do what you please.'"

Frank cleared his throat. "You know, I speak a little Spanish myself."

"What are you talking about, Dad? Where's Mom?"

"Buying ibuprofen. Her headaches, you know."

"The Joan Didion of Bayside, my mother," Lyle said, adding, "minus the writing, minus the California and the *Vogue*."

"A smoker with migraines."

"And minus the cigarettes."

The paper program from the event was still in Frank's hand, rolled up. He smacked it against his thigh, a signal to go, but

Lyle did not acknowledge it. In his peripheral, Frank shifted his weight from foot to foot.

"You look at the internet and here is an opportunity to make information free to everyone except the advertisers. That's something academics've never understood. They always think the higher the markup, the more knowledge means."

Bri snapped open her lighter, another cigarette tucked into a weird miniaturized smile. "You ever miss it?"

"So I can spend years writing the conference papers, the journal articles, and who will read them: eight and a half people if you count the one who doesn't finish?"

An ironic eyebrow. "You think all eight would read front to back?"

"Not even my mother."

A wing of oversized shirt spread as she drew on the cigarette, paused, then with maddening languor said, "Don't ask permission or forgiveness. It's your choice. But don't insult mine either."

"I didn't mean," Lyle said, and stopped. He looked away. He looked at the ground. He looked at his father. "Why don't you go wait for Mom at the truck?" Lyle said. "I'll catch up with you at the house later."

"But I'm just getting to know your friend," Frank said.

"Bri's specialty is sixteenth- and seventeenth-century Ottoman expansionism," Lyle said, very stiff, formal.

"Ottoman. So what *are* you?"

"Don't answer that, Bri," Lyle said, and to Frank, "What is wrong with you?"

His father threw his arms up in right angles of surrender. "All I want to know is who I'm talking to."

CHAPTER 4

The next afternoon, Lyle watched Bri Freeman undraw borders with the names of the past. Her hair was smooth, and one of her fists was a port and the other palm, skimming the air, was a ship, and she was talking about a time when most people had never seen people from other countries, other towns, and here is a cosmopolitan city. She was telling the story of a new human consciousness.

"Maybe mountain was only a word you could conceive of as a large rock," she said. "In the technology of traversing space, the imagination changes. There is more to hold in it."

After the conference, he took her out for drinks at a place that served booze in plastic cups. He brought back blue drinks, drinks with schnapps and curaçao to torture her. They sat at an uneven table pushed up against the wall paneling in the back of the bar. He apologized again for his father the night before. He explained this was a guy who hung an Italian flag in the living room above the television set, and he'd never even been to Italy.

Bri shrugged. With her mother, too, the notion of home was complicated. The disgust was complicated. Her mother saying of politics there, the villagers with their witchcraft. Bri said they'd never been religious. Her mother had come to the United States and gone to business school. She worked in HR. "And she was always trying to prove her transformation," Bri said, eyes going distant. "I didn't learn the language until college. But I suppose anyone wants to belong."

"And look at you in spite," Lyle said.

She shrugged again. He reached across the table. There was spilled wax hardened and greasy on the surface. "You were always the more gifted academic," he said.

She squeezed his hand. "Never was," she said, "a competition."

He withdrew his hand, stared hard into the jukebox under shitty overhead lights. He thought of her at the conference that afternoon. He thought of how she'd always been so sure. It had never been in grad school that the explanations, clauses of qualifications, questions of whether one was or was not an internalist would cause Bri to lose track of her conclusions in the recitation of the facts that were her premise, all those pages blurring as they had in him. The massiveness of his admiration made him frantic, but he took a sip of his drink. "You're a success," he said.

CHAPTER 5

When Lyle Michaels called, Alexandra said: "It's early your time."

"Which is right on time for you," he said.

"Seven, Friday the fourteenth?"

"Friday the fourteenth, seven," he said. "My time."

She placed the phone on the coffee table, returned to the laundry. This had been a choreographed call. *Phone me at ten Sunday. I'll be home.* And of course, so would Jeremy.

From his place on the sofa, he put down the newspaper, looked at her.

"No interesting news in there?" she said, smoothing a shirt.

"Very interesting, but you are more attractive than the PM."

She thought of something said by Shakespeare: "But love is blind, and lovers cannot see / The pretty follies that themselves commit."

Kant: "We are not rich by what we possess but by what we can do without."

"The substance of my life," Murdoch said, "is a private conversation with myself which to turn into a dialogue would be equivalent to self-destruction."

So Alexandra kept, for preservation, her thoughts to herself, or at least from Jeremy. It would keep their life resolved as in fixed, not the chemical way that meant undoing into parts, becoming quotients. Out the window, the sun threw ballsy colors through the sky, and she said nothing of the Forrest or her brother, strange now and furtive but back, back, even if not here.

Jeremy edged toward her on the couch, upsetting a tower of folded clothes. "I've got to get to the crisis center," he said. "I should leave soon."

"Then who will leer at me?" Alexandra said, a pair of his underwear crumpled in a fist resting on her hip.

"You could at least *pretend* not to be pleased," he said, passing a pair of argyle woolens.

"*I'm* not going to a crisis," said Alexandra.

On television, people in the audience of *The Jeremy Kyle Show* gasped together. There was the leaving of chairs. Cameras down passageways backstage. Teary returns. A woman slashed a pointing finger.

"I could still buy a ticket to New York," he said.

"It wouldn't be fun for you," she said. "It will be old college friends and inside jokes."

"I could go to the galleries, walk around. It wouldn't have to be every minute together."

"Don't you know the movies say, if you love them, let them go?" she said.

And of course, she *did* love him, but she had promised silence. It was the one thing she could give Shel.

Jeremy pulled his arm down off the back of the couch. "Want to get rid of me?"

"I've hired a hit man. You'd better watch your back. I'm in it for the life insurance."

"You can only get life insurance if you're married."

"Lucky for you, then," she said. "I have no reason to kill you."

CHAPTER 6

Define need, Jeremy sent as he walked from the call center.

Since he'd quit Strategic, he had rarely met Wright, but now Wright wanted to choose a loud bar where they wouldn't be heard. A nightclub would be best. Sloppy dancers would let them alloy with strangers, and in splintering green strobes, most cameras would fail.

Month of fools '92 on our hands again.

Jeremy deduced Wright was referring to April 1992, when every headline was a failure. On the day Gerry Adams lost his West Belfast seat and a bomb detonated by the IRA at the Baltic Exchange sent scenes of stained-glass angels spraying, there were three dead, ninety-one injured by the blast. "Not by the blast. By the Provos," One Rock had told Jeremy.

Impossible now, Jeremy responded to Wright. Or implored, perhaps.

He chose a long route by foot. He'd take the way down Bayswater Road past Hyde Park through the wakening city. There was something to watching the earth wind around past a rotation, the day unfurling into the moody quiet of night listening, and the sky softening again dark to light. You can believe then that time revises trouble.

Is it her? Wright wanted to know.

It's history repeating is always too clever by half.

Because already in 1992 it had become difficult to remember where sides cut. In theory, the Intelligence Corps' FRU worked to support the RUC Special Branch. De facto, Jeremy had seen that sometimes what they gave RUC were cursory scraps, and suspicion rooted beneath intel companies. Language had ceased to mean what it meant. Silence evidenced guilt in the Diplock Courts. Faith, Hope, and Charity tracked suspects. Radiation from British Army watchtower antennae had poisoned South Armagh locals, Sinn Féin claimed, and maybe it had been true.

Hence requisite rendezvous.

Jeremy let his hand skim hedges. He was already sweating, halfway home. The sun was being sucked up slow into the sky. He supposed it was only a meeting, an instance of logistics.

The fourteenth then, Jeremy thumbed, while she's away.

CHAPTER 7

He thought about Wright's message. Month of fools '92. He thought about it and knew there was nothing good to come of it. The last time he had believed any good could come of Northern Ireland was 1991.

When Jeremy landed in Lisburn that year, they gave him a name to follow. Gunner. In retrospect, a poor alias. Facile. He arrived to Jeremy as paper before flesh: a file, text. Date of birth, criminal record, address. He was a Belfast arms liaison, moving lethal technologies to the republicans. Gas-operated guns from Estonian radicals. The PIRA sweetheart special: M16s. Then the British had caught him with a shipment of Degtyarev bullets powerful enough to leave a victim looking exploded instead of shot. On capture, they told him silence was the sound after a dead child hit the earth. Your boy is old enough to know fear, they said. Your boy with the condition. Secrets for the boy, they said. And it had been easy to turn him because the mother of the child was eighteen months in the grave. The first time he met Gunner, Jeremy stood in the basement of a fish shop in Shaftesbury, the smell of sea flesh clinging. There were boxes everywhere, an agony of newsprint. In an icebox, black fish eyes stared over gaping mouths. You could see the moment of recognition, the startled look that would stay forever. He slipped ice chips in his hands to clean them of rubbish.

Gunner had selected a crate stacked over a pile of collapsed cardboard cartons, plunked down, and Gunner had brushed the metal wheel of a lighter with his thumb so that small blue flames hiccupped in his hand. "Got a clinker seat for the show. Will you not take one too?"

"I prefer to stand," Jeremy said, but something about Gunner's smile made him feel foolish. Jeremy had not expected Gunner to be so boyish. The photograph in his pocket that day, small and grayscale, showed only a compromised head against cheap paint.

"Like making it hard on yourself, do you, Allsworth?"

"We've got business to attend to," Jeremy said.

"Protestant work ethic will fetch you supper, but it won't win you time to eat it."

"I'm not a Protestant," he said, flush running up his neck. "Or a Catholic for that matter."

"Everyone needs someone to pray to, Allsworth, even the English," Gunner said.

Jeremy had not known what to make of the man. He had groped for the tongue of someone in such a position. He had thought of what someone else, someone who did not turn red as jam, would say.

"You talk a lot for a tout," he said.

A freezer groaned in the corner. "I suppose that's what touts do."

Now, many years removed, Jeremy remembered how that one word had knocked off patina, and Jeremy remembered how when Gunner had finished snitching, he stood, face wrung out. Gunner had rubbed his thighs, straightened. He had a way of inviting looks with casual vigor. Jeremy remembered thinking it was a poor quality for a man with secrets. And Jeremy remembered the thought to touch his hand. They had not shaken on meeting, but his own swampy palm remained in his pocket. Do not extend to the informant, the trainers had advised. He will swallow kilometers.

That afternoon, Gunner crossed the room. He paused at the door out of the shop basement, turned back abruptly so that the upstairs light bristled around him.

"Cecil's his name," Gunner said, "my boy."

"I know," Jeremy said.

"And he'll not be harmed now."

"I'll make contact again soon," said Jeremy.

"Already he's company. I burn a toast and he shouts, 'Own goal.'"

"You're proud."

"Don't have one of your own, so," Gunner said. Jeremy bent down to lace his shoe. "You're not a bad man, Allsworth. But are you decent?"

Jeremy stood again. "Who would believe whoever it is a person claims to be?"

"I'm original but not creative, Allsworth; I won't lie to you."

"You already did. The boy isn't speaking yet. The specialists say he's nonverbal autistic."

Gunner shrugged. "I figured you for pitiless, but I thought you might be charmed."

In that moment a prickle began, perhaps not yet the knowledge that nothing good could come of Northern Ireland but some consciousness of how little he knew. He would not until then have known the inertia of divisions. Nor would he have known that one day he would go around his home turning lights off, Alexandra already dunked under sleep, that looking at her, he would want to blot out the information of his life until she'd arrived in it.

CHAPTER 8

He did not know what to say, so he said that there was nothing to tell. He did not say that he'd forgotten facts were less dense than all the thick fictions, that facts pushed against the surface, bobbing. It was the night before she was to leave for New York, and now she was circling on what he could not say.

"It's just you never said you were in the army," she said.

"I haven't known you all that long," he said. "Whereas I am very old. The math of it is skewed."

"So catch me up, old man," she said, bright and campy with something.

She'd ceased eating. He reached across the table for a crumple of lettuce and tried to think up a quip about how she was allowing her salad to get cold. They had gotten to the moment because she liked war movies, not cowboy movies. They had gotten to the moment because he'd burned the roast. They had gotten to the moment because he'd wanted them to have a very nice dinner before she left, and they *had* been having a very nice dinner. He saw her glance at his hand holding an oily green. "I was in the army at the end of the eighties, in Germany, and I went home."

Alexandra made her voice dramatic, ironic. "Did you kill anyone?"

Jeremy cut into his steak carefully. He finished chewing, said, "I drank like a young man for a while, and it made an old man of me. I used to have a hairline in the proper place, you know." Jeremy searched for more true things to say. This meant stick to Germany.

In Teufelsberg—translation: Devil's Mountain—the air then was Dylan and *Klassenfeind* radio, *Bitlovka* jackets and the class enemy who comes in the night. By the time he had arrived, old ladies across the wall were watching *Dallas*. He had been eighteen and buoyant with army money, a fortune compared to the sums available in the gray mines at home. The Siggies had three days of the week off, and so when he was not listening on the radio for words that meant war games, he'd read E. T. A. Hoffmann or left Field Station Berlin to buy champagne for young Germans who sang songs about the state where hop and malt did not lose. The final days of the Cold War arranged themselves like a holiday, and whether it was Schabowski's mistake or his stratagem, what everyone accepted was a few words and the war was over.

"That's what you did in the army?" Alexandra dangled her fork over her plate. "You read stories and sang songs?"

He raised an eyebrow. "Why do you think I've got dirty little secrets?"

"I don't entirely, but I want it all," she said. "Don't you?"

He thought of how he loved that she couldn't sleep without music playing on the stereo, how because of that sometimes he'd wake in the middle of the night to Bach. She had never known her father, but she said because he'd owned a grocery, she thought of him when she saw a misty globe of lettuce. She was quietest in mornings. She left vitamins on Jeremy's toast plates. And, simply, he thrilled to look at her clavicle, her cheek.

"No," he said. "I don't. I like you just the way you are."

Alexandra's mouth drew into a wry little bow. "And what if there is more?"

"Is there?" he said.

He set his knife down. His fork. He lay both hands flat on the surface of the table. Steady. Symmetrical. One side of him, the other. Heart, skin.

"I used to have secrets. I was a fifteen-year-old with a forty-year-old boyfriend."

"You nearly still do," he said.

Her hands were brisk on a cloth napkin, folding it, setting it on the table. Done. Alexandra wobbled a glass of wine, circling it on its base. He could see she was a little drunk. "Did you ever think of one thing," she said, "did you ever think if you could only fix that one thing, you would fix it all?"

"Once," he said, "for a few years."

"And then?" she said.

"And then I grew up."

"My friend Lyle Michaels," she said.

"The journalist."

"The journalist," she said. "Lyle says when you learn someone's secret, that's when you really know them."

Jeremy swallowed. Jeremy raised a finger. "It is my turn for a question," he said. "Tiramisu or flan?"

CHAPTER 9

When she'd bought the plane ticket to New York, she had not imagined receiving his words on a screen, but perhaps it was better than all the years of no Shel whatsoever. Alexandra had walked through the fish smells, wafts of fried dumplings and garbage, windows of golden, hanging poultry. The New York storefront had a cardboard sign on its glass door: LUCKY SEVEN WEB COFFEE. Inside, she'd bought a spongy cake with a frosting mouse and given the woman behind the counter a ten for internet minutes, receiving in return a piece of paper with handwritten numbers, a log-in code.

A square of light appeared on the screen, words blinked and disappeared. Hello, it said, and then it didn't. Announce yourself, it said, and then it didn't. Hit the keys-ies if you pleasies.

Alexandra, she typed.

You alone?

I'm alone.

All the way, one hundred percent, to the bottom alone?

No one but the lady with the code. She kept her hands on the keyboard. She wanted her minutes, seconds.

Xiaoliang is all right.

Where are you?

I can't tell you that. I've survived this long on being only what I told.

You told me if I came here, you'd name a place.

New plan. If you want to obviate classes of problems in coding, you need to be able to anticipate hypothetical miscalculations.

The cake's glassy, unblinking eyes focused on her chest. Alexandra hadn't taken a bite. A girlish laugh came from behind the counter. Xiaoliang was watching a soap on a small screen leaned up against a jar of change and holding a piece of spongy bread in between a folded paper napkin. The woman's face was screwed into a knot, and she turned it into her elbow, sneezed.

How did you know I'd log on now?

I could explain. At the same time, learning the difference between dog and cat when there are wolves can just equate to all the better to be eaten, my dear. Tell me. Did you get out of that job?

Alexandra did not know why it, her life, did not transmit to her brother, why the good feel of it didn't seep through. She blamed it a little on the thin developments of telecom that tendered silent shouts landing afar. But it was also the way his virtuosic fear rattled the settled substrate of her life, upturned the glossy surface she had mastered, so that what was left was the halting thinness of a teenage self.

Not yet, she typed.

Yet is a human arrogance. It implies you can predict. Today there's a seventy percent chance of precipitation in Reno, Nevada, and that you'll wake up tomorrow. Laughable.

She suggested in smaller increments. Not a dinner but lunch.

Not lunch but ice cream. A cup of coffee. There was a place nearby. They could sit in a place where the only thing between them was a jar of flowers. Instead he was saying hedge fund managers would become subscription computer programs. The AP wire would be written by robots. Half of what she saw on Cathexis was generated by shadow governments weaponizing complacency and impulses.

The symbols on the screen began to seem strange to Alexandra, ancient. The sounds stopped coming into her mind from them. They were just twenty-six motifs shifting in light. Her stomach was curling in on itself, and she didn't know what he was saying, but there was a feeling to it like the moment before a dropped object hits the floor.

CHAPTER 10

Without Alexandra home, Jeremy needed to think through a problem with his hands, so he went after the broken watch. Online, websites said this is the gathering pallet, the stop-lever spring. This is the warning wheel. There are pieces to the mechanisms. Fix one, fix them all. But that was a lie. It was one piece off, nothing works.

I want it all. Don't you?

Month of fools '92.

He could not make out what Wright was getting at.

Wright who had been too enthused when he told Jeremy the Five Techniques were not torture but that it was known they worked because the Chinese had broken their own that way.

Wright who had told Jeremy the ways to step that would kill you involved ammonium nitrate and fuel.

Wright who had advised the less you speak, the less you lose.

I want it all. Don't you?

She did not.

Now, Jeremy turned the screw, the appliance reconstituting in his hands, but the numbers didn't come. The lights didn't. He arranged the nest of watch circuitry in a drawer.

He checked his phone. It was nearly time.

CHAPTER 11

Alexandra appeared at a bar in the East Village to meet Lyle Michaels two hours after leaving the internet café. She was sick with cheap noodles and sick with her own stories, but to see *a* friend from NYU mitigated the lie, approximating a reunion of sorts, she thought. She told herself that.

Lyle's foot was propped on a brass pole lining the floor beneath the bar in an Irish pub, and for a while they sat together on cracked stools, looking at pictures of the baby. They exclaimed. They spoke of how it used to be that he'd have taken out his wallet.

"What are you doing here anyway?" Lyle said.

Alexandra returned the phone, watched Lyle raise himself from the chair a little to fit it in his pocket. She set her face. "Seeing an old friend," Alexandra said, "who I think is in trouble."

"When you say trouble."

She chose her words. "Maybe needs in-patient."

"Because."

"Because I can't tell you."

It had become clear that her brother was losing his mind— odd sentences, odd paragraphs—and she didn't know where to retrieve it. What she knew was that he had been a boy who smoked Pall Malls. A twelve-year-old with a pack-a-day habit. Not menthols. She knew he had been pushed out of home too young.

Lyle pulled noisily at the bottom of a drink that was over already. "You're having a friend committed."

"He's not a danger."

"So he needs to surrender himself to treatment," Lyle said.

A squeeze of lemon into her drink. A stir. Jangling ice. "That's the problem." She did not understand his eyebrows, their puckering now. She turned up the corners of a napkin so it clung to her sweating glass. "He needs to think it's his own idea."

"And you'll feed it to him." Lyle leaned toward her.

"I'll help him."

"Well, if I'm ever in trouble, don't help me," Lyle said.

"What's that supposed to mean?"

"He really that far gone?" Lyle said, tapping a straw against his head. "Because to do that to someone."

"To do help."

"You really believe that?" he said.

Alexandra rubbed her cell phone with a thumb. Overhead, a woman on television was deciding between three choices to prevent her elimination. She trusted the knowledge of those she knew. She made the call.

"I believe everything he says doesn't match everything I know."

"Maybe he knows something you don't," Lyle said.

CHAPTER 12

Alexandra had been told his name had once been Allsworth. She had not, of course, been told Bill was Wright's alias for Jeremy when they met these days, a riff on Wilhelm, the real third name of E. T. A. Hoffmann. Jeremy called Wright Ray. And it was from Ray, or rather Wright's former name Wilmington, that Jeremy had learned in Lisburn how secrets could thicken a man, accrete rings so that one was not diminished by the work, worn by it. In invisibility, he had expanded like hot air, but in recent years, his hands shook except when he spoke of Northern Ireland. "The voices of bureaucrats dismantle years of our life," he said. "It is all cartoon legitimacy, redeemed outlaws. Terrorists don't get better. They must think we're stupid."

Jeremy looked at his feet. "It's other fish now."

"The other fish they know to be sharks. PIRA painted pretty pictures of Basques. They would cry about rubber bullets and human rights. Meanwhile," Wright said.

"Fertilizer and Barrett Lights."

"Thinking shock to be astonishing. Thinking martyrs to be saints."

Jeremy spoke slowly. He stared into the white pane of a

cocktail napkin, skated it on the edge of the table. "But that isn't why you asked me here. That's old news now."

Wright flicked his hand in and out of his pocket, pushing a folded piece of newsprint toward Jeremy. It was a short piece in the financial section. An AP bite. According to the story, Cathexis had moved its headquarters to Dublin. Then an Irish subsidiary of the company moved to Bermuda, a tax haven. Jeremy read it twice to see if he'd missed something.

Wright agitated his hands, vibrated. "If you're seeing what I'm seeing," he said, pointing to a line in the clipping, "you're seeing this goodly American running the show is the same goodly American who made the call on a number of crises. You're remembering that these crises, they were addressed with coups."

"And," Jeremy said.

"And you see the connections or you are naïve. I smell fish, Billy. Mackerel, salmon. Our American friends are demanding from private enterprise weaknesses in the software they can exploit for surveillance, digital weapons R&D, misinformation campaigns, or all of the above."

Jeremy's knee began to pop like a sewing machine needle. "It isn't the worst idea."

"They can't control this kind of warfare, Bill, because they don't understand it. They don't understand the science of hitting buttons in a room."

"Maybe they are not card-carrying Luddites, Ray."

The surface of Wright's face peeled back, gleaming, gray teeth peeking out from thin, tense lips. He arched his neck back. "If you're talking about that adorable little idea out of the Weapons Intel Unit."

"I have no idea what you're talking about."

"Tried to bug PIRA weapons to snatch the dirty talk. All the techies thought electronics were going to win a deathless war, but what happens? Republicans get wise to the jarking, sussed out all the funny gunnies. It was as though the WIU had given the Provos a list of touts. A load of executions caused by the fastest-fingered secretaries in the army."

"That was then."

"Private companies though, Bill. How do we know *they* are secure? Or, how do we know they don't sell the same technological weapons to terrorist groups or hostile governments? Security. Mercenaries. Go ahead and say it's not a woodchuck. It's a groundhog. No, it's a whistle-pig. But it's all the same squirrel. Every agent thinks he is offering the best of all possible worlds. Find out the mistress is everyone's mistress, but you cannot trace the beds because these are black ops. Because there are no checks on men like us."

Jeremy couldn't quite keep up, follow the progression of conversation. What he saw looking at Wright was a hunger for action that made the air vibrate, that hunger that would find any opening. It made Jeremy's ears ring or maybe it was the music they ducked into to cordon off their words to everyone but each other. He took a long drink so that the heat spread in long fingers through his chest.

"This is not even to speak of whether actors *within* governments can be trusted. Think of all the Sinn Féin TDs in the Dáil or Seanad, the NIA, lapsed PIRA with their ballot box legitimacy and their old friends. People don't change, Bill."

"*You* don't change, Ray," Jeremy said.

"In Lisburn, Lawrence wanted to believe entering information in intel databases was multiplying knowledge, that it would skim away inefficiencies in interagency sharing. Trust MI5, RUC. Please. We might as well shout secrets through microphones. So where does that leave us?"

"In new lives, Ray." Jeremy meant it gently. "You're paranoid."

Wright reached over the table, flicked a speck of something from Jeremy's collar. He peeled back slow and uniform as the second hand of a clock moving from ten to twelve. "What if I were to tell you that a Sinn Féin councilor had met with someone on the payroll of that pinguid little security firm Tyle headed by Lawrence?"

"Are you?"

"And happens to be Tyle've gone very deep into cyber."

Jeremy inspected the collar Wright had undirtied. "How would you know who meets with Lawrence's men?"

"You don't think that's interesting."

"I think there are a lot of reasons for contact," Jeremy said.

"You're not listening, Bill. Lawrence. Irish. Public-private. Cash flows. What's the sum?"

Jeremy worked over logic, refutations, but these were useless devices here. He knew the prolonged pinnacle of danger was the last bastion of reality to Wright.

"Lawrence is playing both sides of the pitch, Bill."

"There's no way to know that," Jeremy said.

"You know what Wittgenstein said about the human soul?" Wright said.

"Ah yes, Professor Wright."

"Don't be cruel," Wright said. "Be smart."

"It doesn't matter how many wit's ends you've got, it doesn't make a knot."

Wright sucked his cheeks tight to his teeth. "And would it be tied in a pretty enough ribbon for you if I said Lawrence had also personally met with your old colleague Gavin Thomas? That there was some very interesting talk about capital flows from Belfast?"

"How would you know that?"

"You asked, Jeremy. You came to me for help with Thomas."

"*You* said he was just another hedgie."

"And you convinced me otherwise, Billy."

"Jeremy," someone said.

He turned, squinted. Two women. One unrecognizable. The other saying his name again. His throat was dry. "Genevieve."

"What are you doing here?" she said.

"What are you? Decide against the reunion?"

She put her drink down. The other woman was smiling, looking back and forth between them. She reached to shake Wright's hand.

"What reunion?" Genevieve said.

"Yours."

CHAPTER 13

The whole way home, all he could think was perhaps his problem had been that he was too quick to surmise. Of a person, action. He would catch the angle of lift in a conversation and take it past the trajectory. He would see the beginning of a pattern and believe it a rule.

But change was what she'd done, and there *had* been something odd about Alexandra lately, as when you looked from only one eye and then from both, and what you saw was perceived as the same object, only somehow different.

At one point in his life, he'd been a listener. The listening had deepened his shadow. He'd heard the world shrink through radio waves that brought distant voices into the close quarters of machines, then learned how to be a man for whom sentences appeared on the tongue, ready-made as text. But he had not heard her lie as a lie. He had heard her words as any given schedule.

He had forgotten that listening is not alone opening the ears. It is quieting the mind. Jeremy could not quiet his mind.

Change was what she'd done. He had blamed it on the sleeping pills she'd begun taking, but the change was neither drowsiness nor sleepwalking. Sometimes, he asked if *she* knew what it was. But she didn't think anything was different except his imagination. She asked if something, perhaps, was different in him.

"Is this your way of leaving me?" she said.

Which was exactly what someone would say who wanted you to believe that you were the one deciding to leave. So that it's my idea instead of yours. She must think he didn't know much. Certainly, she didn't know he knew about the reunion.

And another thing she didn't know he knew: sometimes, she prayed. She didn't kneel or make the sign of the cross, but her hands folded, her eyes closed, and he knew she was asking for things she couldn't do herself. She did not do it often, perhaps because she didn't need to. Lately, though, he would see her pause before the closet, gazing onto trousers, and her face was less occluded then, then there was a silent word in a gesture of her mouth, and it was, he believed, *please*.

She was sad and lovely in those moments, and he'd need to draw on a sweater, and he didn't know what the fear was wadding up in his stomach. Sometimes, he was sure she caught him staring too long at the white of her wrists, the petal of her earlobe, that she could see the question in his eyes. But she did not answer, and all he could do was watch her. He watched and knew if Alexandra was a liar, he did not want the truth.

Perhaps, he thought, it was like the time he'd urged Gunner to accept a prison sentence so he'd not be suspected a rat. The idea had been to cloak him in punitive action, make him the republican martyr, an innocent. The idea had been Gunner would return home decorated by prison, the *oglach* who gave his freedom for the cause, consummate. But Gunner had wanted Jeremy to assure him there'd be gentleness in lockup.

"There is nothing I can say to console you that isn't an empty promise," Jeremy had said.

"So lie to me, Allsworth," Gunner had said, "and learn to mean it."

Jeremy would accept Alexandra's lies. He would accept them as long as one day she meant them.

PART THREE: DIVISOR

I said I'm in a hurry for freedom. He told me freedom was coming.
It was like a boat coming to shore and my rushing into the water
would only get me wet, not bring the boat in faster.

—Kwame Ture, born Stokely Carmichael

CHAPTER 1

On Christmas Eve, Jeremy offered what he could, which was distraction. He offered it when Alexandra's aunt Irene said she missed Shel, the only of them who'd ever sung carols. And he offered it when Mrs. Chen said that Irene had been held back a grade and couldn't understand why it had only been once.

When a song about rushing fools came on the radio, Mrs. Chen put down her cigarette. She caught Alexandra's face in her hand as she slurred that Mr. Chen loved Elvis, and she wished they could see his hips go. Pelvis Elvis. Mr. Chen would do the Elvis Pelvis because he knew how to make her laugh.

"Alex," she said to Jeremy, still gripping her daughter's chin. "My beauty, always was, look at her. She has that good Oriental skin. Orientals always have that clean look. You can see it in her, can't you? Just like Mr. Chen."

"She is very beautiful."

Mrs. Chen's hand dropped. "He was baby-faced her age too, and then he was dead."

Throughout the day, Alexandra whispered to Jeremy about what she couldn't wait for, which was their departure, but as the evening settled, he told himself he would remember all the awful decorations, things cast poignant by their position in the home where she had been a girl. Irene and Mrs. Chen sat on the striped couch in their pilling bathrobes and graying slippers like old stuffed animals. They sucked striped candies, and beneath the tree, packages were still perfect. Something that Jeremy had never noticed: Alexandra's hair was the type of black that expressed its environment, red in the Nevada sunlight, but bluish in the living room near the strung garlands. He was still discovering her angles, and yet, he was afraid it would be their last Christmas together, so he tried to encode it all in his memory. Tinsel. Holiday tissue box. She turned on a video of *The Nutcracker*.

Alexandra on the floor, chin resting on his thighs, there was quiet amongst them, and Jeremy could see the dancers abstracted on the screen of her face in pink and blue puddles of television light. This was not the Hoffmann *Nutcracker* with the fever dream of doppelgängers or doubles or deceptions. The dancers looked like pieces of jewelry animated by light, and there were the animals too and the nutcracker prince's sword cuts arcing in long, benevolent, lovely lines. For some minutes, Jeremy thought maybe they could stay that way forever. Maybe they could always be watching ballerina rats and families articulated in tulle, Alexandra leaning her cheek into him. Then it was over.

"I haven't enjoyed something so much without laughing at it in a long time," Alexandra said as the video ejected.

The fact of her face was honest but soft. The night was ending. Jeremy fumbled with the lamp as she raised herself from the carpet, the puddle of a long skirt stretching up.

"You liked those sweets shaped like hamburgers at the gas station."

Alexandra shrugged. "Ironic food doesn't count."

"Dancing-in-one's-head sugar plums aren't ironic food?" Jeremy said.

"There's something you should know," she said. He could not see her eyes. He wanted one more look within this moment, this night. "I accepted a job in New York."

Jeremy stood then, as though it were an answer, though there had never been a question, some soft part of him vandalizing his own mouth. "It's sudden," he said finally.

"Everything is sudden," she said.

Over, under—every turn of the weave of the blanket expressed itself in his hands. Jeremy set it down beside a heavy green dish of potpourri. He looked at Mrs. Chen with the breast of her shirt crumpled beneath her face. Irene reached for her, and Mrs. Chen slapped her sister's hand away.

Nodding, she was nodding. Fingertips thrust white through her hair. "There's no way around it," Alexandra said. Alexandra said, "You understand you'll have to marry me to come."

Jeremy moved a stunned hand to his throat. On the sofa, her mother was choking on God, gasping rapid rhythms. There was a queer feeling in his foot as he stepped.

Alexandra did not blink, said, "Stay in my life."

CHAPTER 2

Their final night in Nevada, they went to a bar where half the jukebox songs stole quarters and paper snowflakes still bent at the creases hung from taped-up string. They drank beer cold enough frost hugged the bottle. When a slow song drew to the floor by the pool table couples, Alexandra let him lead her, sway. And in the light of cheap lager neons, a drunk man hooting in the back, folded against Jeremy's wool shirt so his bergamot smell touched her face, there was a private, spacious feeling.

That night, Alexandra and Jeremy held each other in her thin childhood bed so that neither would fall off, but also because she wanted to remain tight to him in whatever way she could. On a small table beside the bed sat a green glass vase and scratchy fake flowers, always in bloom, touched with clear glue dewdrops.

She remembered out loud and quietly. Her autobiography returned to her in old jean jackets and corduroy dresses, the edges of which she could see in the closet, in a black backpack drawn over in Wite-Out. They bent around each other in her cartoon sheets, never after grade school replaced. She rubbed on a type of soda pop chapstick she'd not bought since high school, and turned her eyes over a white window panel intimating wild birds in lace.

The next day at the airport, they discovered their seats had been, without cause, upgraded. She leaned her hip against an information kiosk.

"But why?" she said.

Jeremy accepted from her things passed she didn't have hands for. Holiday pattern bags. A child ran by, rippling blue cape behind. To use her hands, she put on the sunglasses that made everything lavender.

"When the luck is good," Jeremy said, pastel and happy, "the answer is not why. It is yes."

CHAPTER 3

Returned to London, they made calls. To Genevieve, to his parents. Their cheeks pressed together over one phone, and in the telling, the news became sleight.

"I've tricked him," she said, "into marrying me."

Jeremy caught on to the act, would say that he was not a credulous man and enumerate his cynicisms. He declared himself worldly to the work of black cats crossing ladders. He said the only certifiable things were bad British weather and scheming politicians, and no one believed him. They observed he was a dupe, but Alexandra's dupe, and radiating good fortune.

In the days that followed, Alexandra involved him in choices that didn't matter. None of it mattered. The costumes, the place. But one day Mrs. Allsworth was very small and hunched as she showed Alexandra a photograph of her own wedding day, her eyes big with need. She offered, then, an ivory silk dress. And though it would never fit, they pretended for a while, made the motions of tradition.

CHAPTER 4

Alexandra rested on the couch, illuminated by useful machinery, and Jeremy read Hoffmann's "The Sandman." He had given a vintage copy of the *Night Stories* to Alexandra for Christmas, and she had given one to him, both knowing he loved it.

The other phone in the inner pocket of his robe was vibrating. He did not need to glance at it for the name. Instead, he looked at Alexandra, the lean silk of her draped on the couch. It was already the time when she had taken her sleeping pill, began drinking drowsily, when the feeling was that sleep was sinking slowly as through water. These days, she liked to get drunk in front of the computer or television until her arms went swimmy. She'd speak to him with her eyes half-closed until she faded. There was in the flat a sense of the edges bleeding. After-dinner smells ran in from the kitchen: coconut and curry, powdery dish soap, a sandalwood candle.

Alexandra adjusted a pillow, gave a sigh without resentment. He saw her seeing him rise from his seat, laying the book mnemonically. He turned toward the kitchen, where he took calls from his mother. He switched the phone carefully. In the doorway, he was already saying, "Mum."

Alexandra's eyes ran dreamily over houses in the computer on her lap, gray marble and circle fixtures and windows onto vistas of cement ordered in cluttered grids. "I will not catch cold," Jeremy said. "I wear a hat *and* a scarf." He leaned against the counter, angled such that he could say silent things with his face to Alexandra. She laughed. "Soon," he said. "We'll visit very soon. We'll be thinking about your roast."

To her he returned, tall glass of whiskey outstretched. A tinkling of ice on glass announced him. "Am I a psychic or a charlatan?" he said.

Her upper lip curved over the tumbler's edge. "Depends," she said. "Is the future pretty?"

"I will be in your future, which is the bedroom," he said.

Through a doorway, he released music composed fifty years before from a radio. He adjusted the volume so that a dead woman's voice urged toward the living room. She sang of what a man didn't need to say, pled to be believed. Drops caught drops in the liquid run down the window. Alexandra came in, lay on their bed. She pushed socks off with her feet: a familiar message.

Cool fingertips reached through the dry, cottony air. A new old song vibrated against their scalps. Her shirt was in his mouth, then her ear. He looked down at her cheek flushed against a sheet, lavender fragrance turning mineral as the warm moisture came up off swoops of back and the round of thighs. Under sounds beyond language, he searched for the secret folds and wisps of hair lifted up off skin, and the room was shot through with bathroom glow come from the parted door that illuminated the tiny parts of her. A bird feather somehow at the neck, and then her hips rolled upward. Gasp like reaching for life.

Their chests rose and sank slower and slower. It was the time of night when dark gathered in the corners spread, sleep insinuated. "Love," she said like a discovery.

"You do?" he said.

She was beginning to slur. Her eyes had stopped fighting for real pictures, sleep pill settling. "Sometimes I think about everything we don't know about each other, and it is more than our life."

"We met each other after every time else," he said. But she was already asleep.

Jeremy covered her, closed the bathroom door. He waited until the numbers on his watch signaled it was time. Outside, he dialed.

"Son will not follow Mum at twenty-three hundred," he said. "Everything is fine, Mum. Everything is great."

"Son," Wright said, "we need to talk."

CHAPTER 5

In the apartment, Alexandra pursed her lips, tidy, but her pulse was elaborate with wanting to know where he'd been. She was in one of her old college T-shirts, and her legs were moist with lotion applied with the productive fervor of not knowing what to do, where he'd gone. He came to her. Got on the couch. He put his head in her lap, and she didn't touch him.

"I just needed to speak to a friend."

"You needed to speak to a friend in the middle of the night, outside."

"It wouldn't work to speak in the flat."

"Because you can only speak secretly, in secret places?" she asked.

"Yes," he said.

In the standing, her knee knocked his chin, and even then, there was a flicker of wanting to reach out, apologize. But she did not apologize. She watched him touch his smarting face.

"What are you hiding?"

"I'm not."

"You're not hiding as you speak secretly, in secret places?"

He rounded through the spine, fingers laced. He leaned his

forearms against his knees. "Maybe I was nervous," he said. "Don't be sore."

"Nervous."

"We're getting married," he said. "It's normal."

She braced her face, swallowed. Holding the doorframe stilled her hand. It *was* normal, his feeling, and it opened an eerie hole she did not want to peer through.

She looked at her hands, now wrung smooth. "I thought we were better than that."

CHAPTER 6

In the days that followed, she reviewed lives, the long scroll of them on Cathexis. Sometimes they were only sentiment without eloquence, but sometimes they were stunning little quadrangles recording seaside champagne occasions or a mother's recipe produced by her son, and Alexandra's gestures on the screen expressed her Favor numbly, unstoppably. It was research for the new advertising job or it was a very good excuse for it, the cough syrup haze of minor curiosity softening whatever it was between her and Jeremy. Jeremy had decided to pursue social work in New York, and he would sit working on his graduate school applications, and she could think, across the room from him on the sofa with all these snips of celebration held in an electronic that it was not so difficult to live well, and she would crack open the silence, say, "No one's told them only celebrities canoodle; everyone else hangs." He would have something not quite unkind to say that separated them from everyone else, that made her believe that he was not so unsure after all that they would keep on together, clasped.

There were, too, groups she didn't Cathect into entirely. She was a lingering eye, a reader. They were people with addicts for daughters or alcoholics, and they would write ragged accounts of their hurt, tell each other they knew how it felt, they did because of their father or son. Better was the outcome sometimes, and she liked these strangers with bettered families best. She was sure she was not so miserable as the rest because she only looked and because, too, though Shel would miss the bugles of stargazer lilies in her hands as she took the aisle, the popcorn fuzz of baby's breath in her hair, they would be closer in America. They would not be so unredeemed, centrifugal.

The night before the wedding, Genevieve brought Alexandra to a restaurant with fat, seeping steaks and velvet curtains. The waiters wore starched garments. They replaced forks. For a long while, Genevieve and Alexandra remembered being younger and stupider, the romance of even ordering a drink. Whiskey and Coca-Cola.

Someone cleared the dishes. There were flakes of light in the rounds of their wineglasses. Genevieve spun the delicate stem of a flower between them.

"Never thought you'd end up across an ocean, married," she said.

A squat, tense pyramid of panna cotta came, served on a plate with mint leaves and berries. There were two little spoons on the plate. Alexandra concentrated on pulling a neat scoop. "Who says I've ended up?" She winked. "Maybe this is just the beginning."

"The beginning of your husband spree?"

"Yes, serial wife Alexandra Chen on the loose. Authorities say Chen is unarmed and dangerous."

"They will put you on the channel with the face-eaters," Genevieve said.

"There will be terrible reenactments."

"They'll call you the Spousal Slut of the West."

Alexandra scraped a bite of panna cotta. "And you'll call me?"

Genevieve reached across the table for her hand. "Often, and also my most infamous friend."

Alexandra wished then that there was an architecture sophisticated enough to breach latitudes between London and New York, that distance could be miniaturized for more than representations: words, images. She would be unable to corroborate the substance of her friend's hand on another continent.

Inside the pub, everyone was shouting, and no one was heard. People crowded around them in the charade of feeling young. He found Wright with a beer and tried to slide beneath the noise. There were fists in the air around them. Glowing halos. They nodded, hissed under the crash of metal, and a woman slithered atop a table. Wright began pacing.

"Mum's got a secret admirer," he said.

Meaning: he was sure he was being followed ever since he'd started scratching away at the ties between Sinn Féin and Tyle. Ever since he'd begun looking into Thomas for Jeremy. Wright's thought was the IRA memory was long, and now they could retain the mercenaries from private security firms like Tyle, firms populated with men of their own training. He had disappeared, and so he'd be simple to disappear. In the bar light, his teeth glinted blue.

"I am not so lost I couldn't be found," Wright said. "Bill, it's them."

Jeremy began to look at everything except Wright. Wright could exact sanity from you. He bore newspaper clippings, waggled rumors, advanced theories. He thought the one thing to

trust was there were ways men like them were questioned that
could leave you in a padlocked room babbling.

"What they can doesn't augur what they will," Jeremy said.

"You want to sleep at night; you don't want to see in the dark.
Gerry Adams can shake the hand of an American president on
camera, but in the background, *Tiocfaidh ár lá*, our day will come,
Sinn Féin is saying. There is someone following me, Bill."

Too long Jeremy had thought he could keep a small compartment for Wright, the odd, ruined brotherhood of *semper vigiles*
carried around a clean life with a well-appointed flat. But that
was when it had seemed she would not be willing to follow him
entirely into the desirable clichés. Somehow, after the night she'd
caught him letting himself back into the flat, he and Alexandra
had recovered in days passing and speaking nothing of their fight,
the silence stretching out discontent like an image pulled until it
blurred. He behaved as though nothing had happened, and the
hard outline between them thinned, and he needed only to stand
with her tomorrow, speak aloud the promise already deep in himself that they'd not end up quotients.

"Appropriate would be request new cover at HQ, then,"
Jeremy said.

"We're classified, Bill. We don't exist. Not in declassified documents. Fifty-fifty, it was someone *in* HQ that leaked."

"Were it, you'd be dead already, Ray. You said you knew it was
former PIRA."

Wright's fist hit the table. He folded his arms, looked over his
far shoulder, back. A song like machinery came on. Right hand
to pocket.

"I said it was *them*. When the borders have fallen between

public and private, between countries, them can be anyone. By the time you find out who someone is, it's too late."

"Only adversaries."

"Vetting fails, Bill."

"Especially when there is no one to vet."

A snort that appeared to throw Wright's head back with its force. "Don't play cover ID with me, Billy. The hedge fund naïf turned do-gooder. There's no way you believe that. You've got to be not looking if you don't see it."

"And now a tautology from the philosopher of the mind."

"Think of Gunner."

"That was Belfast," Jeremy said.

"Everywhere is Belfast with a different flag."

Now, Wright looked at Jeremy, but Jeremy did not return his gaze. He should not have come.

"Do you remember when we first met?" Wright said.

It had been breakfast at the barracks. He remembered Wright, Wilmington at the time, saying, "They're terrorists, but they're our terrorists now. You make sure they're eating right. You don't keep them alive with a foot out the door and a soft heart." Wright was grayer now.

"I had to tell you eyes went three hundred sixty degrees there, that we might call ourselves the Fishers of Men but we were in an aquarium, right down in the depths with them trying to pretend we weren't getting wet."

"I didn't understand what you were saying," Jeremy said.

"You needed to know your knickers ought to be soiled. You didn't know a good informer for the RUC was gunned down by men at his door dressed in RUC uniform. You didn't know the scope could slink out. You were wearing the white sheet and still were spooked. Do you remember what you said to me then?"

Jeremy shrugged.

"You said, 'Be seeing you,' Bill. That's what you said."

"So?"

"So here it is, Bill. Here it is: I told you you'd *have* to see me. I told you there's nowhere to hide from men like us. And it's still true."

The night was intolerable. It didn't matter that they'd been parallel handlers in Lisburn. Ninety-eight, ninety-nine percent of the time, the tours had been counting minutes, running down hours in Thiepval Barracks muttering about Palestinian flags on republican houses. A reasonable man would have left the deprivations behind by now. Wright was a man deranging.

"Sometimes what looks like spying is only the company of men," Jeremy said. "The man marooned on an island doesn't have privacy, Ray. He's only alone. I'm leaving."

"But the night's so young, Bill."

"Leaving wider than that," Jeremy said. "New York. For her."

He would not wait for Wright to finish his drink. He would not finish his own. Even the night was lighter than here in the bar, and he could feel it pull him away from Wright back to her sweet coppery smell. Long, thin shins. "I can't help you, Ray."

"You forget there's an us in this room," Wright said. "You forget that if they know about me, they know about you."

In the bar, the clothes were black and the music was loud growling. Green light cast over a barkeep screaming what she was owed, the cloy of fry oil rising from somewhere in the back. "We are not important enough to be followed," Jeremy said. "Only paranoid enough."

"Or maybe it's nothing to worry about for you. Maybe you've got contact with Lawrence."

"He is as to be found as any of us."

Wright leaned over the table. "You're getting privileged information. Else how is it you're always out just in time? You leave Lisburn before Thiepval is bombed. You quit Strategic before Bear Stearns or Lehman goes down. Terror. Markets. How is it nothing touches you, Bill? Too late for anyone else is just the beginning for you."

"I guess I'm lucky," Jeremy said, standing in the shuddering light, looking diagonally away from Wright, in the direction of home.

CHAPTER 8

Too late for anyone else is just the beginning for you. Jeremy could not understand the sentiment. He walked home, and he thought of how he had always been too late.

Even Gunner had known it.

He had warned him.

Impossible Wright had forgotten, for example, that they were too late for the woman shot dead in her driveway at Dortmund. Impossible Wright had forgotten that they were too late for the family optimistic enough to have repainted their walls before the lot of them was gunned down at home. Impossible that Wright had forgotten that they were too late at every turn.

Jeremy thought of the afternoon Gunner had warned him not infrequently. Gunner's hand long and white on the horseshoe latch, the tension around the mouth. Jeremy had agitated something hard in his pocket, change or keys, as Gunner said, "There's a witchy air around our rooms these days. I've a mind to disappear, Allsworth."

And because, at the time, he had not known they were too late, Jeremy had slid an unimpressed screen over his own unnerving.

He had returned warning with warning: they'd find him. They had before.

"There are places you won't follow." Gunner had grinned, then let the smile fall off his face. And was it memory or some retrospective flourish: that space between Gunner's eyes closing like a fist, how something had passed overhead, drawing a shadow? "There are few places to begin anew and many to end, Allsworth. Maybe I want to do the democratic thing and die."

Jeremy could not unconvince Gunner of the sense blood remembered, that he was born knowing to scream for air, ancient indecencies—so why not the other thing? His sense was his father died so his son would be a freedom fighter who'd die for his son to be a freedom fighter, death his antecedent. "From wee boys on, it is sixers in our streets, vehicles of war driving by our doorsteps. We were *Fianna Éireann* when we could walk."

On that afternoon, they had volleyed. *Morbid sentiment. Official craic. Irish platitudes. You were not born a soldier. An alibi. I will not have someone thrown in the ditch for my body, and you're somewhere in London drinking gin and tonic. No one asked you to smuggle Barrett Lights. Sure of that now, are you?*

They had gotten tired.

They had reached a point that Gunner had laughed quietly, or shook noisily. His eyes squeezed and his jaw hinged, a little askew, and Jeremy had stared.

Gunner had been quiet a moment, thumbing a fingernail beneath the edge of his lower lip. "Feeling's not right, Allsworth. It's nothing you can put a name to, but I feel it on my neck, in endless smiles. The circumference constricts. You could get me out of here."

Too late for anyone else. Yes, Gunner had known it was too late.

And of course Gunner had been right. Gunner had known the push of history was already beyond them.

Because too late was just the beginning. In those days, One Rock had had a mostly unrequited penchant for information on Terrence Feeney, a Sinn Féin man with ties to the Social Democratic and Labour parties and a proselytizing touch. Feeney had shown himself dangerous at the last *ardfheis*. Feeney could light fire through a microphone, that big voice that made ideas big, individuals big: you can be a terror of a hero with a homemade spectacle and a free heart. He was less careful than Adams, presented as the great stylist of street warfare with his everyman pathos and dirty fingernails. But it was still unclear whether Feeney was only a starlet party whip or whether his orations included operations commands, still unclear how directly he killed.

One Rock had pressed Jeremy, and Jeremy had pressed Gunner. He had told Gunner the way out of informing was bringing home a human trophy. There were tactics passed from One Rock. Jeremy looked at Gunner and told him to bait Feeney with botched ops. Lay on the rue and missed opportunities. Shake your head. Feeney will say next time. They are so hopeful, soldiers. The soldier will want to have learned better. The soldier will share a new plan.

"Or he will think I've turned tout," Gunner said.

And so it went, the regular argument over whether Jeremy was trying to get Gunner killed. How they do it: You lose your sight first. They just drive you over a border with a bag over your head. Maybe over the radio Phil Lynott is singing. Maybe you hear the car door slam or open. There is a sound to the end of brotherhood coming out of a gun. Feeney was too beloved, Gunner believed. Mistakes are seminal in his proximity. They cascade in the gazers and fans.

"He's protecting Feeney," One Rock had said. "His own fear being the alibi."

"He was quaking."

One Rock tilted his head. "They could have been movie stars."

In the quiet notches of days that followed, Gunner had repeated party lines, and Jeremy had called silence an insult to the deal. He had offered scant flattery for the rumors that trailed off, and he had bottled up his face so that it emitted no light. Air compressed, released. Someone was always holding his breath.

But no matter the approach, no matter the slices of persona Jeremy applied, Gunner had become less reliable. Sometimes, Jeremy waited at the tree or the lot or the back room, and Gunner didn't show. Later, Gunner would ask how he'd have explained why he wasn't at the garage or the shebeen.

"Use your artistic sensibilities," Jeremy had said.

"Like Patrick Mayhew's as he declares Britain neutral on Northern Ireland?"

"Or the ones involved smuggling guns," Jeremy had said.

There had been, too, the time that Gunner changed the place of their meeting to Andytown, placing Jeremy on the same block as the May murder of a Sinn Féin member named Alan Lundy. There was the time a bullet smashed through a window less than a meter from Jeremy's gullet; they both dropped beneath the desk, Gunner's face blank as milk. And there was the time that, waiting in the alley behind a hair salon, it was not Gunner who came but Brendan Kelly, mouth curled like sideways question punctuation.

"Of all the places in all the world," Jeremy had said the next day, speaking quickly to mitigate the tremble.

"This isn't Casablanca," Gunner had said.

"What reason had Brendan to be at the salon where you should have been?"

"Yourself is not the only one who wonders."

The ominous matches persisted. It was a time of echoes. It was a time of double down. It was a time death came cheaper with big bombs, those bloody protest fireworks rearranging the composition of buildings. It was too late. Wright must remember that it had been too late.

Now, almost two decades removed with London beneath his feet, what did Jeremy remember though? Jeremy remembered that when, on television, they watched the president of the Republic of Ireland shake Gerry Adams's hand, Wilmington had spit on the floor. He remembered that Gunner's step lost its buoyancy. He remembered that one afternoon he had gone to St. Malachy's, found himself surrounded by all that brightness, the thick white filigree that seemed to drip off the church ceiling, and he knelt and did not know whether to hope there was or was not a god. He remembered that. But most of all, what he remembered was the green philodendron falling down behind One Rock as he said that Gunner was dead, that Jeremy was too late.

"Was it fast?" Jeremy had asked.

"Dead on arrival," One Rock had said.

"And the boy?"

"Went home with the grandmother."

"And painless?"

One Rock had tilted his head. "No one ever does report back."

Jeremy had been too late.

CHAPTER 9

When they had their quiet wedding, she kissed him, her cheeks bouncing up in a smile when she pulled away. There were minia-ture flowers white against her hair, as Genevieve Bailey popped a loud, cheap cracker that smacked the smell of sulfur into the air. His parents drank their sherry in the restaurant with them after, and after that, in light linen clothes, he and Alexandra took a weekend at the sea. They looked out on the ocean pulling away from the shore, returning.

In the weeks following, she took to the planning of the move, and the performance of everyday life gave him something to believe in. Morning coffee. Side-by-side teeth brushing. Any-thing on the couch, and most of all, food. Here is the slice with preserves. Young raspberry unspoiled. They would be preserved. After a bad movie, she said, "That was not a rip-roaring good time, but the gladiator will live."

Now home, theirs, he said, "Hungry?"

"You cooked?"

"No," he said, "but I am very clever with a knife, preserves, and a piece of bread."

So they went to the kitchen. He told her to choose. A carrot.

Lettuce. Box of biscuits. Anything. He would give her anything. And once she had her toast and milk in the living room, washing dishes was a good tedium, round motions, elements on the hands. You could assimilate good patterns with the slip of sponge, circles. A vague citrus fruit scent rose up with the steam. Hot faucet water.

"If cozy is tiny in the code of realtors," she shouted from beyond the threshold, "what is 'shabby chic'?"

"How many screens do you have open?" There was an intimacy to shouting through doorways, trust. You believed your message would be delivered to the person you couldn't see, that they were there without verifying the body.

"Ruins, right?" Her voice. "Or this one: 'One bedroom with your *very own* bathroom.' Your very own! No need to find a public restroom in your own apartment!"

"Television, computer, phone. Am I right?"

"The more screens the fewer minutes. The more screens the fewer minutes. Repeat the mantra, Jeremy."

"I should think you could just click quicker."

"The connection is slow. The pictures lag for days," she said. "One and a half rooms. What is a half room? A closet?"

"Likely a cabinet."

"Windowsill, Jeremy."

"When there are windows, they say views."

"What about none?"

"Intimate. Private."

His phone vibrated, an organ exterior to his chest. He twisted knobs, grabbed towels.

Water finds water, said the message. The code to meet.

Jeremy knew trust was like murder. You couldn't do it halfway. He didn't trust Wright entirely anymore, and what, after all, did he know of Wright except they had been men who collected secrets from the side they intended to destroy?

Wright had buried himself in hypotheticals, guessed connections. He saw in systems, secrets. The St. Andrews agreement didn't mean the war was over. It meant Sinn Féin had its teeth sunk in the Police Service of Northern Ireland. Someone had followed him. If they knew about him, they knew Allsworth was Jordan. He could be right. His head or tails? A coin flip. And a coin flip, too, whether Wright had been only angry, desperate, desperately angry when he accused Jeremy, accused him, he couldn't quite make out, of what.

Alexandra came in with her china smeared red. He could smell her shampoo. Lilac or that other purple flower. Jeremy turned away from the faucet, sopped up. What was spilled could be recovered in civilian life. He needed the quiet bide. Evoke nature.

"Why didn't you invite Gavin to the wedding?" she said. "I never asked."

"Why would I?"

Alexandra leaned an elbow on the counter. "He was your best friend at Strategic."

She was speaking and he didn't look at her. His head was noisy. His face was red. Red as jam. Purple flower. Jammed.

"*I* was my best friend at Strategic," he said. "That's why you have a rich husband."

He did not want to believe that a single decision leaked out into forever. But a desperate Wright might act. A desperate

Wright would strike out before stricken. He must convey that they were of a side. Together.

"And a joke without humor is only an evasion."

Another vibration. Flick of metal: Precipitation north to south. The Gulf Stream warms the waters of the River Lagan.

And because somewhere deep and animal where it was fight or flight she preceded every thought, gesture, he hardened his face against collapse. "So is going to New York for a reunion that your classmates aren't attending."

"What are you saying?"

"I ran into Genevieve while you were in New York," he said, turning back, "or wherever you were."

Her face looked slapped. She sucked her cheeks in, released them. "She was in the School of Arts and Sciences. I was in the B-school. It wasn't her reunion. It was mine. Just like my time, Jeremy. Not yours. Mine."

The metal flutter in his breast pocket again. He turned. Forecast: continued showers followed by lightning. It's not a question, was the message.

"I'm *talking* to you. Shouldn't that take precedence over someone typing to you?" she said.

"You take precedence over everyone doing anything," he said. "Why haven't you got that in your head yet?"

CHAPTER 10

Jeremy paused by the entrance for a moment as his eyes adjusted to the depressed light of the interior. A man stood half in shadow toward the back of the room. He was working at something with a small, pointed knife and the pips of his whistling competed with a low ambient hum.

"Come to see the good doctor Boswell for a medicinal cocktail, have we?" came his voice.

Jeremy watched the man scalp an arc of skin off a great yellow orb. Boz busied himself with gestures structured around glass and tin. He passed a menu. "We have a special going," Boz said. "You buy, I pretend to fancy the company."

"Christ," Jeremy said.

"You don't believe in God," Boz said. "You probably only believe in economists."

"Categorically, no. Occasionally, yes."

"So what does that make you?"

Jeremy passed the menu back to Boz, pointed. "A misanthrope with a 401(k)."

With a quick flick of tins and ice, Boz poured a drink and slid it toward Jeremy. He held his hips, cocked his head. "Something wrong?"

"Why would you assume something's wrong?" Jeremy said.

"Because you're drinking at two on a weekday," Boz said. "And because you look like a popped piñata."

"Half three. What do I look like normally?"

Boz returned to slicing lemon rinds for martini twists. "Wary and waiting."

"You might know me better than anyone, Boz."

"How did you fuck up your life enough that a bartender knows you best?" Boz said. "A bartender who isn't fucking you, I might add."

It was a good question. It was a fine drink. "By having very little of myself to know."

PART FOUR: PARTITION

I adore a moat.—*Henry James,* The Portrait of a Lady

CHAPTER 1

Once, Lyle's sense was the internet was reorganizing the world. Third world cell phones connected to everywhere else, so where you stood needn't be where you were, virtually. Technology was only half of it. The ethos reached deeper. Pedestals were falling, boundaries drawn by nationalists. And most of all there was the thought that democracy means elites get the media they deserve.

But his undoing was swift. Maybe it was to be expected. Lyle's boss, Greenie, had always said there wasn't time for long stories on the internet; there was time to be first. Break before the others. Lyle had broken faster and faster, found the complacent hypocrites, gunned for traffic. Once a week, Greenie would gather them for editorial meetings and show them their rise and fall, so Lyle published the address of an internet troll sent by a tipster. He published hacked emails proving racial targeting by predatory lenders. He published screenshots of the *New Left* editor James Hausman's engagement of a male prostitute via an online classifieds page.

But it was this story that had made everyone who was and was not paid to think on the internet opine that his work was malicious and unnecessary. James Hausman was a good editor of important, progressive pieces. James Hausman had not been ready to come out, and people were calling Lyle Michaels worse than a reckless blogger; they called him a homophobe. Then there was the speculation that the hooker who'd provided Hausman with oral sex had been paid by conservatives. Maybe Lyle had. When nine months of unemployment checks had passed, he still hadn't found a job.

At times, his daughter, Marina, placated his anxiety, just looking at her. A scalp freckle that one day would go secret with hair. Sequin of nail. He had never felt the athlete impulse until he had first carried her outside, one defensive arm blocking the crush of city torsos. She fell asleep clutching a fist of T-shirt on his weekends, and for a while, he could forget to catch up to the person he had decided he ought to be as he held his daughter.

But lately, paper stating debts had begun arriving in the afternoons. Lyle could hear the postman's keys from the apartment as he stared at an endless log of horrible jobs. Chink of cheap metal, the clamp of shut doors. He dreaded envelopes. He got a second credit card, and then he was denied a third. He had to ask his father for money when Ingrid pressed for late child support. It was one of several humiliations.

Still, when he thought about it, which was not infrequent, he figured the worst of his termination was missing the financial collapse. Late 2008, he'd watched the web of stories grow on the internet. Lehman Brothers. Bear Stearns. The drama of subprime-backed CDOs. This was everyday terror: bogus credit ratings, profit on people who still believed in the American Dream.

In graduate school he had been meant to come to conclusions

about advances in the printing press or the television or the phone, something about the utopia of a connected world getting caught in de facto monopolies, that there were only two ways to be—powerful or fucked—and that every unchecked politician perpetuated the naturalization of capitalism. He'd left graduate school for journalism to peel back all the undifferentiated apathy, exposing corruption. He had wanted to knock the egos out of powerful men. Yet somehow what had happened was people who professionally defaced former child stars in Photoshop were telling the generational story he had been circling around most of his adult life. It only made him resent Greenie more. He obsessed over Noze bylines. And when his replacement, Saul Vaughn, published an investigative piece in a major legacy magazine about a Monsanto ghostwriter who'd placed articles in peer-reviewed science journals concluding their weed killer was not carcinogenic, absolute lies based on fabricated research, he called Bri Freeman, something jumpy inside.

"So he's got weed killer," she said. "There's a pesticide scandal for everyone out there."

"Actually," Lyle said, "there is not."

The line was dead a beat, then: "And that's disappointing to you."

It was, he supposed, the sort of condescension afforded someone preternaturally successful, a view from on high, where, once you'd deserved it, that position, you could see everything else as small, small-minded, petty considerations.

"How's my old pal Frank?" Bri Freeman asked finally.

"He says the Micellis always worked."

"And you say?"

"I say I'm an entitled white male, and I intend to preserve my energy for intellectual labor."

"Some people would say the thing about irony," Bri began.

"Some people would be all right with sustenance."

"But you."

"I'm not all right with being less than who I used to be on the way to becoming." He moved his phone to the other ear. Shift ears, shift what is heard. Shift something of the conversation.

"There's a woman in my department," Bri began.

"I wish *I* joined a department."

"No, you don't."

"No, I don't." He scratched his beard.

"But you know you always *could* come back, if you wanted," Bri said after a while. "Stand in front of a classroom, get chalk on your pants."

And because he did not know how to go back, he said, "I spill coffee on my shirt. Isn't that enough?" It was more bitter in the utterance than he'd anticipated.

"I'm asking," she said.

It seemed on Cathexis that everyone he knew was always doing something that occasioned wine and cheese, and he had begun to think the only way back, the only way out was a book, a book bigger than the internet, more important and lasting, a book that would make the think pieces look as small as they were. Not weed killer, but something else. Something other than not even reading the book on weed killer, not even the glowing review, but the title on a list of books notionally connected by quality that the list-maker probably hadn't read either. "It doesn't work like that. There's an order of operations."

"Since when is happiness math, Lyle?" Bri began.

"Since Jeremy Bentham," he said. Then he turned to the window. "What I took from studying history is you make certain decisions at certain moments, and they compound through time, and then that's your life. It's how you invent the weapon that ends the war. It's how you become the leader of the free world or are too late for victory."

"But sometimes it isn't too late."

"Sometimes it's too early," he sighed. "You die from diphtheria still."

CHAPTER 2

It was New York, and it was a starting over. It was, after all, the first home they had chosen together. Jeremy looked at the appliances with the factory gleam still in them, the walls that meant the guts of the place had been renovated, and everything was clean. They peeled plastic off furniture straight from the store, and he bought a machine to juice oranges silky, all the pith removed in the morning.

Alexandra had given him a sense of newborn adulthood, a second chance, or some other ordinal of luck. It was somewhere between her lying against him in the gentling night and the graphite dust coming off sharpened pencils, fresh notebooks with the pages still huddled tensely together and the streets with their sweet nut smell. It seemed to Jeremy that with his name on an attendance sheet and a fine, modest home he had wedged himself away from a country where men followed him. Even when the walls were thinner, they were thicker here, secure borders. They kept out. Returned at night, he closed the door and called her name, and he did not hold his breath.

He had, after all, held off Wright.

It was simple. He had wire transferred seventy-five thousand

dollars to Zurich to be rerouted to London. He had allocated
an additional ten thousand for procurement. There had been
a veil he operated under, careful language, neither affirmation
nor denial that he and Wright shared a hostile follower, neither
direction nor rejection of whatever means. Jeremy had reiterated
that weapons exports applications in Germany were maintained
confidential. He had reiterated that Heckler & Koch did not
make fair-weather friends. He had reiterated: on you, Ray. He
had reiterated what he gave was advice. He had reiterated, keep
this many miles away. My help means we cannot make contact a
long while. He had reiterated the silence drops off the trace. He
had reiterated in the covert channels that there would be no more
reiteration because that's how men like them were caught.

And so, in icebreaker exercises at social work school, he told
what he could, as he'd once told Alexandra. Edwinstowe. Robin
Hood. In classes, he raised his hand. He took notes. The authorities stood in the fronts of rooms. Here, there were supposed to be
no hiding experts. In twelve-point font, they honored the living
and the dead flamboyantly.

Cite your sources, the professors said.

It was a regular life. He made a friend at school named Robert,
who had a baby son he wore like a soft, knobby necklace on his
chest the days the wife was working at the hospital. Jeremy found
restaurants that served picturesque dishes, and after, when the
sky was dark, Alexandra wrapped her legs around him in an act
known as man and wife.

In the mornings, at his clinical internship, Jeremy sat with
people for whom life had become difficult trips to the bathroom.
Or else sometimes the people Jeremy spoke to were in trouble

at school or in trouble with drugs. And he didn't mind the new listening. He took in the volumes of sheer narration and tried to make less of a story of it. You could fit an individual into a service, name a disease. Reduce. Quiet the noise. It is not you. It is a pattern we call a mood disorder. We would like to recommend dialectical behavior therapy. It is a therapy to skim the habit of drama from the top of your life.

"The fuck accent is that?" a client asked.

But Jeremy found himself soothed by his own words. In the utterance, he became; he was convinced by the script.

CHAPTER 3

A book idea: write about the explosion of a Bayer pesticide plant in Institute, West Virginia. Put it to the page, and you could see the failed promise of safety everywhere. People worried about crop contamination had driven demand for pesticides, but the plant played fast and loose on manufacturing the chemicals. A tank burst. Two died. And the corporation went on. It was still associated with aspirin, healthy bodies. Consumers trusted the brand logo with the heart and familiar font, even though the betrayals traced back to the mid-eighties. What you saw if you remembered 1985, though, was a toxic cloud over Institute. This was man-made. And a year before, the company's Indian site had been scene to the worst industrial disaster in history. Five hundred thousand people exposed to the very same toxic compound, methyl isocyanate. The cycles of toxic clouds hung over towns little more than plants with dorms, but the reliable Republican voters continue to say the company puts dinner on the table, even when they are coughing up the company's transnational fumes.

But another idea: information is only cheap when it isn't expensive. Reporting costs are not the sort of thing Frank Michaels will write checks for. Lyle could not afford to tell this story.

CHAPTER 4

The stories from Washington were the stories from Iran or Afghanistan, and they were in their living room, and these days, she told him she felt as though she was always behind, even when she'd arrived. Alexandra was haggarded by stories. She told the stories of vegetable juices and pens that didn't drag ink; goal: accrue in them the aura of hitting Cathexis Milestones. It was a time when that mattered, hitting Milestones.

And didn't he know it?

Jeremy had thought he would be appeased by marriage, but happiness was like drugs. Once you had it, you wanted more and more. He drew a knot tight and pictured a family beyond two, a house thickening with people who were theirs.

And so, as she unfolded aluminum takeout containers, he was making the geographical case. A small campaign of information. Latitude, longitude. He said, "There is that Montessori school a few blocks away. It's very creative. They don't treat the children like ticking time bombs of failure. There is painting and movement class."

She raised an eyebrow. "Why don't you get a puppy?"

"Naturally, I would train the child to pee outside," he said, "and sit and heel and fetch."

"And what is your stance on leashes?"

She dolloped food, handed him a plate. From the other room, he could hear someone who thought his career into perpetuity was the first priority of public service. Jeremy held the plate with both hands. "We can't get a puppy. So-So and Jill would not consent."

"So we must have a baby for old cats' sake," she said, and she was smiling.

They went to the living room and turned off the television. He wanted them to love someone together, not the compromised love of children to parents but parents to a child. Their love would expand into time, a child persisting when they were gone. She would have in a jewel box the ring that Jeremy had given Alexandra the day they made promises into infinity. He looked at her lips now, careful on the fork, closing. Out loud, the logic he gave was the spices they were eating had come from around the world, the recipe had survived history, so what would be so crazy about a child?

"You don't even *like* family," she said, and he could not determine if the tone was joking. "You barely speak with yours."

"I like family. I don't like *my* family," he said. "Yet."

CHAPTER 5

Not yet, Shel had decided. Not in person. But he taught Alexandra a way to speak that was supposed to remain hidden, encrypted technology, and she was sure that what he told her of himself meant something, or that he did. And when she thought of what would happen if he was too preoccupied to notice an oncoming car or overdosed, if he raged too openly to the wrong person, it comforted her to think of her brother the way he described himself at a time she didn't know him.

The narrative she thought of most was how he came to computers. He'd won an old Apple II in a poker game, and he hadn't then known how to use it. But one night, he brought a girl home from a party. "I used to love that," the girl said, drowsily running her hand over the monitor. "The turtle graphics."

And so, he watched her type, how the keystrokes made a circle of white stars appear as though drawn with a thick white marker on the screen, graffiti produced by buttons. The material was only the stuff of regular traffic signs and candy wrappers, letters made mobile and reshaped, ordered in rows across a screen. But he had never seen such small gestures transform anything. Taps. Strokes. "Show me slower," he had said.

The girl did not carry into his life after that evening, but sometimes when he was home and there was no one in the night, there was something mesmerizing about that wreath of stars. He'd light up and watch the stellar run forming a zero. Already then the computer had been surpassed, but it still had seemed like the future when the loop lit on the screen, and he had wanted to describe more perfect circles.

They shared that, Alexandra thought, refulgence fat in her chest. They were people who wanted to transform.

CHAPTER 6

To become a family, their hands filled blanks. There were the numbers that identified them and the numbers in their accounts, names and dates and copies of documents, the requirements for which were meant to weed out unfit people. As she leaned over the counter, her pen rapid, Jeremy poured a sleeve of chocolate biscuits onto a plate and something fizzy in a glass. That they were applying for a child imbued actions with the future; one day, he would prepare a snack for his daughter like this, he believed, the motion in his mind now straddling time.

Alexandra was a natural at applying. Lists came from her hands. She gave recitations of rules, organizations. And because their credentials for the future were the most presentable parts of their lives, she reminisced pragmatically. She made calls. You knew us when.

Scant was the need, he was sure, to worry about his past. There was a network of references pointing to a life in the open. Stamps, passports, degrees. The institutions believed in language. There was a good deal of faith in testimonial. Words would be delivered on behalf of them by Genevieve and Alexandra's coworkers and Robert. And to Jeremy, their home clarified with every stratum of narration, time reorganized to reveal imminent roles, as though they were inevitable. He could believe that the lousy luck of Ireland could be held off, that some skin had grown over the liquid spread of history, containing it in the past.

He returned to the living room and touched Alexandra's hair. He watched her mouth, soft on a cookie, and her hand, small and tense with precision. There were freckles only on one cheek, inexplicable as love.

CHAPTER 7

In her work, she could distill the senses therapists worried about, clean pathos, make it useful. Something that wasn't an emotion, a directed stream, charged through her body and, blinkered, she saw only what must be done. It was a reliable need. She must convince.

Post-celebrity was the word she used when she walked into meetings. She had a handheld controller, and when she pressed a button an *X* appeared over stars endorsing sports drinks. She talked about the hunger of real people for real people. In better-looking people, consumers could see themselves. She said, dirt under the fingernails. She said, everyone has a story.

They are telling them.

It is time for ads to imitate life.

She shone Cathexis profiles through a projector. Look at the success of just-like-us, models in their frumpy PJs. There is a pleasure to seeing images of myself—but. As though recognized by the screen.

We are post-critic, take back the ratings, consumer-driven relevance come in thumbs north and south.

What does your neighbor have?

We call this democracy.

Let's look at the Oscars. Based on a true story. Memoirs. This spike is personal essays. We see unfavorables on the media.

But in blogs we trust.

The woman who slept with her biological father. Those metrics nearly took down the server.

Who are you? is the only question. They are saying, I am here. My voice matters.

We are seeing unfavorables on "the system."

They are airing laundry. Having a lifestyle is a lifestyle. They are skeptical of what isn't ironic.

Who are you to tell me?

We have an ethos. Unfiltered stories. These markets are amenable to narrative. They are desirous of life.

They are afraid of being tricked, but they are more afraid of missing out. We are seeing the possibilities of bottomless stories.

Chekhov said the gun hung over the mantle must go off.

And of course, she thought, standing in that loveless office room, their daughter would come, and then she and Jeremy would be comprehensively a happy story. Her daughter would not feel that family in her life always tended to fall away into silence and disappearance. She would not worry that she could not persuade into being intimacy that persisted. They would give the girl beautiful picture books and bears, nighttime tuck-ins and advice, and their daughter would always know she belonged.

CHAPTER 8

Because he no longer belonged to an organization, in the long, empty days he accumulated notebooks full of hearsay, collected situations. Lyle had a sense of time spreading out, looked for how whispered hunches became history. There were index cards limning city councilmen, things he heard in bars, on buses. Rumors jotted. On the wall, a city map stabbed with colored pushpins marked unsolved crimes, meeting places. He knew his precincts, seedy bars. He memorized the names of people too successful to be innocent.

Still, fists of crumpled paper accumulated by the waste bin. There were leads gone nowhere, notes that never added up. Words went uncorroborated. Situations didn't become stories. The sweep of big ideas furnished him with hope, but he couldn't make the granules build an arc. He abided rejection, exhausted more index cards. A headache formed from the construction below, a new bar being drilled and hammered where once was a pawn shop. He pushed at his temples, couldn't think.

Except of course, without the constraints of a workday, he was thinking quite a bit. He was thinking of things he hadn't had time to think of for some time. He thought, for example, of Ingrid, how when he'd met her over the dollar bin at the thrift store, her eyes were angry, which he had taken to mean intelligent. They had gone to a filthy place around the corner where half the jukebox songs wouldn't play. They'd discovered they worried about child labor. They worried about the strife in countries other people forgot about. They knew other people forgot about everything that mattered. Death was new then to her, or rather to her father, and on her behalf he was angry that the insurance company had denied exactly who needed treatment, her father, the coverage he needed to live. As she kissed him, the Polaroid around her neck had hit his chest. Even through closed eyes, he could sense the white flash of light like how people described near-death.

"Cheese," he'd said.

And she had said, "Or love."

When, later, she'd asked for the annulment, she'd said that the marriage was an accident of grief, and he did not say that it wasn't to him. He'd said he was, at least, good for something. Good riddance.

But there were other worries now.

And so, on his phone, Lyle looked at pictures of family and ex-girlfriends, former colleagues and people he'd met once at prestigious parties. To thumb through beautiful acquaintances on Cathexis, to see the sheer regularity of them, made him angry enough not to break down, sink.

Alexandra Chen, he noticed, stayed light in posts. He thought of how women like her were never disappointed. Success came to them like oxygen.

He could see it in the sheer volume of validation visible on her profile.

CHAPTER 9

A red dot was someone approving of some limb of her life on Cathexis, but Alexandra did not answer her phone. She was searching so this time she would not fail him.

Once, she'd predilected secrets. The way they protected you from yourself, your own shame. Or sometimes just the contained thrill that carried through the day, all that tabloid inside. But now there was diagnosis. There was typing Shel's symptoms. There was checking results. There was seeing the overlap, the match, and there was seeing the names explode out into more websites, dissenting opinions. She moved through variations of the body. She was, for her brother, finding an illness with a cure.

Stress or depression was always the least dangerous. Or the most. She wanted to differentiate in language, zip up a disease, because if a formless wrong broad as time crushed her very small, a rattled little thing with an overheating phone, it stood to reason the certainty of a name would invert it, would give her something to stand on.

Alexandra thought of their last conversation. She'd asked him if he needed money, and he'd laughed, continued with his inexplicable speech. He'd told her people ardent for numbers sometimes needed to be reminded that zero had to be invented. But zero was intractable. Logic slipped off its rounded form. Its multiplication of another digit diminished the value, yet it adhered to each. It was a clingy void once feared by the West. Boethius concluded evil was nothingness, but that was before A-bombs, weaponized planes. Shel said he refused to make the mistakes of his hemisphere. It was the East that saw zero's value, the cipher bridge between debt and plenty. Muslim conquerors carried the uncountable to the West from India, where the word then was *sunya*, empty. And now, Shel said, he'd found a way to teach America to fear the nobodies, to take inventory of the void, so in all the numbers they cleaned and crunched, the bytes of data grown tera, they would not seek to find the nothing yet in everything. He would hold ransom all their irreproachable numbers. Shel had laughed again then. No, he did not need her fucking money. He had sounded insane.

She turned off her phone and shifted into the living room. Jeremy sat on the couch with a textbook, his neck both bent and stretched. It was a reassuring shape, his. She kneeled nearby, seconds swelling with silence until he looked at her.

She spoke symptoms, let the container of a few syllables close around the weedy tangle of what Shel had done, said he had. She enumerated what was factual as though hypothetical. She spoke about Shel without saying his name, and she was not sorry.

She became impatient. Jeremy was explaining the difference between a prodrome and a regular symptom. A prodrome was a precursor symptom before an acute onset of an illness, but sometimes what looked like a prodrome was only a precursor to a healthy life. You would find that it was an aberrant event, he said. He said and he said and he said.

"And what do you do if someone you know has it?" she said, when finally he ventured an illness.

"Stay far, far away." Jeremy winked.

He returned to reading, and she closed her laptop. She crossed the room and slung one buttock over the arm of the couch, so that her left foot touched his. "You wouldn't do that."

"Once," he said, laying down his book, "I had a friend like that. He was very dear to me, and then he wasn't. This man clamped on to anything he didn't know and saw murder in it. And there were many things he didn't know. So no more, I decided."

"But what if this person was lodged deep in your life?"

He looked over his reading glasses. "Then I would have gotten rid of every part of my life he was in until he was eradicated."

"What if it was most of your life?"

"Then I'd have started over," he said. And when she didn't say anything, he put his eyes back behind his reading glasses.

She remembered now a story he'd told her once about his first merger arbitrage deal. Rumors had made their way to him that Vodafone, the British mobile company, would make an unsolicited bid on the German mobile company Mannesmann. Mannesmann's chairman might play angry at first, might even *be* angry. But he'd know it was accept the offer from the English raiders or suffer total stock carnage. Jeremy's job had been simple: Push to take a fifty-million-pound position long on Mannesmann and short Vodafone. Work the spread. Prepare for windfall. He had told her this, and she'd thought it meant he was a man who understood what must be done. But now it seemed callous.

She went to their room and turned on Stravinsky. As a college student, Alexandra had thought this was what collected people did to mollify their nerves: lie in bed listening to classical music. She had not known the hopped-up urgency of Stravinsky, the near doom. People who'd grown up with violin lessons told her it was strange, and still she listened, still to her it was not doom but imminence, and it was the sound she turned to when she needed to brace up whoever she was to be strong as she ought to be. There was something very true and beautiful to it that Stravinsky, this dead man who'd never known her, could fix a clear note of anticipation to her life, and if that was possible, of course it was possible, too, that she could bring Shel to haven.

CHAPTER 10

As she packed, it was difficult to differentiate whose was whose, though the chargers were not precisely the same. One charger had been lost. One was in her hand.

"It could just be ours now," Jeremy said.

"I do not want to be one of those women who can only talk about a weekend by beginning 'We,'" Alexandra said.

Jeremy took her in his arms. "I wouldn't dream of calling it anything but your weekend," he said. "But I want you to be able to call. Take it."

"You are giving me what might already be mine because of what *you* would want, so we don't need to discuss whether *you* lost *your* charger."

"Yes," Jeremy said. "That's empathy."

"No, it's not," she said. "Let's not fight before I leave. Don't go to bed angry, or on an airplane, right?"

"Then I guess you can't leave." He smiled. "Or maybe I need to come with you, strictly to continue the conversation, of course."

"You mean the fight."

"A square is a type of rectangle," Jeremy said. Then: "You will call me if you need anything."

She turned from him. "I won't need anything."

"Except for better plane food," he said.

She conceded to homemade frittata before the flight. There were fresh-cut flowers arranged between them, white and short blooms, plush almost to the touch. For her, he knifed a mango so that it resembled a dome covered in an armor of golden cubed fruit flesh.

"Oh, Jeremy," she said, like it was an emotion.

"You like it?" he said.

"Where did you learn to do that with a mango?"

"It's called the hedgehog technique."

"This table would make a very good advertisement for marriage."

"You're the expert," Jeremy said.

"I know you don't mean on marriage, Jeremy."

"And hard on yourself."

"And late. Kiss me like you like me."

"But I love you," he said, bringing her face to him.

He leaned back and held her shoulders between his hands. He angled his face down to see hers in the shadow.

"You're nervous," Jeremy said.

A twist of lip. A shrug. "It is an important presentation."

She left, and he dawdled with his books. From a bowl on the counter, Jeremy took his keys. And then he saw it: Alexandra had forgotten her briefcase by the door. And he felt odd, baffled. He went for a walk, and as he thought of all the possible things that could be out of place, maybe it was an impulse— he took out his other phone.

To Wright: Shop much in Germany?

Response: Good value.

To Wright: Seen that friend in London around?

Response: I don't kiss and tell.

To Wright: Didn't think the romance was that serious.

Response: Only three wee visits.

Jeremy replaced the phone in his bag. It was not supposed to have gone that far, if he was correct in his reading of Wright's text.

CHAPTER 11

Someone he'd not thought of in some time: his other informer, Pearse Campbell.

"I'm not here because I want to be," he had said the first time they met. "And I'll tell you as much."

"No, you're here because you solicited underage prostitutes."

"They were covert British operators and you know it. We both do," Campbell had said.

Jeremy had looked straight out through the windshield at the fading lines in the cement. "We'll protect you," he said. "Not because we want to, but because we're covert British operators." He did not want to be anyone's friend. But his demeanor did not help, and Pearse pled ignorance to every question. "Then what the hell do you know except how to go on a pull for little boys?" Jeremy said.

"I know that bombs sometimes end up in funny places, Allsworth," Campbell said. "I know that sometimes even handlers aren't jammie. They are on their way to meet an informer and they end up in five hundred little pieces of bacon. Fancy pigs, but still crispy."

Jeremy had told Wilmington about the meeting, and the next

week Campbell was found shot in the stomach. The man who had since been given the name Wright had been irritated by the investigation into Campbell's death, had said, "Quite a lot of water to boil over news that disappoints no one."

CHAPTER 12

It was a period of offensive suggestions. He'd received, for example, a lead on a pharmaceutical company copywriting job from Alexandra Chen that was so ludicrously outside his ethical standards that he would not reply. Was this how far he'd fallen, he wondered, that his own acquaintances imagined him part of the psychopharma hegemony? It was not something he wished to ponder.

Instead, in the corners of the apartment, Lyle inserted sticky traps and waited for a sighting of bedbugs. There were bites, itches all along his body. He'd think he felt them on his skin, check, and the only time he saw them was when they were disappearing into a crevice. He began to house his clothes in trash bags. He searched for the entry points, cracks in the wall, holes. He could see a way in everywhere, so many testaments to the insecurity of his home.

Lyle began to knock on doors. He asked neighbors if they'd bought used furniture, traveled. He asked about their guests and where they'd been.

"Ever thought it was *you* they came from?" the man next door said. This was the second offensive suggestion.

But the third, the third had come from an unexpected source. It had come from Bri Freeman.

Sledgehammer was one name. There was documented evidence. A plan for two: two mosques. Two explosions. We are talking both ends. Assassinate Jews. Assassinate Christians. Erdogan and his people would blame the shooting down of the Turkish plane on Greece. They would point to Gülen behind the conspiracy, if it could be called a conspiracy at all.

"This so-called coup is going to so-called trial," Bri had said. "It's getting almost no coverage. This is your book, Lyle."

He ran a glass of water out of the sink. He drank it, and somehow the water was white before it was clear.

"There are echoes of 2007," she had continued. "What a lot of locals are saying is it's a fake plot. Get critics out."

On his knees, he plucked white cards inscribed with story ideas from the floor. He fluttered dust off each. Bar fight. Raised rent. "You know I won't get a US publisher interested in that," he said. "Too expensive to report. Too expected. They expect that part of the world to be a shitshow."

"This is classic authoritarian optical illusion. They will say they must protect the regime from the radicals. It could happen here."

"To Americans coups happen elsewhere," he said. "We expect moderate politics, liberal Republicans, conservative Democrats. You know that."

"If we can believe terrorists are radicalized online," she said.

"This isn't my book."

"It is. It's good, Lyle."

"So why don't you write it then?"

"I'm working on a project already. Historical contextualization of Western websites outsourcing comment moderation. I'm busy. I have students. I have a mortgage."

"But I have the time to tell your leftovers."

A blur in the corner of his eye was probably a bedbug. He stood too late, knelt back down. He was on his knees, and he was tired but twitchy. The tingle on his forearm. Ankle.

"Do you need a loan?" she said. "Just to get the reporting started?"

"Jesus, Bri. I don't need anyone to take care of me, least of all you."

"Isn't that what your dad's doing?" she said. "That is not a provocation, by the way."

And he had, because he knew she intended to help, done the counting thing in his head. He counted down and before he responded imagined taking off, that he could depart himself.

CHAPTER 13

At Dulles International Airport, she waited in line for a taxi. A car stopped, and she gave the name of a big building. Alexandra brought her fingers to letters, made half-witness of Jeremy from afar.

The Eagle has landed, she typed. Or the pigeon, anyway.

His response was quick. Catch the worm.

Now arrived, she peered around. It was a bare place inside, black walls and bluish coil bulbs, a leather couch belching stuffing from one seam of the upholstery. Glossy magazines with smiling dogs on the covers fanned over the coffee table, a glass and brass thing with no fingerprints showing. Spelled out on the bottom of the ashtray: THANK YOU FOR NOT SMOKING. It did not look like the home of someone who'd irrevocably lost his mind.

Shel took her phone battery to a corner, where a small locker opened when he pressed a finger to a small square of glass. She looked for a place in the room to fit herself, hung on to cursory gestures: the closing of the locker door, return to the folding chair. He reached for a box, lit a cigarette with a contained blue flame, and leaned back.

"I have penetrated atmospheres of acronyms, Lex," he said,

ashing. "Learn the layers of bureaucracy, and the design's brilliance is its inefficiency. You crowd the truth, make the grain disappear in the shore."

"Acronyms?"

He did not seem to hear her.

But she had telephoned a lovely place, where on the way out people functioned. She would tell him there was an outside, green expanse, tulips. The pictures: they were mansions set atop their own fields, lawns anyway, and there were, according to the website, hours for sporting. The testimonials spoke to newly unbroken people. They said, we got him back. And she wanted to get him back before her daughter came, so her daughter would always know her uncle as he really was.

"They say you build the formula for what can be found," Shel said, "you are better than five thousand boots on the ground. The agencies are afraid. They are looking at Nine-Eleven, Seven-Seven, and they are willing to believe in automated fortune-tellers, big bang event auguring."

Looking at him. Listening. She did not know how to start.

"You wouldn't believe the stuff being developed. I'm talking programs that can ID you by the rhythm and force of your typing. Facial recognition. Software matching social security numbers to gait. Can an algorithm know? Can we program peace? The dork warriors say yes and yes and yes. They say they need geo-location. What they mean is, they need to divine where to kill. They gain legal okays to seize our data, comb our Cathexes, all in the name of saving American lives. Just halt terror picking up on the ether, same as advertisers targeting customers."

"Cheers, Lex," he said without waiting for their glasses to meet.

She had practiced how to settle her face. She settled it.

Because fact: Shel as a boy could trick you into believing the sky rained flowers just for you, just for a minute, just by leaning out a second-story window and dropping clipped blooms.

Because fact: Shel had practiced snow angels, in the dirt.

Because fact: when once a purpling woman shook Alexandra in a shop, she did not have to confess the strawberry pops she stole; Shel yanked the shoulder strap of the woman's purse and when she turned, Alexandra ran the whole way home, and they watched TV on the couch at home, breathless with what they wouldn't tell their mother.

Because also a fact: in sum, the facts meant. Reality did, and the professionals at the lovely places with visiting hours would help him remember that.

But now, Shel was talking about a National Security Council vet named Barry Cain who'd wanted meteorology for spectacular bloodshed. Cain had hired a young guy named Sean McCreight who'd invented for casinos a program that culled the connections of criminal ecosystems using Relationship Assessment Prediction Engineering. Shortly after McCreight signed on to develop a program for counterterrorist use at DARPA, word of some other questionable efforts under the newly named Comprehensive Risk Assessment Program was leaked outside the Senate Intelligence Committee. There were some very unhappy Democrats, and some very embarrassed Republicans. So it was a bipartisan maneuver: get Cain out. The committee members knew how to reach across the aisle when there was someone to run off a cliff.

But from the first it was clear the risk assessment program wouldn't disappear with Cain. There was ugly intel on legislators, and there were an idealistic few senators who still imputed safety to analytics. They made calls, revised language. They figured every knot can loosen to a loophole. When it got to appropriations time, the project moved over to the NSA from DARPA, assuming the project alias Glen Close, a reminder of the valley of death always proximal, the valley of death they must close. The legislators had not destroyed it; they'd sent it under the auspices of classified projects, a place safe from journalists and political repercussions, a place with black protections. Now Glen Close was operating with almost no oversight.

"That's why you're here. That's why I asked you to meet," Shel said. "That's why I came to you in London."

Alexandra lifted her gaze. "What do you mean?"

"Why I wanted to see you," he said, a hand on her shoulder.

It was like being folded between space. Warm air pressed all around her. It made it difficult to think, and when she looked at Shel, his features were strangely pointed, as though all the bones in his face had risen. "I don't understand," she said.

"Because," Shel said. "Sean McCreight is Shel Chen. Sean McCreight is me, and I've left the agency."

"Shel," she said. "We're going to get you help."

CHAPTER 14

Alexandra had not yet made it from the airport to Murray Hill, where Robert and his wife, Cassandra, lived. Jeremy took the stairs two at a time, the smell of family dinners in the hallway, and at the door to the apartment held a bottle of wine in the style of demonstration. "You made it," Cassandra said, wiping her hands on her pants to accept the bottle. "What's cooking?"

"Take this. It's an old family recipe. Toss the grapes in a crock, get your feet going with fifty others, and then it is a piece of cake."

"Robert never told me you came from vineyard stock."

"Every man needs his secrets," Jeremy said. "Do you drink red?"

"I drink whatever color's in front of me."

"My good-time gal," Robert said, come from a deeper room and holding his wife's waist from the side so that their hips touched.

"It's bad luck standing in a doorway," Cassandra said, "The devil takes in the indecisive."

"And what's more, there's cheese inside," Robert said.

In the apartment, they leaned in various positions in the

kitchen as the wine was poured, then moved into the living room, chewing on slices of Manchego. There was public broadcasting television playing, and the screen shunted between pictures of men in fatigues and men praying, tanks and regional maps and close-up shots of people with blurred-out faces.

Robert lit a joint, closed his eyes, blew out. He leaned back on the couch.

"PTSD treatment," he said, stretching the joint toward Jeremy. "It doesn't count."

Jeremy waved him off. "What's the trauma today?"

Robert moved his laptop to show Jeremy a video, grainy and cast in green light. There was a cloth bag atop a torso. Then there wasn't. A beheading.

"But why did you click?"

"It was everywhere on Cathexis. I was positively *surrounded*. Terrorism was all anyone was Cathecting in today."

"I wouldn't know," Jeremy said. "I don't participate in the twenty-first century."

"You don't feel like you're missing out?"

"I don't."

"But if you don't Cathect, it's like you don't even exist. You miss invitations."

"I don't know about that, Robert," Cassandra said. "I happen to see two eyes and a nose myself."

"And you invited me *here*," Jeremy said. "What more could I want?"

The boy could be heard on the baby monitor. Robert went for Wally in another room, returned with the child held over his chest. He was humming a song.

"It's a good thing you're not single," Robert said. He pressed his mouth to his son's stomach, kissed it. "These days, I don't know a woman who trusts a man who doesn't Cathect."

"It *is* a good thing I'm not single," Jeremy said.

"You're like my sister, Marissa," Robert said.

"Sensible? A smart dresser?"

Robert reached Wally overhead. A laugh. "She thinks it's undignified to emote online."

"Meanwhile," Cassandra said emphatically.

"Meanwhile, she's a test subject for an experiment on virtual reality treatment for PTSD and claims the algorithm is a better listener than humans."

"Of course, what kind of person isn't ashamed to talk to a computer, if you ask me," Cassandra said.

"Maybe it works," Jeremy said.

Cassandra cleared her throat, put her hands out in the manner of halting traffic. "Marissa's wonderful. Don't get me wrong. Wonderful mother. Wonderful kids. But she is too much once in a while, and that's all, folks."

"I have nothing to hide," Robert said. "I don't *want* to hide. I want my boy to grow up knowing it's fine for men to express feelings. That it's good to. That good men do."

"And that's marvelous you do," Jeremy said. "Better you than I."

A few minutes later, Alexandra arrived in a sleek black suit with small gold knobs in her ears. Cassandra's face bunched up with friendliness. Wally was crying, and she was bending her knees rhythmically in soothe as Robert poured another glass of wine.

"Cuh-yute shirt," Cassandra said.

Alexandra emitted a startled "Oh." Her eyebrows quirked, and she seemed to search a moment. "Cute phone?" she said. Her face was turned to the baby, and it looked to Jeremy like a falling building.

CHAPTER 15

He did not quite know why today was different from any other, sadder, but he knew her palate, and so they walked until ice cream. Under glass, the swirled peaks were pink and white and brown. Jeremy and Alexandra took large pleated paper thimbles, and in the night air, when she was done with her little cup and her little spoon, Alexandra began looking at her phone, walking blindly again.

"Tonight stars Chang and Eng, you and your mobile. Who are these people interrupting us, and why is everything they say urgent?"

"It isn't," she said. "But the machine makes me compliant with communication. It isn't my fault."

Jeremy disposed of the ruined paper. He looked at his wife, standing away from the waste bin on her phone. She was taking it hard, the wait for the child. Their whole lives it seemed the waiting had run, and maybe it had, but he wanted to make his own hope spill onto her, and he didn't know how.

"Berkowitz had the demon dog Harvey. You will say, 'The phone made me do it,'" he teased.

Alexandra thumbed on, silent and busy in the eyes.

"They're so happy now," Jeremy said. "Robert and Cassandra."

"Of course they are. They're reaping the benefits of social currency," Alexandra said.

"Robert says the baby has a party trick. They say 'the media' and rub the baby's belly until it farts. It works for 'bureaucrats' too. A joker already. A critic."

"Now everything that passes gas is a critic?" Alexandra said. "It's an intentional fallacy."

Jeremy put his arm around her. She let him for a half block, maybe more. He was her eyes while she attended to her phone, let out all the discourse in her fingers. There was a ring around the moon indicating the presence of ice crystals, refraction, tiny mirrors glowing circumference into the sky. He wondered what she was typing, but he did not look at her hands.

He decided to make a joke. He said, finally, "Everyone who passes gas *is* a critic."

"Only on Cathexis. Cathexis doesn't afford neutrality."

"I wouldn't know anything about that," Jeremy said. "They're only proud."

"Social currency."

"Or love," said Jeremy.

"Because who hates parents?"

Jeremy shrugged. "Their children sometimes."

"Or their friends."

"Our daughter will come," he said. "We'll be so happy. Look at Robert and Cassandra."

"We aren't Robert and Cassandra."

"We are far better-looking," Jeremy said, "and less religious."

"Our daughter," she said, losing track of the sentence. Maybe testing the words.

PART FIVE: OR QUOTITION

I'm Nobody! Who are you?

Are you – Nobody – too?

Then there's a pair of us!

Don't tell! they'd advertise – you know!

How dreary – to be – Somebody!

How public – like a Frog –

—*Emily Dickinson*

CHAPTER 1

Tyrell was supposed to call his mother if he was going to be late, but the boys were crowded up on the corner with their breaths clumping in a huddle, and he was calling bullshit on triple-doubles. The game was this weekend, and he was looking to push clarity. His, theirs. Derek had his headphones swung around the back of his neck and his hands in his pockets, and Omar was popping his hands low to the pavement, a torso pumped in and out of the circle, step back, set, shoot, score.

"Like that," Omar said. "Right off the glass but easy."

"Look like an elf."

"Elves's tall though."

Derek sucked his teeth, crossed his arms. He squinted at Omar. "How would you know? You been to fantasyland or whatever?"

"Because I saw the movie," Derek said, "and elves's lanky."

"Lanky and short."

"No such *thing*, Omar."

Tyrell was waiting for the pause, opening. But the talk showed no seams. His own concept shook in his stomach, and he was edgy and he needed to say what needed to be said before it was time he was expected home. Ever since they'd left school, Derek and Omar were saying triple-double, triple-double, it was always triple-double on a guy. But Tyrell had thought about this. There were better ways to do the numbers.

"Point's nobody better in the paint, D."

"What *I'm* saying is why is that *your* stat when assists are half on your boy?" Tyrell said.

"Paint's small and the court is long. And elves are tall with bows."

Tyrell hit a fist into his other palm. It had started as vengeance. He wanted to demote Jason Kidd in history. Tyrell hated his face. But it was bigger than that too, the whole system of it. "Which is like okay, so how about we think about sometimes you pass a ball and someone's butterfingers meltdown change *your* stats."

"Okay, Tank Top," Derek said.

"Because the number isn't yours. It's never just yours," Tyrell said.

"We heard, okay."

Derek made a long imaginary shot. "I'm saying, all I want to see from him is some shooting from downtown."

"Why are you changing the subject?" Tyrell said. "It's wrong. One hundred percent, all the way, twenty-four-seven wrong."

"You don't even play, Tank Top."

"I know math."

"You heard? He knows math," Derek said. "Little tank top bitch."

"What I'm saying."

"How about stop saying, Tyrell. Just stop."

"Boys."

They looked up. Mr. Abiola. A tall man, all right for a teacher and on the younger side. "All right over here?"

"All right, all right," Derek said.

"Tyrell?"

"All right," he said.

"You need a ride?"

"I'm good," Tyrell said.

"You two?"

They got in the car fast. The car shuddered and pulled off, and when it had turned the corner, Tyrell began to walk home. He thought about Kobe, and he thought about LeBron. He thought about how you could come up with a whole different set of numbers that was smarter. He was thinking about how he'd vote in any system to downgrade Jason Kidd.

He got the key out, and when he'd gotten upstairs, he got the other key out. He had a mnemonic like for planets in school. Triangle for home as in the building. Circle for home home. And when he turned the key for home home, he could smell the night-before's stew still.

At the kitchen table, his grandma was talking about all the excuses she wouldn't make if her younger daughter were murdered. She was saying all the warnings she was going to repeat. She was saying how she'd tell how many times she told her younger daughter not to do it and wouldn't cry.

"Everybody does it online now," his aunt Rhonda was saying.

"Maybe *this* century." Grandma raised her eyebrows. "When I was young, people met waiting around like staring dopes, just hanging around a spot looking at everyone who came in, in case someone special happened to them."

"Oh, okay now. Touché, ma." His aunt turned to Tyrell. "She's competitive with history, you know? Always it's she's got more history. I give her that, I do. Credit where credit's due. I'm about to make a sandwich. You eating a sandwich, Tyrell?"

He shrugged.

"You don't even like sandwiches anymore?" Grandma said.

His mother came in the kitchen with her scrubs still on, wiping her hands from the bathroom and her head the degrees to one side that said sarcasm. "He's still upset about the overnight."

"Am not."

"Are too. But I'm saying what kind of man wants to spend a night at the pool with a bunch of boys."

Grandma was shaking her head and pressing a pink fake nail on his aunt Rhonda. His mother put her hands on his shoulders, kissed his cheek. In the mornings, he could smell her shampoo even if she'd gone to work already. Sweet like fruit out of a bottle.

"It's unnatural is what," his mother said.

"But every day you hear."

"Mr. Abiola's okay," Tyrell said.

"Wasn't born yesterday," his mother said.

"When you were a girl, I didn't care uncle, cousin, grandfather. Could be anyone."

His aunt was blowing her nails. She was shaking her head and blowing.

"A grown man in a locker room overnight with boys in their shorts."

"I'm hungry," his aunt Rhonda said.

"Every day it's another story you hear on Channel One."

His mother filled up her mouth with a mean little voice. "*Mentor. Community.* Not my boy."

She was still leaning over him with her shampoo smell and her scrubs. Her earring was blinding gold, and sticky stuff was on his face where she'd kissed him. A too-sweet scent. Vanilla.

"*Just looking out,*" his mother said, still in her impression voice. "Please. Just please." And he didn't know why, but he yanked hard on her earring. It was just an energy in his hand, like someone lit up a lightbulb. He grabbed fast and pulled down, and it was quick relief right like taking a leak after holding it three school periods.

But then her voice changed again, and it was saying his name like a tragic question. His grandmother was talking to Jesus, and when he looked up, his aunt was holding his mother's head.

"Why don't you know how to act?" she said.

CHAPTER 2

It was nothing anybody could see on his body, but knowledge improved Lyle's blood flow. How it happened, the story—his— had been nearly like the Noze days. Lyle had received a letter with a phone number. An anonymous tip. He had been curious enough to use it. Just see. And what came back was something more important than anything Lyle had been a part of in a long time.

On the phone, they talked about agencies. They talked about terror. They talked about why the man whose tip it was had chosen Lyle: the suppressions and delays of legacy media. You have the *Miami Herald* killing their Bay of Pigs story in deference to Dulles. You have the *Times* sitting on Little Bush's surveillance program over a year. You believe the institution that held a story all those months has told the whole, you are sweet or stupid. You aren't sweet or stupid, Michaels. You know that. It's what you were getting at in that CUNY panel. I saw the video online. You took them on. You take them on. It's been your prerogative your whole career. That's why we're here. The story was his generation's *The Jungle*, and Lyle was going to break it.

Now Lyle could feel the life in his hands organizing paper piles, fingers following the lines and fragments. He sat in the crumbs of bodega sandwiches as he grafted events and thought about men who daunt, how their shadows angled off points of suggestion. He was reporting on something wonderful, that is, secret, and the code of it gave him quiet substance. In his notes, his source became M, and though he knew the official name, he thought and wrote in a language of his own that made being in the world outside possible again.

There was an aquatic name. TIDE. The Terrorist Identities Datamart Environment watch list had grown to half a million individuals. TIDE, a drowning by data. All the emails, geo-tagged photographs, credit card purchases, comments, and preferences announced indiscriminately. The phone conversations of diplomats in the Middle East and northern Africa went straight to earphones in a Georgia listening center. It was strange, Lyle thought, to think that he'd been so disappointed over the subprime crisis. It felt like a sound you could hear but couldn't find the location of no matter the strain of the ear.

What M described was snatching scaled larger than numbers you could imagine. And it circled back completely, drawing a circumference around anyone. Fat politicians who thought they were infallible. Soccer moms. Shadow brokers. His potential audience had never been so enormous.

It was M the book would revolve around, M who had an affinity for granules. He could point to the smallest thing, make it cascade back into thousands of decisions: how to take the filth off data, the rhetoric of the code, epistemologies of the algorithms, all the aspects that led to the number telegraphing threat. He was a man with chapters in him. Did Lyle know what had happened in Iran? M had asked.

And yet, it was difficult to pin down M. Insider, outsider, ethnographer, native, histrionic, recluse. It annoyed M, Lyle's ignorance, but he enjoyed lording knowledge. He took Darwinian pride in his intellect, but he believed no one got what they deserved. He had a teenage show-off's penchant for the offending remark, but he liked to hide.

Lyle thought of how he'd portray M—an architect of something terrible, perhaps, but not like the career baskers who liked nothing better than to sit on leather furniture alongside important people calling them by their first names. M didn't have urgencies for cigars or praise. He was in it for proving others wrong. It was why M had used the organization's own tools against them. The weapon is swapping numbers.

CHAPTER 3

Tyrell kept his hands going like solving, but in fact, his math went back into seasons. Seventeen thousand seven hundred and seven points. Average 19.5 points per game. Restrict to playoffs, restrict to 1990 playoffs, and the number is 25.2. He was a free-throw man himself. That is where the variables pulled off, information clear and present, pure. You didn't have other players poking into the percentages.

Mrs. Prince was walking around the room. She had everyone in fours, and she was saying, "I'm watching you."

The problem he'd done for his group already, and they were rapping Young Jeezy, *The Recession*. On the table, there was graph paper. Questions at a level he was answering three years ago.

Joe rolled his shoulders and cocked his head. This way, that. Left and right. He had the beat stored up in his torso. "'My president's black.'"

"'My Lambo's blue.'"

Blue was his free-throw color in the mental graphs.

Tyrell was deep into something bigger.

He looked up with his hand on his chin. Thinking, thinking. The whole catalog of facts could be rearranged like Tetris. He was cooking new rankings. In his own body, he was clumsy. But his head was Magic. His head was Bird and LeBron. His head was Oscar and Michael. And he liked to watch. He liked to keep track. He would go on the computer on after-school program afternoons and look up the latest numbers, incorporate. He made tables. Pie charts.

Yellow rebounds. Pink assists. And other colors too.

"'Bush robbed all of us.'"

"'Would that make him a criminal?'"

"That gum I see, Mr. Williams?" Mrs. Prince said across the room. "Okay, that's what I thought."

Of the young guys, he was liking Russell Westbrook. This was a guy shooting fifty-four–eight at the free-throw line year one at UCLA, then seventy-one–three the next. Tyrell was thinking, this is a guy who will keep throwing the graphs.

He rubbed his hand over the carved-up desktop. FU-Q. Colored in blue.

Blue was also an OKC color. He liked blue. He liked OKC. He liked Russell Westbrook. And he hated Jason Kidd's face.

He was trying to remember the MPGs.

"Stop looking at me," Crystal said.

"I'm not."

"Then who, Tyrell?"

"Russell Westbrook."

She had her hands up and she was saying, "Nah."

"Hold up, hold up, hold up," Joe said. "Crystal looks like *Westbrook*?"

"Not like that."

"Like what?" Crystal said.

Like what, he couldn't say. There was nothing to explain it in the room. It was just another PS with its whiteboard glare and dried-out markers. It was just another year of two-digit fractions.

"Like what?" Crystal was saying. "Like what, Tyrell?"

Tyrell rolled his pencil on the desk. One edge and another and another. Hexagonal. Five, six, seven, eight sides.

"Saying you look like a man," Joe said.

"That it, Tyrell?"

"Awful quiet now," Joe said.

"Like what? Like what?" Crystal said.

He saw Omar turn around. He saw Derek pointing. He saw Mrs. Prince with her slow walk, meaning finish it up before I get over there. And where there were so many numbers, he couldn't find the words, and the search of it swelled in him, pressed out from inside. He was tapping his foot. Tap, tap. Tap, tap. But the sound doesn't connect. Something in him's unplugged.

"Like what, Tyrell? You stupid?"

Joe was snapping fingers in front of his face. "Fat boy about to cry."

His mother was always saying he should stand up for himself. She was always saying it feels good. But he couldn't get a word in for anyone. He couldn't find a silence.

"He's about to blow," Crystal was saying. "Look at him."

"Miss Muñoz, Mr. Wood," Mrs. Prince said. "Is that you volunteering to show us your work on the blackboard I'm hearing?"

"Sure is, Mizz Prince," Joe said.

"Well then. I'm waiting."

He watched Joe reach for the paper, but he was quicker. Tyrell slapped it up, stood. He ripped the paper and threw it on the ground. Throw down like someone just won the playoffs.

He could hear their vowels lengthen, all of them, every single and all together, and he was glad to hear the moan of a scene. It is the sound of him returning from the outside, from all of them. He was up high like a sugar rush until he felt someone clock him from behind.

"Who stupid now?" Joe was saying.

Then a game came back to him from somewhere deep, old retired voices. There were ways to measure the angles, the arcs. The fingers follow, suspended, even after the release. Fists in the air. Sunk shots. And the crowd was cheering.

CHAPTER 4

Glue was the scent of the room. Glue and onions, and it made him cranky for a snack. Thing was, his mother had stepped her business-meaning walk the whole way, so when he pointed out the hot nuts truck, she hadn't noticed, and when he got into how it was not that long to buy a bag of corn chips, she said he *knew* what he'd done that he needed an appointment and ought to have thought of that before. Why is she getting calls at-risk this, at-risk that? Why is it they're saying three strikes in the computer system means automatic appointment? There were supposed to be no strikes. Zero. And because he didn't know how to explain it was him struck not making strikes, now he kicked at the rug like he was pushing off on a scooter.

"What do you mean a *man* social worker?" his mother said.

The waiting room door was open. There was a smeary picture right by it on the wall. "That's who we have," the lady at the desk behind the window said. "Are you rejecting services, ma'am?"

His mother spoke slowly, the way she did when she was trying to seem like she wasn't upset. "I was referred by the school's STARK counselor, Screening the At-Risk Kids. They are saying there are some very serious prodromes."

"Our next available is next month."

"My child got prodromes, and you're saying next month? Do you know what a prodrome is? It could turn serious any minute."

A skinny man in the doorway cleared his throat. "I want to assure you," he started.

"With the door closed?" his mother said to the man, almost like she was winning. "An appointment with the door closed?"

"It's whatever Tyrell wants," he said. "Tyrell?"

Tyrell did not speak. Tyrell looked at his shoelaces. How many shapes? A triangle there where the lace cuts. A teardrop and another. Four triangles up the tongue equal a rectangle. A rectangle is a type of square. He missed those things in school. Tangrams they were called. His mother grabbed his shoulder.

"All right," she said.

Tyrell's mother told him she'd pick him up in an hour, no funny business, but really she was talking to the man, he knew. Wait for her right in the waiting room. If he did, he could choose a snack on the way home. For *after* dinner. Tyrell nodded.

"It's a pleasure to meet you, Miss Owens," the man said. "My name is Jeremy Jordan. You can call me anytime."

His mother took the card. She lined it up nice in her wallet. "My son eats organic," she said. "He was doing times tables at seven. We had the talk when he was eight. That's the kind of parent I am. I am not an ignorant woman, Mr. Jordan. Don't think for a minute you won't be watched."

CHAPTER 5

Jeremy had the sense that he was watching with future retrospection. There was a sense of something having already happened imprinted in the unfolding present, an aura of story, once upon a time. He was not American after all. He was from the part of the world where inevitability was still expected. You were your father's son. Or at least your mother's.

The symbols for sounds were black on his screen, bold. When news carried the potential to change your life, it seemed as though it should be served with some physical weight, even if only the weight of a sheet of paper. But that wasn't what was happening. It came through with the department store coupons and day center memos. He opened the email.

"You've been matched," it said.

He was going to be a father.

Borderless Children, the letter was signed.

The agency communication stated that the child was not a girl, as their preferences had been listed, but he didn't remember preferences. An image of spiraled metal appeared at the bottom, an attachment. He didn't want attachment yet, though. He didn't want to look at the attached photograph of the child. Jeremy didn't look. If somehow the adoption didn't go through, there would always be that little face, that face he'd have to remember as the one that should have been his family.

They'd been matched.

He removed his sandwich from a paper bag and laid it on napkins, but his hands were their own animals. Fatherhood rooted you between past and present, walls of time streaming in and out, the people who gave you life and the person to whom life came from you. He could be someone's history. He could be someone's fate. They could. They had asked and they had waited. He had waited so long.

"Ham and cheese again?" Lily Framer asked, tapping his cubicle on her way out to buy lunch. "Live a little, Jeremy. Nothing worse than regret."

He was hoarse with the morning, with the psychoeducational script used at the day treatment center. *Who here hears voices? It's a disease of the brain. There's no reason why people get it. There's no reason to it.* "Still thinking about the roast beef sandwich that got away?"

"Atlanta, 2006," Lily said. "It's why I got into this line of business. You know what they say: therapists become therapists because they want therapy."

"And that's working out for you?"

"You've known me how long and you're asking? I'll see you in group, Jeremy."

He stared at the sandwich. Someone is offering the impossible life.

His telephone shivered against the desk. It sounded like a quiet automatic. He stared at the words. Matched. He thumbed glass. "Have you looked at the picture?" he asked.

"He's ours," Alexandra said.

"I didn't look. Couldn't."

"But we're doing it, aren't we? Parenthood."

He switched the phone between hands, put it to his other ear. He could hear the street surrounding Alexandra, a weave of voices and car noises. The sounds were the same as any other day, but they landed with new weight. "It's the only clear good thing I could ever come up with."

"You make a good toast," she said.

Lily Framer held up fingers expressing dwindling time. He would need to run a harm reduction group.

He said a thing he needed to do. He took the stairs to the room for group. The walls were vibrating with a failing bulb. There was verification in this, the simple motion of ascendance. You decided on one foot and then the other and somehow it meant that you rose in the small hoists. It was not that the room shifted without your motion, and that was a miracle. He turned into a room rimmed with people in folding chairs, nodded, went to the back where Lily was shuffling papers.

"If it isn't Mr. Ham and Cheese," she said.

"You know me."

"You make it easy, Jeremy."

She was talking. He could see her mouth. She was telling him there were bagels in the break room from the Risperdal drug reps. But the break room seemed very far away when there was his boy. The letter said his name was Han. They would promise to love him. They already did. The feeling was so big it was strange to think that anyone looking at him would not know he was meant to be a father.

CHAPTER 6

Jeremy began to doubt his eyes into his own life. The apartment was brightly lit and impeccably clean, with a wide view and bookshelves, all in all, as much as he could surmise, from the outside a lovely home. Except that it had no bedroom for a child. Tilt it one way and there it is: property of the professional couple. Tilt it another and it is a failure to project home into the future, or negligence. That was the way of these things. They could be disqualified for what they hadn't thought to think.

The adoption people would be looking at all the sharp corners and doorframes of their life.

Several months before, they'd sat in the office of people who controlled the ebb of children. She was very beautiful in a navy sweater with a knobby vine running up the center and gold strung around her neck and her ring from the day they promised until the end together. Maybe it was the application they shared, or maybe it was the command of heart thump— home, home, home—he could perceive her peppermint in his throat, something unflappably bright coming off her, and it was as though she was in his lungs, wintry and vital, sweet in vigor. What he had heard that day were the approving murmurs of the woman making decisions attended by a smile that suggested it wouldn't be long. "Everyone who talked whispered when we met," Alexandra said. "We met in a library." Jeremy could see himself and Alexandra through this woman: thin and neat, accomplished or stable maybe, well though not fashionably dressed, a timeless two, time-honored, family. They fell into the notch. He could feel its periphery fit tight around them, and it seemed to him, as they exited the building, that when he looked up, his self somehow compounded with his Al, his child on the horizon. There had been something bigger than the workweek in the air. He could wrap around the world.

He did not want to lose it all over a protruding nail, sharp corners.

So he hired a small crew to build a new wall off the den to form a second, smaller bedroom for the child. The boss gave estimates on the new seams of the home, elbows rested on his own enormous gut, and Jeremy waved his hand, whatever number, whatever it takes. He could hear the beat of the hammers in his chest as he slept, like loud footsteps of a child coming home. If they were turned down for the adoption, Jeremy didn't know what they'd do with the new room. He went to the hardware store and held paint chips up to the light, sky and seafoam, Atlantic, every element of earth, and he stood there waffling. They had difficult decisions to make.

"There are second acts in paint," Alexandra said.

"But not in the home study," he said.

And she laughed. She told him he was crazy. She told him he was a therapist who needed therapy.

The other difficult decision involved the riots.

Because during the riots, Jeremy's mother called. She wanted to tell Jeremy that his brother had been arrested. "He was in the street with them in Tottenham, and he was running off, but they got him with some trainers."

Alexandra, on speakerphone, said she was sorry. Jeremy, on speakerphone, said of course.

"The police killed a colored man, Mark Duggan," Mrs. Allsworth said. "They tried to fake the circumstance. They pointed out a bullet on a police radio as the dead man's, and it was police-issue ammunition. Your brother was protesting."

"So you smash up a store and run away with arms full of trainers," Jeremy had said. "Tell me what's the message in thieving Nikes."

"He told me it was undercovers who started it. To distract from the real issue."

But Jeremy knew Shane was an opportunist. He knew what his brother would look like to the adoption people. And so he told his mother they could not have Shane round next month, never mind if the family had all already bought tickets.

"The ballistics test proved it, Jam. Just the once can't you believe your brother meant well?"

"No," he said. "I can't."

Alexandra gave him a silent look across the cell phone between them, but he didn't revise his position. He had made difficult decisions before, and he knew there was always a cost.

CHAPTER 7

One day when the paint had dried, he received a call from the home-study social worker, and she was in, and she was out, and it was a new wait, a wait again. The study had been fast as a bubble bursting. Then an evening went long and loose again. They were waiting again, sitting through time.

He began to track time in clients. He would write them down and cross them out like days on a calendar, and because there were more of them than days in the week, it began to feel as though their family was closer.

He met with his client Abraham.

He met with his client Maria.

He met with his client Tyrell.

"Because a pupil is rightless," Tyrell said. "That's why. And I'm, no please. Do not. Do not say that word one more time."

"What word is that?"

"College."

"Does that word offend you, Tyrell?" Jeremy asked.

"Sure do."

"And why is that?"

"Because it's a scam," Tyrell said.

"A scam."

"That's right, Mr. Jordan."

"You think college is a scam."

"No, did I say that?"

"I'm sorry, I don't understand."

"Damn."

"You seem to feel frustrated, Tyrell."

The boy shrugged. He was a big boy, but young. It made his hands look smaller as they wrapped around each other, twisting in his lap.

"Why do you feel frustrated, Tyrell?"

"Because it's a scam."

"What is?"

"Saying it," Tyrell said.

"Saying 'college.'"

"That's what I said," he shouted.

Jeremy tried to think of what a father would say. He would need to have more words for his son. He needed them now.

CHAPTER 8

She already knew what to say in finale: They are you. You was everybody who loved mutually. Alexandra had won the bid to make the life insurance ad, and now she needed to make people think of a happy ending after a happy ending.

They are the couple who decides if it's "One if by land, two if by sea" to stick to their sailboat. They are the opposites attracted. They are the ones who can finish each other's paragraphs. They are you.

"Paragraphs aren't sexy," her boss, Carver Ellington, said.

"They are in love letters," she said.

"Give me sexy. Give me fun. More boats, less prose."

"Sexy boats," she said.

"Exactly. Float my boat. And for the record, that's not a euphemism." He shifted in a seat resembling a perfect red potato chip.

"Got it," she said.

And in a circuitous way, she *had* gotten it. She had come to America for what it refused to give, thinking there were quick tunnels to the complete picture. In its place, she'd been given a new picture, not that family again but a new family, a son, and he was beautiful, and she was in love. She wished she could show Shel the picture of the boy who'd be her son, that the world still surprised.

Shel could be anywhere, one place in all the places. It was impossible to know what he would do, or had. But she decided he was alive because, historically, when he disappeared, he had not been dead. She knew that everyone was historically not dead until they were, and still she was sure she would know it if he had died. Her hand would cease to clasp, or she would find herself sleepwalking all the way to Nevada. Her own existence was totem became the way to think. If she could live, he lived. She only needed to continue as though nothing had happened for nothing bad to happen. And nothing had. Besides, Ray Gutierrez said he could do better this time. Now they had an address. The world was furnished with reason to hope. A son, and perhaps soon, too, a brother.

CHAPTER 9

They lay on the floor of the room that might belong to a son and tried to imagine how he would see it. Is it large? So large it is frightening? They tested nightlights. The brown rabbit here. The little polar bear. He would have a favorite animal.

"I think he'll favor a clam," Jeremy said.

"Definitely a lion guy," Alexandra said.

"Or snails."

"What kind of kid's favorite animal is a mollusk?"

"Children like an octopus, don't they?" he said.

In the corner of the room, they attached three small glowing stars. She looked at them. One for each of the family. She rolled over onto her stomach and propped herself by elbows to look at her husband.

"What if his favorite animal is shrimp, and we can never eat scampi again?" she said.

"Then we'll hire a babysitter once a month."

"And what if he wants a dog?"

"Then we'll attach longer ears to So-So and Jill."

"You are very wise," she said.

He raised his eyebrows, turned on his side. "A fortune cookie amongst men," he said.

"And what is the secret to happiness?"

"You."

"And how do we solve war?"

"Sterilization."

"And what is the meaning of life?"

"The opposite of sterilization."

"And now for the soft pitch: How do you make an angry person not?"

"Sometimes you can't," Jeremy said.

"Then how does he get better?"

"Sometimes she doesn't."

"It seems too meager to be Jeremy wisdom when you say it," she said.

So-So swished in from the living room, a pale orange body climbing over Jeremy's torso as though it were any other terrain. He lifted the cat, detaching claws hooked into his shirt, and replaced So-So on the floor.

"Do not mistake discrete for meager," Jeremy said. "The distinction is what maintains my mental health when clients quit."

Alexandra lay back on her back. Her hair was splayed beneath her. "But what about the ones you work with for a while? Wouldn't it be impossible to see them leave when you know what could happen?"

"Why would it?" Jeremy asked.

"Because people over time," she said to the corner stars. "Because you're used to them, and it isn't easy to remove someone from your life."

"We live in New York City. Every day doing errands, buying milk, on the MTA, I see hundreds of people I'll never see again. That is the grammar of the universe and nothing more. It's normal not to see people again, more normal than continuing to meet for the rest of your life. They are only the laws of time and space that never again will we coincide with almost everyone."

"If you love them let them go? Is that what it is?"

"Don't," Jeremy said, "love them in the first place. I think that is the point. Let's talk about the animals again. I liked the animal conversation."

Alexandra closed her eyes. "A discussion for the birds."

CHAPTER 10

He popped a noise from a bottle, filled flutes when Alexandra came home. She was very serious, he was.

"Open it," she said. "He's coming home."

A new law of the universe: look at a photo, and the information is son. Strange that that is what it meant. Jeremy followed the patterns of light. What can be known? You must know the measurements of at least one object to attempt to scale the rest. Something behind Jeremy's eyes quivered.

And there he was, this little guy, with black hair and dimples, standing in pajamas dwarfed by a white teddy bear the size of a large toddler. In the background, another little boy flopped on a mat. Han looked into the camera, confused. His gait appeared uncertain, or perhaps it was the gravity of his world that was shifting before the lens. Han's hand was extended, reaching, maybe, or else thrown out as a counterbalance. Jeremy couldn't contain himself; he emailed the photo to Robert and Cassandra.

This is him—this is our boy.

Alexandra was sponging mascara from her eyes.

"Who is he?" Jeremy said. Then, "We are going to raise someone who has emotions we can't see."

"Why wouldn't we see them?"

She held the device with the picture, the one from which he called her, the one that connected him to the world. He stood behind her, and they looked at their son, a stranger in a picture taken many miles away.

"He will never have seen a white man probably," he said. Jeremy rested a hand on her shoulder, a cheek on her back. "He will think I'm a monster."

"What are you afraid of?" she said.

"It's exactly what I want."

And he couldn't explain that for so many years his one belief was that a home could not hold. He had believed in having a tighter life so less would be undone.

CHAPTER 11

Across from Lyle, M was speaking, his hands in constant motion. An erect index. Then fingers splayed in roots, pushing something, maybe doubt, down. Their relationship had advanced enough that Lyle could ask about the background, the textures and turns, he'd elaborate in the book, that led to M's brief career with the agency.

Online, M had discovered there were message boards full of names who had loyalties to Linux, channeled hearts full of anarchy into fast type. There was an elasticity to the boards; language sprang back. Someone could respond to you, wherever you were, if you spoke through fingers in downward patter. They called themselves RabbidUnicorn, CommanderUnix, or LordNowuSemen. They were brash, and they were civil. They wanted to keep the internet free, but their mores were practical—don't file a bug report, you enable crises. They were principled haters, generous in advice and criticism, pointing, always pointing to new directions, thinkers, and most of all, they were, even when degreed, anal autodidacts with fuck-you attitudes and enthusiasms for building, dismantling. RabbidUnicorn had even been part of DoS attacks that crashed credit card websites, jabs at the market.

Recess, he called them.

RabbidUnicorn had a mean sense of humor.

And from RabbidUnicorn, M had learned the language you worked in telegraphed your identity. Ruby or PHP: soft. C or Assembly: brawny. So on. He wanted to be legitimate, so he had spent hours tinkering with the least efficient codes. You could do that there, mean what you wanted by taking the long route, do what meant who you wanted to be.

He built programs to model poker hands and made pages of famous maneuvers. He showed his work to people he knew only by prose style. They began to call him the one-eyed king, a Cyclops or Oedipus programming strokes of fortune. The King of Diamonds. He was invited into an internet relay chat channel. The name of the channel was dynamic, fit to lock out malicious intruders. He wore their name for him: OneEyedRoyal.

Late night, he had stayed up in the screen of ideas, the electronic breath of vigilante dialogue. He got in arguments over whether a line of code should contain more than eighty characters. Sometimes, RabbidUnicorn would give him word problems to solve in algorithm. He was testing M, or it was the way he played, or both. It was training or it was evangelizing or it was ritual, and maybe it didn't matter because M liked to listen with his eyes to RabbidUnicorn's ideas about human rights: Most people deserved pursuit of happiness; major party politicians deserved to be pursued by anthrax twat napkins. The freedom to usurp. So on.

But M had wanted to perform addition, create a sum. He thought up ways to bring everyone from the boards into four walls. He thought of establishing a software company or a custom computing service. They could build precise inventory systems, genealogy trackers, systems that counted all the expense and profit accumulated. They could turn detective computers, matching frauds with crimes, find the people who opened credit cards and never paid.

They would need capital to start.

Big games, official ones were the way, he had believed. Vegas. Tournaments. The polygraph detects fear; not lying, he read, and so the intrepid liar could beat even machines. He decided to be fearless in order to lie well enough to win. This meant hedge his play with a series of identities. A person was only a pattern. Inanimate objects were animated by these repetitions, life by logical shapes. If, M thought, his self was only a well-formed series, he could resequence it, iterate.

He multiplied within in his own bones. In frumpy T-shirts, under the names he'd taken, Jack Heart and John S. Pade and Raj Diamond and Mack Sean, he won and lost big at the casinos. They were winners and losers on a mission. He paid losses under ten grand. Otherwise, he'd shed a name and avoid the casino property for a while. He imagined a circuit of computers strung around an open office like Christmas lights.

But a streak hit him. He lost big. He lost bigger. At home, he watched television. He read up on tech companies, how they moved from garages to offices to publicly trade. He read about Vodafone and Mannesmann, MCI acquiring Sprint. These were large companies becoming huge, some rich men becoming very rich.

One night, M told RabbidUnicorn the new proposal. He watched the letters come up on the screen, backtracked, typed again, riled. He stayed at his computer waiting for the time when RabbidUnicorn would answer in his window.

It's like if you knew which college ball players would put on weight in the pros. Hack the merger lawyers, you can buy who's becoming a giant before anyone trading. Then, when the stock price shoots up after the merger, you sell.

Why would we do that? RabbidUnicorn said.

It would be a disruption.

He remembered how even as he had typed those words, something had shifted. He remembered RabbidUnicorn's last words to him.

You don't know how to disrupt anything. You only know late capitalism two point oh. You're a slave, OneEyedRoyal. A house negro, but still a fucking slave.

"That must have hurt," Lyle said. He did not look up from the blur of his own hand taking notes.

"Is that what Ingrid would say?" M said.

"Ingrid," Lyle said.

"Marina's mother. Ring a bell?"

They looked at each other. M's pupils were big black caviar in his face, and Lyle swallowed a tight, dry swallow. He lay his pen down.

M raised his eyebrows, winked. "She's one in a million, kiddo. The Micellis used to know the value of family."

"You hacked me."

"Laugh, Michaels," M said. "It's funny."

Lyle's head was ringing. He closed his eyes. The red behind his lids was vibrating. His chest was. He opened his eyes and M's eyebrows pulled together, and he was crossing his arms.

"Your phone, Michaels," M said.

His fingers fell into the normal choreography of the answer. Bring device to ear. No answer.

When he finished the call, M was gone. Lyle had not seen him leave.

CHAPTER 12

There was an explanation, and it was autonomic. It was neuro-endocrine activation. Jeremy was thinking thalamus, amygdala, hypothalamus. He was thinking noncritical system go down. It is all very sensible, the body. Efficient. Delay digestion. There is danger.

But it was not danger. It was just a room of middle-aged people, expectant and holding pamphlets. There were so many pamphlets here in China.

LOVE IS A TWO-WAY STREET.

QUESTIONS ARE GOOD.

WHEN STRANGERS BECOME FOREVER FAMILIES.

During the adoption orientation at the hotel, all the couples sat in a circle, talking about their current and future families. Dan and Amy from Texas. Steve and Betsy from Arkansas. Jen and David from San Francisco. They were thick, kind people, and they called children blessings. They talked about God, what God had done for them, and it was always family.

That afternoon, they went to the Great Wall as a group. They went to the Forbidden City. All Jeremy could see were the cameras. The cameras in phones. Everywhere there was sound, and nowhere was there a signal. The signal was simple.

We are here for him.

And so they followed the two tour guides, Chinese-Americans who'd been adopted by the agency themselves. They smiled at people. His eyes were wide and unseeing. There was a study of rats. Evidence of activity in the prefrontal cortex long after the physical response to danger. The stimulus might never be rubbed completely out.

The tour guides were clapping their hands. They were telling the group to clap their hands if they were listening.

CHAPTER 13

To listen was to animate the evidence in time, bring it to now, carry the audio files into the moment of knowledge, Lyle had to believe that. He had left the apartment to clear his mind, just a meal, knife and fork, this technique of survival in the cutting and spearing at which it was simple to succeed. Roast chicken.

Back home, his parents whispered their beautiful grand-daughter was sleeping God bless her. His father said it was not so far to Queens that a visit once a week would be too much. His mother promised to take Marina shopping. She urged just call and she'd do the shopping for supper. And when they were gone, when he had switched on the light that spun stars over the walls and ceiling where Marina slept, and Lyle had checked that the door was locked, he dug into piles and files.

The dates divided the interviews. The sentences differed. Yet somehow all of it together is supposed to answer who is M? Can the man who hacked him be the one man who will tell the truth about US intelligence?

He looked at his notes, and he knew it had been foolish to refer to M as M when Lyle knew his name. But the code had given the project weight, secrecy. It was a gesture that imagined eventual subpoena, that the book could reverberate that much, displace an order. Marina lay sleeping in her bed, and that her face was true was something for Lyle to remember, but his breath caught in his chest: a thought inflicted. And he was terrified suddenly of the day when he could first catch her in a lie.

Believe the facts are thicker than paper. Authenticating details.

Lyle wondered now whether he'd misread M from the beginning. Perhaps Lyle had missed something.

"I've met your type," M had said that first time they made contact. "You think adversarial journalism is ipso facto moral high ground. You think the more adversarial, the more it's a public good. Whoever stirs the most anger is the most meaningful. The biggest spoon you call impact."

Lyle had shifted in his seat. He had wanted to show M around his ethics like a museum. "It's more complicated than that."

"As complicated as you're messing with my sister, I'm guessing."

"I don't know what you're talking about," Lyle said.

"Pee-pees and vaginas, Michaels. Fitting and separating. Birds, bees. They breed babies that way, communicate the drippy diseases. You said you're a 'friend' of hers. I'm not such a shut-in I'm too shut-in to be a cynic."

He'd not thought the antagonism would extend beyond the night. He'd thought it was a test, or the performance of a test. M didn't talk, exactly. He orated. Speech bleak as the ramblings of a failed actor, and always stringing code.

The second time they met, M had brushed the bottom of the bar with his hands quickly, knelt to peer beneath the chairs. He had sat down and took a long sip of tequila. It had seemed to Lyle that if he could only break past the first barrier, no more would be erected.

"You think what I say I remember is evidence," M had said. "The beakers are clear, but bent glass warps if you know what I'm saying. You forget it is harder to prove the truth than to tell it."

That should have scared Lyle. But Lyle had only shrugged. "You know better."

"I am a lie."

"The liar's paradox," Lyle said.

"All Cretans are liars, says the Cretan."

"To begin, I believe you."

"A man of faith," M had said. M had sneered.

And Lyle had figured autobiography was part of it. M had grown self-sufficient with secrets, back channels, pretend profiles and counterfeit cards, a whole network of corroboration, reference on reference pointing both nowhere and only to him, just like any other fact. He had manufactured reality so easily, it was nearly a joke.

"You were a good poker player."

"Are. Is that what my sister told you?"

"She didn't tell me anything about you. She doesn't know we're here."

"Then who's the liaison? Two strangers in a room. I want to know what got us here."

Lyle had selected his words like grocery fruit. "I think Glen Close is exciting work, all that intellect in a room, the opportunity to stop pretending instinct is empirical."

"I do miss intellect in a room. What chips do you bring to the table?"

"To begin, I know who knows what you've been up to." A lie. The tip had been anonymous. "I know who knows you have a story."

M had sounded his own knuckles in his fist, efficient cracks rendered with a blank face. "Ten minutes, Michaels. Your move. Are you diddling my sister?"

"I'm not fucking her. She's married."

"So's any executive with a secretary on the side," M had said. "But you wonder because you see she is becoming one of them. They will steal your attention in every direction they can, so everything you know is something the architect of search engines decided met the metric of relevance. Sweaters in our communications, between swiped lives! And somewhere, eventually, we aren't needed for thinking. They have automations, convenient as a microwave dinner, one-click shopping. They want to keep us at our desks, complacent and clicking away."

"You're angry with her."

M had bit a lime, leaving a deflated fringe of cellulose attached to the rind, dropped it right into his already empty glass. A swooped finger brought two more glasses. He had looked over a hunched shoulder, leaned his elbows on the table. "That your opinion, Michaels?"

"I'm a journalist."

Lyle remembered M's eyes then, glossy and large as black olives. "You're an ex-blogger, Lyle, Lyle, pants on fire. Please don't play make-pretend objectivity."

"I will write this book. Question's who do you want to tell your story? The Senate Intelligence Committee?"

"The politicians with a direct line to media can't," M had said.

"They have no idea what I did. They don't understand the mechanisms, the rhetoric embedded in the code. All they know is the fairy tale that Little Red Riding Hood isn't tricked. What gives away the wolf in the sleeping bonnet, Michaels?"

"They greenlit the project."

"They greenlit money for science," M had said. "Numbers. They think quant's the prefix for self-evident in Latin. I gave my declamation: after a terror, the signal is always clear. Hindsight is."

"But you signed on anyway," Lyle had said. "Why?"

"Because if I did it, I'd have wrung out a paradox," M had said.

Lyle had followed M's words with a pen on paper. "What does that mean?"

M had put his glass down. He had neatly fanned a jacket over his shoulders, as he turned away said, "Tell Lex I said hello." Lyle had perceived then that M must feel that Lyle was his connection, not hers, if he were to allow Lyle to report the story. He had believed trust would somehow pass between him and M so long as he did not speak of their meetings with Alexandra Chen.

Alexandra and Jeremy did not speak. Mahogany tables topped with bottles of water. Parquet floors. What is there to say? They waited in a conference room. They were living in an era when there was not even the ticking of a clock. There was the mute shift of light.

And then there, there he was: a little boy, bigger than he'd been in the photograph, a fat lollipop bulging from his cheek, outfitted in small shoes, one with a picture of a giraffe on the toes, the other with leaves, and both affixed with rubber squeakers in the soles, there, here really, was his son. This was not the image he'd returned to again and again. It had not occurred to him that Han was someone who would be aging as they waited for him to become their son. He had been two in the picture. He would be four now.

For one horrible second, there was something in Jeremy's throat. This beautiful boy with the cheek full of lollipop, his tan, squat little legs and his chin tucked in—he, too, would die.

Tether to now, he thought.

He wanted to stop time.

A woman spoke his language. Han twisted his torso. There

was an emotion to it, the torque, and he ran behind her leg, but she was waving her palm to herself, waving Alexandra and Jeremy closer.

Han began to cry.

Something in him cracked, carnation petals in his chest, and when he looked at Alexandra, he realized he'd never before seen her afraid.

WHEN THEY LEFT the orphanage, Han cried for hours. They sat in the hotel room with the red bedcover and a boxy television. There was a cot set up, and there was Han in his blue T-shirt. His striped pants and the shoes with flora, fauna. Inarticulate in his language, Alexandra held his hand. Alexandra picked him up. Alexandra bounced him.

"Bouncing is the universal gesture of consolation, isn't it?" she said.

"What sound does a giraffe make?" Jeremy asked, and Han cried louder.

Alexandra smiled. "What sound *does* a giraffe make?"

Jeremy looked at Han and Alexandra with helpless love in his eyes. He ventured a soft word sometimes, but mostly he was shy. He would feel energy in his hand, a directed fidget of affection, and then something in him would be arrested with the maybe-mistake of it. He would do it right with his son. He wouldn't falter.

The rats with the fear in their cortex.

The rhesus monkeys, with all the ACTH levels like their mothers.

"What is he feeling?" Alexandra said. "Everything is a mystery until he learns the words."

"If we're lucky," Jeremy said.

Jeremy turned on music from his phone. It was soft piano, dusky and slow. Alexandra was speaking, and he couldn't make out the words. He didn't know if he was stupid with the child's cries, the endless noise of it, or if it was something else. But all he could think was toy? Or thirsty? All he could think was that he must do better for their Han.

"Should we take a picture?" Alexandra asked.

"When he stops crying."

"You say it as though you're sure he will."

That night, after dinner, after the revelation that a child could cry and eat at once, they put him to bed. Jeremy tried to think of a way to say his thought, or his feeling, and by the time he did, Alexandra was asleep. He wondered how anyone could ever manage to return such an expansive thing as love, let alone a child, whether real love meant not caring about the outcome or requite. He thought he could love that love, one that needn't be turned back. He already did.

But that night, Han crawled from his cot, and suddenly Jeremy felt a warmth at his back. He felt a bunching of his shirt—a hand. Jeremy was terrified with the happiness of it, didn't move. And for many minutes, he couldn't sleep. This small breath. His son had come to him.

PART SIX: AEQUUS

Charm is not an episteme.—One Rock

CHAPTER 1

Alexandra began to know him in gestures. The raised shoulders: humor. The dimples that spread. She preserved him in her phone. She showed him around at work. This was Sunday. Thank you. He is. We're lucky.

In meetings, she'd say she had a theory. It was a rote script, hurried off and practiced, mindless almost now. She'd say if fashion is an imitation that the privileged abandon once picked up by others, there was something to be learned by social media. She would say, this is true of words too, stories. She would say, sharing the news creates a social unit. There is a fear of being cut off.

We are seeing tantrums of data. We are looking at the metrics. How many words. When. This is survey research embedded into life.

We have never had so much inner life to process.

At home, Jeremy was preparing lunch or reading books. He was taking Han for a walk. The black hair on her son's head took a burnt-red hue at the tips when the sun was so. It was just one of the ways she'd begun to know him.

She kept a notebook. She wrote: the set mouth before every

bite. She wrote: giraffe. She remembered the day he plucked a flower at the park and ran with it until every petal had dropped, how he cried.

And we are seeing that there is an effect created by the early splash. A piling on. This is partially algorithmic. These codes are time-sensitive. They take the early data, make what is big huge. People like it. Show them more.

There is primal psychology to the fashionable narratives, she said. She said, the stories that can't be missed. What if you failed to be alarmed?

She brought home wooden trains. She brought home the bear with the velvet nose. They would turn on the music and spin. His favorite game was to hide and scream goodbye. That face peeking from behind corners, turned up from beneath chairs. Goodbye. Goodbye! Maybe it was only the joy of a known word. The repetition of adults.

She would not repeat the adults of her life.

Current climate is we get coverage for social justice, and we get coverage for failed justice. Narrative cycle. That is the fashion of it. That is how you sustain attention to the brand. We amplify our advertisement free of charge when the writers think they are Roland Barthes but thirst after tabloids.

She pointed to the graphs. She said, this is the science of winning the online content cycle. She said this is the singles generation. Forget publications. These stories embed in Cathexis. I am talking about insisting the brand into every day.

Her speech was automatic as an electronic clock alarm. She was thinking about Jeremy and Han, playing the game that persisted the longer you said anything but the word. Your opponent was trying to know, and you were saying bread crumbs, blood-stain. You were saying gone.

The missing thing: it is still present.

She had thought the addition of a son would mean she'd not feel the subtraction of a brother, but the desire persisted to say the unuttered thing. She wished she could tell Shel that he was an uncle.

CHAPTER 2

Shel Chen had many names. Shel Chen, OneEyedRoyal, McCreight, and M. But McCreight was the one he told Lyle to call him. McCreight was the one who had built the tools of revelation that both succeeded and failed too much. He was the one Lyle decided to trust because he was who was worth a story.

Over recent weeks, as he'd continued to narrate, deeper and flatter was the way McCreight's voice had gone. Lyle could hear the way the years had pulled him down, just like anyone else, and it made it easier for him to put the hack behind them.

They were both disappointed men.

But there was a sharpness too, he recognized in the audio recording, that blade running beneath. He knew he must be careful. That blade—it pointed at Lyle.

You ought to look at data and say, there is an editorial unit here, a unit being the shape life doesn't have. But I look at you, and you are too hungry to tell data, Michaels.

Lyle had tried to compliment McCreight into returning to the subject of Glen Close. He'd talked about vision, scope. Sometimes what looks like misanthropy is for the potential utopia of the whole world.

You want me to say I did it for heroic reasons, Michaels. You want me to be your protagonist, and I'm not. I wasn't after good. I was after the top.

Lyle said they were not so different. They were both data analysts of sorts.

I buried everyone I was to be who I wanted to be, Michaels, McCreight said in the recording. *Don't do the same. If you don't stop now, you'll become your profile: set, finite. Wait too long, you'll never spread out again. You'll wake up who you wanted to be with nothing you want. Change the theorem.*

In the recording, there was a silence before his own voice. What do *you* want? Lyle had asked. And he remembered how McCreight had leaned over the table, quick as a slammed door.

For you to be someone worth trusting, McCreight said.

The computer spoke again in Lyle's voice. It said that they were not talking about Lyle but Sean.

You aren't the one who will be punished. Comes to a point, I will never be alone of witness again.

Lyle coughed, asked who was witness.

They are.

Lyle again asked who.

Let's imagine they were waiting for someone like me. Let's imagine they've been following me since Nevada. Maybe there never was a RabbidUnicorn, Michaels. Maybe RabbidUnicorn was many shadow operatives. They wanted a loner. I was a body no one would claim, so ripe for them, controvertible. From work to cocktails— you can wear him so many ways!

A guttural sound. A quick four beats of flesh on table.

Of course, Alexandra thinks it couldn't possibly be. Everything ugly is always somewhere over the rainbow. And if it isn't, she'll send it there first class.

Alexandra isn't here, Lyle said. Let's focus on the story.

Crazy would rather think, her own brother crazy she'd rather think than that her government is.

Lyle heard the record of his voice glom on to RabbidUnicorn. Then there was a drawn-out silence, a thinking one.

In retrospect, maybe the whole group was run by them, McCreight said finally. *A quiet game of make-pretend geek revolutionaries. They groomed me like pedophiles. You think there are two sides, that the discontents are disrupting the rodeo, but they've filled in every side. Modus operandi: you teach them to code, wait for something useful. Or you embed in hacker collectives, disrupt service. Then you make the arrests, turn anarchists to work for the government. Who are they? They are Mr. Potato Head with all his mustaches.*

You feel tricked?

The worst way to be was duped, I used to think. But that was because I'd never really been scared.

What is the fear?

One day you are us. The next you're recategorized. Guy I worked with on terrorist finance tracking applications: dead. Three bullet holes. He was thinking of getting out. He was investing in properties. Over fast as three bends of a finger.

"And you believe him," Bri Freeman said on the phone when he called her.

"He's emotional when he speaks. It's not practiced. You can hear that he feels he's being followed."

"Sounds like Gülen," Bri said.

"The cleric."

"He will cry as he lectures about interfaith dialogue, the West. But meanwhile, he prays in the Poconos, the beneficiary of the CIA's hospitality."

Lyle looked at the ceiling. He couldn't see the full figure of McCreight, summarize him. Just as Lyle caught a trace, Sean dropped off. "The entire story will crumble if he's a fraud or a crazy."

"You think he might be."

"And you think?"

A pause. "I think it's hard to tell a true story," she said. "Even for Lyle Michaels. Maybe you need a wider sample."

"Meaning?"

"Who can you talk to who knows the guy?"

CHAPTER 3

Alexandra was lovely against the horizon at the Rockaways with Han. They bought ice cream and corn dogs, dough still hot and trailing sugar the whole way to the ocean. Han used the stick to draw Elmos in the sand. One, two, over and over, until finally as far as they could see it was face after face of smiles made by his hand.

There had been Elmo in China. It was something he recognized. It was a word they shared, the smiling monster.

Elmo, he said, and they knew he meant he was happy or wanted. That, at least, they were people he wanted on the other end of a conversation.

They pointed to the sky. This is bird. This is cloud. This is rain. His boy loved weather. It was nearly a hobby. At home, every picture book, his finger moved to the sky. Jeremy would sponge nimbuses into the blue walls of his bedroom so that Han would know his father wanted to give him more than the world.

They ran back to the car, and he was laughing. They were.

And that's what Jeremy thought of the rest of his life: redeemed weather. The flight and soar. There were droplets clung to the ends of the boy's black hair as he was fastened.

Han turned his face from the window in the car, said, "Baba." And he was pointing. He was pointing at Jeremy, and they were an impossibly beautiful thing, the three, a family.

CHAPTER 4

Because they did not want to wake Han, their sex was quieter now, and there was something about this quietness, this holding sound in, the pressure. She pressed her fingers harder into Jeremy. Something deep inside her was more thrown. From behind it was almost unbearable, but she asked for it. Sometimes she cried into a pillow, and when she felt him nearly forget her, faster and much harder, light spiked behind her closed eyes, and after they came, she was pristine, desireless.

Usually, she fell asleep quickly. But some nights she would lie there, whispering with Jeremy. Some nights, he dozed first, and as she had not since the early days, she lingered on his taut belly, the crease in his pelvis. There were short grays in his hair now. She counted them.

At these times, she would hold his arm, shake him awake, and he would be confused. She would say his name. She would roll onto him. She kept her knees tight to his ribs. And when her thighs were very tired, she disciplined herself from the scream.

CHAPTER 5

It was impossible to go back to before McCreight. This was obvious to Lyle. It was obvious when he thought of the editor with whom he'd gotten the appointment via strings of strings pulled.

The book proposal had been simple: America had always been a culture of fakers, a backlash to the British Empire stretching into the present. This is where it starts: trade imbalances between the Empire and the colonies, gold and silver specie made scarce in the new world, opening up a solution: paper currency. These are bills of credit, people saying, you can't create money out of nothing. Where are the precious metals? This is including John Locke. But then you have Ben Franklin saying, let's try mortgage-backed cash.

The editor's eyes had been blue and cold, but he had continued. There were banks printing money all over. This was not centralized. This was make nice to your state politician, he gives you a charter to print cash money. No one knew how much circulated. No one was saying this is the standard bearer because there were no standards. So the counterfeiter is not so different. He's one of many creating new financial instruments. He is the

American self-made man with his self-made money. He says, freedom is the freedom to make money.

Lyle had pressed the exigencies. He had told the editor, by the end of the eighteenth, beginning of the nineteenth century, you have a nice grip of entrepreneurs printing money to underwrite speculation. It's open season. This money's value is based totally on trust. This is not an IOU from your neighbor. You have bills, you can operate a little anonymous, do business with this paper in which value is supposed to inhere. It is not a matter of reputation. But of course, the value is slipping on and off all the time because there's zero regulation. You see this arc, you see the whole financial crisis of the aughts was in the country's DNA.

The editor had checked her phone. The editor had said his name. The editor had said, "I wish the market were different."

"Who will make it different if you don't?" Lyle had said.

Then she showed him the door.

On the outside of people he wanted to be, he needed a "timely" story. On the outside of people he wanted to be, he needed to parse McCreight. And so on the outside of people he wanted to be, he dialed Alexandra Chen.

CHAPTER 6

It was the sort of hotel room that you could project onto, the walls and soaps and bedding white and lovely, all clean cotton ball feeling. Because of this blankness, the impossibility of maintaining it, Alexandra treated the room carefully, and, more than usual even, urged a personal spotlessness, without residue, scrubbed of aftermath. She flipped the television channel. A voice-over spoke of a Harvard psychiatrist accepting nearly two million dollars from a drug company manufacturing the drug Risperdal; in return, he'd signed a scientific abstract that reported Risperdal's efficacy in treating child bipolar disorder and prescribed it out of a special clinic at Mass General. It might have gone unnoticed, the broadcaster said, if little boys with the prescription hadn't started drooling and growing breasts.

Now, trying Jeremy's phone, she again stared at the television where the stories looped. Alexandra turned the television off. In her ear, the tone intoned. From some months ago, Jeremy's voice through the earpiece apologized that he could not now be reached.

"I miss you," she said, "and you didn't even go anywhere."

She heard muffled fingers on her door. In the peephole scope, a deformed figure stood squinting down the hallway. Something rushed down the inside of her torso that she didn't trust, but she felt her fingers twist on brass, opening the door. Lyle leaned his head against a fist on the doorframe.

"Figured you'd want to know," he said.

Lyle put his hands in his pants pockets. They looked at each other from either side of the threshold until something animated in her stomach, and she had to turn her head to look at an area of the floor.

Lyle began to speak, and she focused on the gray matted in little snatches by his face, the slight paunch in his lower cheek. *To do that to someone.* He had understood something she didn't. It was why Shel had gone to him, not her.

"Are you going to offer me a drink out of a tiny bottle from a tiny refrigerator?" he asked.

"There are only the bathroom cups."

"If it looks like a cup, and it walks like a cup, and it quacks like a cup," he said.

"It must be a goose."

"He doesn't hate you," Lyle said, "if that's what you think."

"All right."

"Talk on the same side of the door like two civil human beings?" he said.

She shrugged but turned. In the refrigerator, there were small bottles of vodka, gin, light and dark rum, whiskey, a green glass bottle of sparkling water, and small red cylinders of cola. Her hot hand clarified condensation on the can. She sat at the end of the bed, and when he did too, she stood. She walked across the room and didn't look at him, stared into a hung masterpiece blanded by reproduction on the wall. Lyle Michaels had said that he needed her expertise, expertise on her brother. It was a competency she wanted to have, and she knew she didn't.

But for a while, she listened. She listened to Lyle say Sean McCreight was rueful on behalf of their century. He kept using that name. Sean McCreight. Sean McCreight could not believe all around them people saw intelligent boxes and didn't want to know what lit them from within, what made them expel nearby restaurants and the sixth president of the United States. Sean McCreight thought these people were fools.

And fool was his idea of her, she knew. She crossed the room. She opened a shade and looked down at all the people she didn't know, would never, perhaps like her brother. She turned back to Lyle. "And why is he talking to you?"

"Because he says he sees now it won't stop. They are beginning to send cops to houses based on predictive policing and to develop diagnostic codes. They will round up people for crimes, for mental illness, and he doubts anyone will fight it because they don't know how to argue with the science of safety. He doesn't like agencies monitoring when you are home with Wi-Fi thermometers. All the unmitigated windows. And I think part of him wants to stop it. Part of him is saying the Fourth Amendment crisis slips into every crevice. Maybe he also wants to prove something simpler: that he was there. That he exists. That he did something bigger than what anyone expected of him. And I think he thinks, you make your life a public document, you can seek asylum. You get open arms in another country."

"I mean why you of everyone?"

Lyle sucked on the inside of his cheeks. "Maybe because of you," Lyle said.

Alexandra took the glass and slid it in small circles on the table. "Do you think he's happy?" she said.

"No," he said. "Will you help me?"

There was something nervy in her body, and there was nowhere to put it. McCreight. McCreight. She thought of what Lyle Michaels would never know about her brother, and it was all of when her brother had been Shel Chen.

"Why would I do that?"

Lyle twisted the top from a bottle. A little gasp indicated the release of pressure. "Tell me I'm wrong," he said. "Tell me you don't want to see him."

CHAPTER 7

The boy did not want to see him. The boy had his hood up. Jeremy sat in a chair and pressed his fingers together. He had been asking the same questions for many sessions, but now, he watched Tyrell pull on the ties at the neck side to side as though milking a cow. In Jeremy's professional paradigm, the question was what was *really* going back and forth? Perhaps this was the moment he'd finally tip, stop weighing pros and cons, speak openly.

"Simple as it's a scam."

"What if it's not a scam? What if it's that they think you're very clever?"

"Nah."

"You don't think you're clever, Tyrell?"

"Putting words in my mouth, Mr. Jordan."

"Why don't you sort me out then?"

"'Sort me out then,'" Tyrell repeated.

Flat affect. Steady eye. His hands were folded.

"And how did this idea come to you?"

"Because it's not literal. There's one way and the other way. And they know it'll *seem* like it's the other way when I know, you know, they know: not even close."

One day Han would be a teenager. Jeremy imagined dinners in restaurants, the three of them. He imagined going to museums. They would come home after a movie, and he would ask Han whether it was tired, the plot. If it was too neat. And he would want Han to think the neatness was how life worked. He would want him to say, it's real, Baba.

"You don't think they mean what they say."

"That's it." Tyrell nodded his head and leaned over to rest his arms on his knees. "That's it."

"So if I have it correct," Jeremy said.

Tyrell sighed. "They say college so it looks like they're in it."

"In what?" Jeremy said.

"*It*, man. Come on. Don't play ESL with me."

He liked Tyrell immensely, and he tried to be patient, tried to see ahead in the conversation, carve it. Jeremy hoped that if something were ever to happen to him, whoever was left to console his son would have something wiser to say than he did now. "There are many its, Tyrell."

"I'm saying the image."

"Which?" Jeremy said.

"They can't wait to get rid of us but talk college so they look like people who care."

Jeremy wrote a note in his pad. "Or maybe they just want to see you succeed."

Tyrell laughed. He had a giggle still. His voice hadn't changed, and it was still the laugh of a child. He put his hands on his knees and took big breaths. He looked at Jeremy square, suddenly, serious. "Then how come they pass people that can't succeed a long division test into the eighth grade?"

"Sometimes we need to believe in honest mistakes," Jeremy said. "Sometimes we need to trust the adults in our life." Jeremy drank from a glass of water. He replaced it on a small table in the corner by his chair. Consistency of space. Consistency of objects. This is the environmental condition for safe sharing. "Do you think this might have anything to do with your father?"

"No."

"Sometimes our brain connects things without us even knowing, Tyrell. Maybe we feel out of control. Maybe we can't make our sick parent better. And maybe it makes us think something about whether we can rely on grown-ups."

Tyrell pushed his lower lip forward, turned his head. His arms were crossed. Self-comfort. The comfort given when it was not anticipated it would be received.

Or else he was protecting himself.

"What would you lose if you trusted that people mean what they say?"

The boy picked a thread hanging off his pants. His nail scratched back and forth on the fabric. "Okay, Mr. Jordan," Tyrell said. He looked up. "And how I'm supposed to trust adults when you don't even listen?"

"You don't think I listen?"

"Not even here."

"Tyrell."

"In your own world, Mr. Jordan," Tyrell said. "No sight of what's in front of you."

CHAPTER 8

They'd married and he had, at times, gotten better, though he had never been best. This, for a hopeful person, might have been a consolation prize. But instead, strange things occurred of his own doing if not—or so it seemed—his volition. There was the mutant yolk cooked sunny-side up, inedible when he saw its yellow doubleness. There was the missed call. Then, he had upended the trash, found what he had not intended to seek, and the hotel receipts were as real as thin was the story.

She had not even seemed to believe the narrative herself. Of course she wouldn't. It was an alibi.

A friend, Alexandra had called him.

And a diamond is a rock.

He could not speak the word that Lyle Michaels was.

Jeremy passed a park shrieking with children, trees imported to gaps in cement. It was a Friday, and a slapping sound was skipping rope. Jeremy kept on. His head hurt with every sound come into it.

Wright had said, listen to everything in case it's something. An Intelligence Corps trainer had said, we trained the E4A, but there are dogs that bite the hand who feeds. And Alexandra, she had said soon she must go to Nevada to hire a home health aide for her mother. From somewhere, the jag of a child's cry cut through the noise, and there was a loss of equilibrium for a moment. In the sky, the sun shone, but even in the light he perceived a loss of center, transitory North Star. There was something rising up his throat. He paused by a trash can to smell the steadying stench of decay.

"Baba sick?"

Sometimes Jeremy forgot where he was in space. But he didn't forget that a body is evidence that you are watched. He must be a man strong enough to be seen by his son. He walked again, and Han was still holding his hand. He walked faster. Just get them home.

"Excuse me," someone said.

He stopped. He turned toward the voice. The voice, he saw, belonged to a young woman in blue jeans. "Excuse me," she said again. "What exactly do you think you're doing?"

"Sorry, what?"

"What exactly do you think you're doing with this little boy?" She knelt. Her hand was upturned, pink fingers spread, extended to Han. "Where are your mommy and daddy?" the woman said.

He looked down at the splash of black hair on his boy's head, looked down at the blond hair on his own arm. "You've got it all wrong," he said. "This is my son."

Black. Blond. This woman's hair was brown.

"I'm Rachel," she said. "I'm a friend. Can you tell me where your mommy and daddy are?" And she was touching him now. She had his hand.

There were explanations, but Jeremy didn't have them. There

were explanations, but his mind was locked up. His son was not speaking. His son whose hand she'd taken. She wanted to take his son. And before Jeremy knew it, he pulled hard, and he was running. He hugged Han to his chest, heard him cry, and ran.

Later, after the matter was cleared up, after the police had been satisfied and Alexandra had put Han to bed, after she'd said the woman with the brown hair and blue jeans could fuck off, the woman with her ratty brown hair and ratty blue jeans could go fuck a hydrant covered in dog piss, her voice was very tight and she had to pour out a glass of red wine she'd filled with ice cubes. Jeremy folded the corkscrew, gave her a new glass.

"But what I don't understand," she said, "is why did you run?"

CHAPTER 9

She did what she did when facts were unruly. She used the internet tracking program she'd downloaded to monitor her mother. Alexandra had saved her credit card information on her mother's computer. Now she could see where the money went, she could see what her mother wrote, and it mollified something to know she could know.

From a store that sold everything, Janice Chen purchased DVDs of her programs. When there were no more of her shows, she bought movies that came up on the screen as suggestions, dramas in which dangerous women threatened to ruin everyone's history with secrets. She bought lipsticks: nudes, reds, magenta. She bought thirty-five-dollar perfume. Last week, liquid foundations had arrived via FedEx in glass bottles, and today, an eye set came at 2:33 p.m. She had not needed to sign for the package.

What occasioned the cosmetics, it seemed, were her mother's emails with "Victor," "Victor" who wrote that Janice Chen was a woman who deserved. He called her things like Princess. He asked, *What is the fashion of your heart?*

It was surprising how much of herself her mother told.

I lost a husband, the most beautiful man I ever saw, and no one knows my pain, least of all my hateful babies, her mother wrote. *It was the stillness I loved about Mr. Chen, the common sense of his long, beautiful hands slicing raw meat. The money from his store went to his sisters, who never approved of me, even though I was the mother of his child, which means certain rights, a fact obvious as a whitehead pimple. My own mother didn't like Orientals or Jews, but she knew the rights of a mother.*

On that topic, I was not a mother like my own, Grace Oliver. I never beat my children, who had to grow up fatherless when they should have had that life with the pride of their own store. My two children are:

(1) Alexandra, who doesn't even bring my grandson to Nevada and didn't have her wedding near home when she married an English. She has that civilized Oriental look but didn't care her own mother didn't have the nerves to fly and couldn't sit on an airplane the length of an ocean without pain in the bad hip.

(2) Shel, who became my son after his father, my brother, died drunk driving the night the United States Olympic Miracle on Ice hockey team beat the Soviets. It was not any different to me that he wasn't Chen. I never treated my children any different, even though Shel was a public rascal once he started school. I always treated him right as my own, proof being it was my disability checks wasn't it that went to lunches, which you only need basic human intelligence to see what that means.

In answer to your questions dear Victor, I have survived on old bread soaked in milk. I am alone, but I don't need much. I know no one will ever do it for you. I raised my babies on my own, I entertained myself, I made up my own mind. That is who I am.

Your princess,
Janice

"Victor," Alexandra saw, had already written back.

I know something you can't do alone, he wrote. That was when Alexandra decided to stop reading.

CHAPTER 10

She thought of telling Jeremy Lyle's proposal, and she thought of not telling Jeremy Lyle's proposal. Not telling Jeremy Lyle's proposal had its benefits. Suppose Shel wanted to be part of their life, Han's. Shel would not then be the person to Jeremy who had once been dangerous, had once been a spy.

Besides, when she tried to formulate her reasons for not telling Jeremy Lyle's proposal, for how she could keep quiet the loudest thought she had though he was her husband, and she loved him, she did not want specifically to lie, she thought he'd forgive her. There was precedent.

The precedent was the time he'd told Robert and Cassandra that he had been raised by a single mother.

Alexandra had nodded along.

Alexandra had not immediately mentioned Carl.

It was only later, after they left and Alexandra had waited until the door was locked, that she demanded an explanation.

Pleaded maybe. But with anger.

She remembered now how Jeremy's voice sped up, consonants stampeding. Carl was his dad, but he wasn't, Jeremy had said. He thought Carl was, but he wasn't. When Jeremy applied to the army, there had been paperwork to fill out. He had listed the man he'd always known as his father as his father. When his mother saw the forms, she had told him he was an idiot. Carl was his stepfather. His real father was a Hungarian doctor who'd employed his mother to organize his life by the alphabet, and though his mother had raised him on her own until he was five, he guessed he'd just deluded himself a little because when he was young, he'd wanted a dad so badly.

"I was embarrassed," he had said.

And she had said, "I don't want to not know you."

"You do know me."

"I didn't know your family."

"You do now," Alexandra remembered he'd said.

Delayed gratification.

She had asked, "Is there something else you're keeping from me?" and in the immediate days that followed they had been a little smaller, a thinner unit. But in time, they'd grown back, become more expansive again. They'd pretended nothing was wrong, and then nothing was.

CHAPTER 11

All afternoon he and Han had been cartographers. There was a cardboard atlas bigger than Han that Alexandra bought at a children's store one day. Han had needed Jeremy to turn the page. Or sometimes he had put it on the floor and crawled over continents. England. Ireland. China.

She could be anywhere now.

And so now he was too awake and, too awake, he paid the sitter, left the apartment building, passing between stone animals guarding their doorway. The streets were drowning with data as he walked. He saw pregnant women yelling for their already born to slow down, police officers writing tickets, and leashes on every corner. He went all the way downtown, past the open stores with crates of produce tilted for display. He turned back near the Manhattan Bridge, and someone was always shouting after a beautiful woman.

He was walking it off.

Or he was walking, minimally.

His legs gained rhythm as they forgot streets, all the garbage bins slackened of meaning. He was able to stop extrapolating off faces. In theory, the stroll was a way to remember the horizon, throw off the buildings converging, the mass of information that was this city. De facto, it was a way to reduce the landscape to the background of a problem called Lyle Michaels, stare through the pinprick.

Gather information. Listen. There is always something more. It is a contest of exhaustion.

The night before she met with Lyle Michaels, there had been an unfamiliar smell in the house. Nail varnish. He had watched her read gossip websites as she painted her nails. Red Dahlia was the name of the bottle's color. She would not have believed him if he said that the flower signified betrayal. He watched the slow drag of gluey polish, the brush spreading. She painted just one of Han's fingernails.

"You can tell the stories?" she had said.

So Jeremy had tucked in Han. He had read the picture book with the fox and the picture book with the duck. He told Han about the nutcracker and Clara. He told him about the rat. He made his mouth firm in the shapes, so his son would learn, so his son would have language and always tell him.

Alexandra was packing in the living room when he finished. He looked at her from the hallway, and it occurred to him there was always a frame. Even together, they were part of a composition that ended. He'd found ways to extend the panorama, but even vistas carried edges. He went to the bedroom to lie down.

When she came to look in on him, he blamed clients. There was a young boy. He would get up in the middle of the night, take every item out of the refrigerator. He set a rabbit on fire. The two parents were in prison, aggravated battery and manslaughter. His aunt wanted to know he could get better, but do the math of his fate. It made Jeremy's head heavy.

"You're afraid for him," Alexandra said.

It was like a Russian book he'd read once, he'd told her. The author said all wrestlers cheated for bookies, but there was a place in Hamburg, a back room where wrestlers brawled in earnest. Only there could you know what a man was capable of, what the Hamburg score was. He thought about that book, and he thought how there was no Hamburg score in real life. He needed to think. He said he wasn't feeling like himself.

"Who are you then?" She smiled.

"Your husband," he said.

She had gone to the doorway, rested a finger on the light switch. "Since when do you speak Russian?" she had said.

Now he took a left and headed west. The sky was clear, and in the streets, women in tall shoes jangled with weekend jewelry. Passing groups was meditative. He thought of what Alexandra was doing now. What she'd done. She had been taking strange trips since before they were married. It suggested choreography, tactics. Maybe she was in love with this man, always had been.

From his research, elementary stuff, Jeremy knew in 1999, Lyle Ross Michaels had taken the same class as Alexandra, *The Odyssey* Then and Now. Ostensibly, this was where they had met. Ostensibly, a visit to Lyle Michaels was the real reason for the trip years ago attributed to the New York University reunion, the one Genevieve had not attended, and the one that was not archived on the internet.

Lyle Michaels was not married. The danger was that he was ready to be.

Somehow, he'd forgotten to snap into the SIGINT stance, the ear turned toward secrets, codes, and clear and present danger—enough to forget the vague dangers of fractionally requited love. But she had not left him. There were actions ahead. Jeremy could secure their life, but he knew this was a time for carefulness. It was a time to ask before answering, consider before doing. He would walk it off until his appointment with Wright. He would wait for the facts to speak.

CHAPTER 12

A problem: facts had a way of hiding other facts. The facts of Northern Ireland had been good water for fish, mild weather from the Gulf Stream. And that it was a temperate place had not meant the sectarians were any more moderate than elsewhere. The last year he was a spy, the whole city was redolent with umbrage turned to blood, hoax peace, and pretty political verbiage. Only driving approached truth to Jeremy, everything flooding by him, the whole country running away with complications of animus.

"An bhfuil feall eile le teacht?" Gerry Adams would ask—is there another betrayal coming?

And Jeremy might have believed it was only paranoia—not paranoia, perhaps, but the logic of sectarian war, fathers for fathers, a country of wrong places at wrong times—if it had not been for Wilmington.

That night, in Lisburn, Jeremy drank with FIFA in the background, the green turf washing down, and in all the legs, he couldn't keep straight the teams. He had lost count of the Guinness. Someone sat next to him. There was a penalty kick. People leapt in the stands. He heard his name, the weight of a hand on his shoulder.

There was the image of all those fans coming to their feet, arms overhead, the embraces. There were numbers painted on faces. There was Wilmington saying his man was there too, at the Laundromat, when Gunner died. Wilmington's man was Brendan, and he could not understand how the UFF, who'd taken credit for the hits, had known Brendan, Feeney, and Gunner would be in The Spin that night without an intel leak. It begged certain questions. Why, for example, had Brendan received at their message-drop a note Wilmington had not sent telling him to appear at the hair salon two months before? In slow motion, a player's hips twisted, quick wrench of torque, deceptive. The goalie couldn't read the intention until it was too late to guard the corner.

"Which salon?" Jeremy said.

"Lost an orange tabby, did you?" Wilmington said.

"Jesus."

"Was betrayed by his own with a kiss."

All fall, after everyone else slept, Jeremy and Wilmington stayed awake. What lodged them to their seats, to each other, to endless strings of Guinness, was the war played out in information. Sentence could be a subject and a verb; it could be punitive, death even. They knew there were names not uttered in the chambers to which they had access, and now, it was not simple to know who killed; it was not simple to know where a sentence traveled or how it amended in the mouths of men who thought they knew how to fix the world.

"Any person is a possible leak," Jeremy said.

"No," Wilmington said. "Everything we suspected was a leak was a channel. You're a good boy, Allsworth. Don't believe that means anyone else is."

According to Wilmington's new informer, someone in the Intelligence Corps had given a UDA charge called Mikey Spring intel that only could have been accessed through One Rock. The killer of Feeney, Brendan, and Gunner wasn't Spring, but it was he who furnished a time and place to murder. Wilmington's new informer had been chummy with Spring. Spring had told him his man on the inside of British intel had wanted to protect him, give him something to keep the UDA questions off. Problem was, Spring was a guy who thought you had to open your mouth to breathe. Spring ended up a dead man with an open mouth, shot taking out the waste one day by his friend since nappies, Wilmington's new informer. Wilmington's new informer, who the loyalists did not know had been turned.

In retrospect, it was obvious to Wilmington and Jeremy. The top Corps officers had wanted Feeney. He was a symbol. His hit was. Lives were weighed. One Rock approved the Laundromat attack. He handed the loyalists Gunner and Brendan for Feeney, for the death of a man who made headlines.

Now in New York, a trajectory became clear to Jeremy. His mother had betrayed him. His father. And the Intelligence Corps betrayal was supposed to be the last. Jeremy had not expected to meet Alexandra, marry. To have a son named Han who drew smiling monsters in the beach sand, trust in four walls called home. He had not expected to trust happiness. The spy was supposed to have learned better.

PART SEVEN: (TRANSITIVE PROPERTY)

The Internet is not something that you just dump something on. It's not a big truck. It's a series of tubes. And if you don't understand, those tubes can be filled and if they are filled, when you put your message in, it gets in line and it's going to be delayed by anyone that puts into that tube enormous amounts of material.

—*United States Senator Ted Stevens, June 28, 2006*

CHAPTER 1

Things he was good at pretending: sleep, hungry. Things he was not good at pretending: not sleeping, relaxed. But he was laid out on the couch while his mother and aunt Rhonda watched television, and he could still hear the actors. Gunshots. Remember not to gasp.

It was a good show even not seeing the blood.

The killer had a time bomb, a hostage, and a hidden location. Tyrell was keeping track, holding the clues in his mind side by side. He had his guesses. He was counting in his head to see when the police caught up to him. His guess: ten minutes, six hundred seconds.

"So we were getting nice," Aunt Rho said.

"No surprises there," his mother said.

There's music now like horror. He didn't know the instrument, but those sounds—you know the reveal is coming. Shoes on linoleum tapping on the way to knowledge. Slow walk, but going away from mystery.

"When he did it to me, I felt it down in my feet," his aunt Rhonda was saying.

His mother cleared her throat. "Girl," she said. "He missed the point then."

They laughed and shushed. He could hear them wheezing like life is a comedy and we can't stop watching. And he couldn't hear the police. They were on the phone with the terrorist, and he couldn't hear. This could be the best part. This could be the moment of a clue.

Eight and a half minutes. Five hundred and ten seconds. You want to hear if the next sound is a creaking door. It can be the killer.

"Point, game, series," Aunt Rho said. "He did the whole season."

"My sister the winter freak."

Aunt Rho began to sing-laugh. "Let it snow," she was going. "Let it snow, let it snow, let it snow."

The detective's teeth cramp around his lips. This is whisper. This is the terms.

"Shut up," Tyrell shouted. "This is the good part."

His mother cocked her head, crossed her arms. "What are *you* doing awake?"

Eleven p.m. He could see Wright ahead in the queue, so he waited. He memorized with a glance as though he were checking the time on the phone outstretched in his palm. Gray tennis shoes with a swipe on the side. Grass-green laces, black stitching. Later, he would find the shoes, not the man. Eyes caught on commodities. People did not say hello to strangers. They said, I like your shoes.

The door swallowed the line in fits. Jeremy showed a card that said his name was otherwise at the door. Wright had sent this ID. Wright had sent a dire code. You'll want to know this.

Inside, the crowd moved him down into a grand basement. The intelligence of the throng was its magnet sense for consumption. He let himself be carried toward the bar through the floor litter of plastic cups. From his vantage by the bar, a form stepped through his periphery. "Nice shoes. Where would I get a pair like that?" Jeremy said.

"Place on Broadway."

"When the thing is shoes, it's always a place on Broadway."

"Name's Ray."

"Bill."

"It's on me," Wright told the bartender.

There was a logic to public rooms that they understood. They moved toward the edges, where the leaners and tables hung in the shadows. It seemed everyone was damp. A human mist rose up in beams of roving light. Wright collapsed a semicircle of lime, hands large and precise on the fruit.

"Where are you staying?" he said.

"Got a little place in Bushwick inconvenient to the train."

"That how the realtor put it to you?"

"The inconvenience makes the foot traffic easier to monitor on my end." Wright scratched his nose. "Warehouses. There are regular workers who eat at the food truck, and then there are those to fret after."

"And what is the fret now?"

Wright laughed his way, strangely, stomach caving, receding farther in the corner. Jeremy let him finish. "Your adopted home base, Bill."

He found a shard of plastic in his drink, picked it out and laid it on a napkin. Wright gazed out onto the crowd, where strobes made moments of faces, bright ephemera. He began talking slowly, musingly, not looking at Jeremy.

"Look, it's like this, Bill," Wright said. "Mid-seventies, British intel given to the US leads to the capture of a gunrunner, George DeMeo. The Feebs cut a deal with him. He wears a wire when he meets with the Irish stateside; he receives immunity and never has to testify against his old friends. Then they'll send in undercover FBI to sell the guns to the Americans involved with the IRA. Simple transaction."

An emcee was on a microphone collecting volume.

If you got five dollars in your pocket, make some noise.

If you got ten dollars in your pocket, make some noise.

If you like sex, make some noise.

Where my two-step at?

"Except while the FBI are trying to pin down Michael Flannery from NORAID, show the money isn't going just to widows and orphans, CIA have their fingers in the IRA gunrunning business too."

"All very plausible."

"So five Irish émigrés go to trial in 1982 after an arms roundup. Does the CIA lie to Congress? Does the CIA arm both sides of an insurgency? Does the CIA run guns too? Of course it's yes and yes and yes, but DeMeo is pleading the Fifth like it's the sole way to breathe any time CIA are mentioned."

"That's a tactic, sure."

Wright turned abruptly. Jeremy felt the pace change, time quicken. "So the defense argues the five Irish didn't sell the guns to the IRA; the FBI sold the guns to the CIA. Flannery and his crew are acquitted. All that British intel flushed out over interagency sibling rivalry. Every one of them wants to bring home the trophy to Dad. But do you think the Americans learn? Of course not. They now think you pay more than any research institution, buy the most elaborate toys, get the best computers in the world doing your dirty work, the result is zero splashback. But the physics are still there."

"And what physics are we talking about?"

If you believe in God, you love God, you get down and give thanks every morning to the Lord our Savior, make some noise.

If you graduated from junior high school and *high school raise your hand.*

If you sexy for no reason, raise your hand.

Take your shoes off 'cause we don't give a fuck.

"I am hearing that the GRU have a hacker stable on payroll," Wright continued. "So this gets me thinking, Bill. I'm really thinking about this possibility."

"The Kremlin will spin any fairy tale just to keep us afraid of our own grandmother."

"But it isn't just the Kremlin. It's everywhere: digital criminals in intel."

"And we bugged phones," Jeremy said.

"And I'm thinking you can't trust these guys, Bill. Hackers like nothing better than putting a spanner in the works. There was a breach in our own databases, Bill, a handful of years back. Someone grabbed us between the legs for ransom. Ransom we paid because the Ministry of Defense is incompetent to the new lunatics. We've already seen American-developed viruses stolen from intel agencies and used on our own hospitals, telecom companies."

"It's delicate with allies."

"What happens when hired gun hackers begin planting misinformation? What will it cost us? Aggressing the wrong region, will it be? A republican seizure after everything we've worked for? And this is to say nothing of the crying over civil liberties once the BB fucking C gets a whiff."

"I left my son at home for this. What is it you have to say?"

"About that."

"I'm listening," Jeremy said.

"There are Int. Corps with kids, families in other divisions," Wright said. "I know that. But our little outfit."

"Not ours anymore."

"Northern Ireland is not over. The Real IRA are still exploding things like it's American Independence Day, Bill."

"When might you realize we're retired, Ray? When will you realize that remembering will not make time run anticlockwise?"

"What if I told you Provos are training ISIS in car bombs? The old radical kinship. You did not think it was only symbolic, the Palestinian flags, did you? You're mental if you think this is over."

"Or Ukip decide an enemy to unite over. And then the fatality is 'not terror.' It's border reform."

"Contact is one hundred."

If you a real roly-poly, raise one shoe in the air.

If you comfortable with your sexuality, bend over for your real friend. This one for the ladies only.

If you know this ain't no place for skinny bitches, make some noise.

"Who is your contact?"

"More like who's yours."

Jeremy began and finished the glass. He leaned back, away from Wright. He squinted. "Meaning."

"Not so long after Seven-Seven your wife goes to Northern Ireland. She is meeting with some very important people, government, developers, big money and the like. Then suddenly she's out of the business of nation branding. Suddenly, she's in a new sector, here, and she's meeting with tech people at Cathexis, Cathexis who has made their headquarters guess where. You see where this is going, Bill."

"I see, Ray."

"But do you?" Wright said.

"I see I'm not the one stupid with theories."

"No, you're stupid with gash, Bill. Our friends in MI5 ordered agents to marry persons of interest. It was tactical relational fabrication," Wright said.

"She is not a person of interest."

Wright pressed his fingertips onto the table, his wrist bent so that his hand resembled a five-legged pod. "Perhaps, *you're* the person of interest."

"You've lost it, Ray. You've really lost it."

"Was there a time," Wright said, finally, "you were going to tell me your wife's brother had some nasty business with the NSA?"

"No," Jeremy said. "Because it isn't true."

"What if I told you I've intercepted communications indicating such?"

"You're spying again now."

"There are no coincidences, Bill. I'm telling you an operative. Has a name for every day of the week."

"And what if he is?" Jeremy said. "What would it matter to you?"

"If you don't see it, it's because you're closing your eyes to the skeleton in your own cupboard. It's been so long since Lisburn, has it, Bill?"

If you got real hair, put your hand up.

If ain't no one can mess with your real friend, take that real friend hand and put it up in the air.

Can I hear it for Brooklyn?

"They're American."

"So is Martin Goddamn Galvin, and he's been wailing for bloodshed decades now."

"You're mad, Ray. I need to relieve the babysitter."

"Of everyone in the world."

Where my Boricuas at? Where my Morenas at? Where my Domin-icanas at?

"What we're talking about," Jeremy said, "is thousands of Americans in these jobs."

"And he left a fat breach for your thousands."

"I feel sorry for you. You need help."

"Don't give me your psychobabble sympathy, Bill. I want the truth. I hear your psychobabble, and I think this man has been compromised."

"I see, Ray. Very nice."

"I want you to tell me how is it Barry Cain, ex-NSC, ex-DARPA, met with Lawrence last week. Tell me how it is that Cain happens to have been the one to identify a young recruit named Shel Chen, who happens to be your brother-in-law."

A woman in a dress like a tight trash bag tripped on the corner of their low lounge table, laughing and apologizing, her purse swinging with its own inertia. She patted the table, corrected glasses. Her skirt was bunched up, and she was laughing. She fell onto Wright's lap.

"Who's your friend?" she asked Jeremy.

Jeremy stood. "He's not my friend." And then he walked off, reabsorbed in the crowd.

Mr. Jordan was explaining that he was not a friend; he was a clinical social worker. He had his palms out, waving little circles, then he made a butcher chop move. If Tyrell didn't listen for a second, he'd have no idea what was up at all, just weird little signs in the air.

"What, you don't like me?" he said because he was tired of trying to listen.

"I like you very much, Tyrell."

He leaned back. "So that's it then. That's gravy."

The idea was simple. The idea was come to the science fair. Soda bottle tornadoes and egg drops and all that. Vinegar-clean pennies and pizza-party afters. There would be other parents, and Mr. Jordan.

Because his mother was not-happy. His mother was not-playing. Came home and he had a safety pin earring he'd poked himself, shouty music thick above the alcohol-rubbed cotton balls—and he knew what words like desecrate, violate, you let me sounded like—and she was getting loud like not-happy, not-playing, and don't think an earring won't be used against us.

And he knew she was talking about the lady in the STARK

office. And he knew when the STARK lady said *predictive models show a lot of boys like Tyrell*, his mother said *not my son*. He'd heard them. He'd heard the STARK lady saying *before it's a bigger problem*. He'd heard the STARK lady say *meds*, and he'd heard his mother: *that's enough*. But also, to him later, there was no TV or ice cream and *you've got to get correct*.

Fine. He did not want her at his fair. He had his people too.

He picked up a pink and blue Slinky toy Mr. Jordan had on the table. Juggle it and it's purple. Clean, good sound. He can get lost in there.

Mr. Jordan looked at his notes. "I'd like to return to something you mentioned last week."

"But that's just it, Mr. Jordan."

"What is?"

"The circles. Don't you get tired of it?"

And Mr. Jordan's face was crooked as he said, "Yes. I'm so tired."

CHAPTER 4

Past the chicken spot and the bodega with EBT, he found the big grocery and tested the tomatoes in his hands. His instructions were choose one flavor of juice box. Juice box. Not fruit punch box. Not high-fructose corn syrup. Not fruit-flavored beverage. His instructions were spaghetti and tomatoes and onions, cilantro, beef. Check the date on the milk. Canned pineapple, chicken thighs, cereal.

"And not one with sugar coating either," his mother had said.

But these were rules he liked overall. He liked to compare prices. Look at the cost per unit and the pounds. He would estimate how many ounces. Test in the silver hanging scale.

He took the aisles with a red basket. Fruit from Chile. Sauce from Italy. He could spray the whole store out in every direction like a map in foods.

The line was long. The woman ahead was arguing about the price of Pampers. She was jabbing old coupons.

He checked the other lines, made estimates. There were probabilities to consider. The chance of hold-ups. He stayed in this line. Also, the cashier was cute.

Her hand touched his as she counted back the difference on his change.

Back home trudge. Forty-eight seven-two. The receipt is in his pants pocket with the keys. Circle. Triangle.

He was studying the receipt as he walked, working up a theory over the numbers under the barcode. There's an order to it. His mother said everything happened for a reason. Like with his dad and how he came back from Afghanistan.

"Watch it," a man in a plaid shirt said. Tyrell had walked straight into his torso. His head in this man's belly button.

"Watch it, *please*," he said, because his mother was a manners fanatic, and he was his mother's son.

At home, the smell in the doorway was fresh breeze out of a can and morning coffee burning on the machine. He walked in through the door to the kitchen, bags bumping corners, furniture. There was a bowl of bananas sitting up top a blue and white checkered tablecloth, and his grandma had her sudoku out, but she wasn't answering in pencil like usual. A thin man waved, loose-limbed and smiling. He wore a red T-shirt with a bulldog face on the front.

"I know you," the man said. "Tyrell. From the pictures."

Tyrell squinted. "Mom?" he said, and she came out from the TV room, nodded.

"This is Eddie, Tyrell," his aunt Rhonda said. "My boy-friend."

He stepped back. The counter was there. "You don't have a boyfriend."

"Oh, but she do."

"Before I was talking to Eddie, I was talking to his persona,"

Auntie Rho explained. "Eddie said we had to meet in person, and I wasn't sure."

"Because you sent a fake picture."

"It wasn't fake. It was squeezed for a lengthening effect."

"I decided no fear," Eddie cut in. "I decided let's stop talking through windows; we aren't in a zoo."

Tyrell stared at Aunt Rhonda. She wore rugs of mascara and a lipstick the color of a Bulls jersey. There were small flowers on her nails, and her nails were on a mug picturing bug-eyed animals. She had always been big-time for Tweety Bird.

"Didn't your *mother* wonder where you were when you missed curfew?" his grandmother said. "How *old* are you?"

"Nineteen going on forty, know what I mean?" Eddie said, rubbing down his own arm.

"You're dating a *teenager*, Rho?" his mother said.

"Age looks backwards, ma'am. I'm about the present, mindfulness. Think how you think. Is it serving you? That philosophy's where I'm at."

"Nineteen and a man," his aunt Rhonda said. She was tearing open a bag of potato chips and pouring them into a large, ugly bowl painted with the words MOVIE POPCORN. She pinched one and placed it in Eddie's mouth.

"Made with avocado oil, plop, right into the kettle. Our hearts love healthy fats," Eddie said, swirling the bowl toward Tyrell. "Try them."

"He could be your son," his grandma said. "You're thirty-four years old."

"It's what men and women have been doing since cave times," Aunt Rhonda said.

"You'd be dead already if we were cave people," Tyrell said. And his mother was laughing crazy. She was crying from laughing and she jumbled her hand on top of his head. She slapped herself and laughed. His grandma did. "What?" he said.

The what game: What color is this crayon? Black. What else is black? Jill. Besides Jill. Hair. Not my hair. Hair. What about just outside the window, Han? Sky. What kind of sky? Night. And what do we do at night? Story time.

"We also sleep," Jeremy said.

He hadn't recently.

Anagrams are the technique. Wright and Lawrence had met at least once, or Wright was making up the Cain-Lawrence connection. Wright and Lawrence had met at least once, and Wright had confected the Cain-Lawrence connection. Cain-Lawrence, it mattered or it didn't. But Alexandra, her brother.

"Story time, Baba," Han said.

Once upon a time, there was a man named Nathanael and his beautiful fiancée Klara. But he fell in love with a doll called Olimpia. He did not know her limbs were wooden. He did not know that when people stared it was because they knew he was a fool. Then one day, Nathanael saw Olimpia's eyes on the floor, and he was thrown from his madness. It seemed for a time that he would recover. But one day, he looked in his spyglass at Klara, and the sight drove him to hurt her. In his madness, he cast himself to his death.

And once upon a time, a man named Aleksandr Solzhenitsyn threw a log into a fire. He did not know that the log had rotted, that it was full of ants. The ants poured out into the flames. They were burning up, squirming in pain, and they fled the fire for the cool sand of the fireplace. But then, as Aleksandr watched, they began to circle, circle, circle in the sand, distraught. They began to return to their home, though there, it was certain they would be eaten up by hot flames.

CHAPTER 6

In the dream, a crack accommodated a slivered view. He can sense Gunner, a focal point.

Jeremy, his body becomes more present in the waiting. Spying is looking at mostly nothing changing except time. How long. Long. That is how it feels, but wait long enough and the revenge of the languid comes. Brendan, Clarence, Padraig—ordinary frames busy with grudges—and, squatting on a dolly in the corner, Gunner.

Brendan is pacing the garage, springing puffy hands. Brendan takes two steps, stops. "It was Chinky Bratty who did it, not a doubt," he says. "Chinky Bratty who we should've gotten in November when we had the chance."

"He wasn't home," Gunner says. "I don't suppose the point was kill a bit of air in the kitchen."

The clock is broken. Jeremy can't keep time straight. The hands on the face say it is night, or afternoon, or all-time in never. Dream time.

Jeremy smells shrimp. He smells burnt bread. Something bright and cold accumulates in Jeremy's stomach. Someone raises two hands on a grip, fires, infringes on idyll. Clumped in the carpet: the slop of meat thrown by a bullet, the body kneels like praying, falls. Life gone before the tax of cordite clears.

Brendan stands, slow and loose-limbed. Something is happening in him, a revelation real as a woman. Jeremy closes his eyes. He opens them.

"Alexandra?" Jeremy says.

An orange cat crosses the floor. "Your bake." She laughs. "Your bake."

And then he was awake, and there was a toy horse staring at him from the bedside table, a light pricking from his phone. Wright. He turned to the flapped-open blanket on her side, empty of Alexandra.

For the poor flames, they blamed yesterday's weather. The sticks remained damp, and their early attempts didn't catch. They burned newspaper after newspaper, days of events curling above the lighter.

And look at him so careful with the graham crackers when she pointed to the perforations, the breaking points. He studied them. He pressed his lips together.

Jeremy placed chocolates in bowls. He reached down to kiss Han's head. She watched them spear marshmallows on the stairs of the weekend cottage.

"You must be very careful," Jeremy said. "They can burn."

"Ants," Han said.

"Fire," Alexandra said.

"Or they can swell up big, big, big like a brown cloud," Jeremy said, "and the cloud tastes delicious."

The fire was dying, and Alexandra prodded with a stick. She added more newsprint, cartoon families and office cynics. A weak little hand came to her knee. He warned her, her son.

"Smile for Auntie G," she said as she took the picture.

A blue lick swerved around a marshmallow, and Han blew it,

told his father to make a wish. She could smell the burnt sugar settling between pine. Their heads were bent together, blond and black.

"I'm so happy," she said.

Jeremy straightened, a green coat stiff around his neck. "Are you?" he said.

CHAPTER 8

She had told Jeremy that she was flying to Nevada to entrust her mother to someone after her mother had taken a fall, which was true. She was also planning to stay in Brooklyn for a day on the return. She was planning to meet Lyle Michaels and her brother.

Lately, Jeremy removed himself from the apartment or else he was a roving camera trained on her body. He turned to her when she said his name, and his eyes were flat black, and he asked sharp questions about her mother's health. She believed if she pretended not to notice, he would stop. A romantic idea: a woman in control, emotions tight to her, all tucked in, administrative almost, capable of being a woman who had it all.

When she got to Nevada, there were ten résumés. Ten curations of history. She had made the calls. But references were strangers too. Everyone with a horror story had trusted someone once.

"My own flesh," her mother said, "can't stick at home for her mother. My own flesh hiring the cheapest person."

"You think this doesn't cost me?"

But there was a moment, Alexandra already at the door. She turned back. Federica, the new nurse, was folding a towel. Her mother was a slumped thing, thick but wilting, and there was black mascara all over her eyes. It would be different when Shel returned and Alexandra brought her son. There would be a phenomenon of numbers, multiplied people. Her mother had never believed a life turned better was common sense. It was not in the evidence she'd accrued, the years, and now she was old too soon, had been some years, aged by small checks and worry and all the disdain from the neighbors, teachers. It would be a shock, no, a surprise, such goodness.

Alexandra looked at her mother with the remote control in her lap and the dry, loose gullet. Her hands were lumpy on the arms of the chair, and Alexandra remembered their tremble on a pencil when once Alexandra had asked for help with her algebra homework. Her mother had copied the problem slowly, begun and then erased and then started over again, had gotten a new sheet of paper and tried once more. Her mother's hands were shaking. Her mother had crumpled the new sheet eventually and stood, told her she would not tolerate a stupid daughter who didn't pay attention in school, didn't learn any better, and as Alexandra watched Federica place a blanket on her hunched mother's shoulders, the pity and rage were fast in her chest.

Her mother was slapping Federica's hands away, but she was very weak now, clumsy with opioids. She was moaning like a child, and Alexandra wished her mother would call out to her. She wished, for a moment, she could with no fear of retort tell her mother she loved her.

"I thank God my husband isn't alive to see his ungrateful daughter," her mother told Federica loudly.

When she'd gotten many miles away from her mother, inside

the hotel, Alexandra could smell the exhaust of expensive food. Fried cremini mushrooms. Aged steaks. She cut straight through the lobby with all its dark wood and leather. Up the elevator.

In the room, she poured three drinks and sat at a table reflecting city light. Out the window, there were windows. Alexandra could see a figure in an adjacent building pacing. She was certain if only there was one more, just one, she would fall into the filled boxes of their life, part of a company, a marriage, a family, all the indices of experience. It was not too much to ask, she was certain, in the twenty-first century.

An alert in her pocket. Unlock phone. Not going to happen tonight.

Lyle Michaels.

CHAPTER 9

Barry Cain was off booze for now. He had a glass of red confection come out of a soda gun, claim of the barkeep: cranberry juice. In the days since the wife's imposition of dietary austerity measures, his belt band was softening off him. Lyle Michaels took in the droopy suit, slid up by a bar stool next to him. Cain grabbed a shoulder and a hand at once, quick gentleman greeting dance and then they hunched up over the bar, leaning on forearms.

"You said you thought I could help verify some information."

"Still do," Lyle said. "I'm hearing a lot."

"And yet the information seems full until it doesn't. For a while, you have everything, a whole theory of the world. Then you are saying, what was the date and what is the model. The facts spread. You did the right thing making the call."

Lyle looked at the chalkboard menu. "I'm going to order."

"It's a better place to go than chaos," Cain said, a cramped little smile turning at him. "My wife hates that joke."

"The animal trainer," Lyle said, finger in the air. The bartender lifted a chin in question. "An IPA. Whatever IPA you've got."

"That's right. Got a ribbon display."

"Confess I looked you up on the internet."

For a while, Cain talked about the structure of competition, all the ramps and obstacles. It was different from regular show, less eugenics to it. At their house in Virginia there was the Australian shepherd–Maltese mix Sweet Tea and the two houndish ones, Jezebel and Secret. His wife had started into dog agility contests when their kid began applying to colleges.

"An empty-nest thing."

"Maybe a little."

"You're visiting your kid without her this week, you said."

"The dogs. There are seasons to these things. It's also that she hates a goodbye. Don't think she even realizes it's part protective of herself."

"But you do."

"I infer, anyway. She knows her own way. Natural survivalist in tennis whites, you know."

"Why do you think she does it, the competitions?"

"The bodies of animals don't perjure, for one," Cain said. "Two, there is making herself a sight. She wanted to be a singer, you know, and then, it's got the verbal aspect. She likes talking to them, giving orders. I think it gives her a sense of control over the natural world."

He needed a few more beats to bring Cain to temperature. It was a technique Cain undoubtedly knew. But Cain was far from DARPA and the National Security Council now, and it made Lyle easier too, the small talk as though they were friends, easier, anyway, than McCreight. He'd ventured rapport work. But try and there was snapback.

Barry Cain twiddled a straw.

"It's been hard for her losing the house," Lyle said.

"She didn't cry when her daddy died. It was Katrina drilled grief down. She grew strong on crawfish boils. Didn't matter we didn't go more than twice a year. Some women go elbow-deep in relief efforts. For her it was pups."

"Wasn't Jezebel eaten by dogs?"

"Only her corpse," Cain said.

Lyle untucked a notebook from the inner pocket of his blazer. He made a slow show of curling the flap back, curling over used pages. He hit the end of a pen against the bar to snap the writing point into protrusion. There was something in the gesture, he was sure, of Jack Burden, the first not the second adaptation, John Ireland. It was a story that had once entered his eyes and stayed there in the place of a question, the rhythm of a nod, structured the way he leaned into space with a stranger under the gaze. He understood the shape he took in the other person's eyes, he, a writer.

"I wanted to ask you about something. A human resources question."

Cain smiled. "Alrighty."

He had a large forehead like a pink lightbulb. Lyle squinted into the light of it and cleared his throat. "Hackers."

"That a question, Michaels?"

"There hackers on the federal payroll?"

"You know I'm not a federal employee anymore. Legislators made sure of that. I've got consulting, of course, but these are private companies we're talking about."

"Private companies under contract with the US government. Your Booz Allen Hamiltons and such get intimate, I understand."

"Given," Cain said. "You having another?"

His hand moved to a thatched wooden bowl gritty with some kind of man-made dust designed for onion flavor. Lyle pulled his hand away, ate a cereal piece at a time, not saying anything. The bartender sat a beer, sailboat etched onto the pint glass, on top of a foamy branded coaster.

"What kind of singer?"

"Singer?"

"Your wife."

"She liked the jazz standards all right, but her daddy said he didn't want his own onstage performing Jew-boy librettos. She has long blood if you know what I'm saying."

"Hence the pups."

"Hence the pups."

"But you wouldn't know anything about hackers. You have contacts but wouldn't know about hackers."

Cain folded his hands, resting his elbows wing-like on the back of the stool and the bar, torso facing Lyle. "What's the difference between a self-taught programmer with a bad sense of humor and a hacker, Michaels?"

"I don't know. What?"

"Sincere question."

"Because I'm hearing things."

"Are you."

A finger circling the rim of his glass. The place was a slow establishment tended by a thick-jawed man who polished rocks glasses and played Irish folk songs out of the jukebox. Now he was sliding quarters in the slot. The slap of song lists could be heard as he arrowed through the browse.

"I'm hearing about malware that can bury itself in systems.

Software, whatever you call it, that can make automated mechanisms fail. Traffic lights. Train signals."

"You're talking about the rumors the CIA planted software that commanded pumps and valves in the Trans-Siberian gas pipeline to operate so fast, build so much pressure, there was an explosion."

"No, Barry, I'm not. I'm talking about cyberweapons being built. Not just by com-sci guys ready to get out of the university and rake real coin for once either. Domestics and foreign nationals. Some of them living abroad, possibly even the same exact hackers caught infiltrating US systems. Possibly even groomed by the agencies in the first place."

Cain pulled a paper cap off the end of a straw. "The Cold War is over, Michaels. I doubt many resources can be gathered to turn green lights red in Siberia. The speed of telecom means radicalization runs from teenagers in their basements to jihadists in *their* basements. A defense strategy would need to go online quietly if that's what you're asking. Foreign governments do not announce themselves as the directors of hackers. That would involve potential punitive action. Diplomatic disaster. But you know I wouldn't know anyway. I'm private sector now, just like they wanted."

"What about a virus to disable uranium centrifuges? Because that's what I'm hearing."

"Hear where?" Cain asked.

"Your old apostle Sean McCreight. Can you corroborate?"

"And where *is* McCreight these days?"

"It's an interesting prospect. It points to other possibilities."

"Another cranberry," Cain said.

The window was streaky, small, and barred, but Cain looked

out at the feet cutting over pavement anyway. His hand lay on a paperback's embossed letters. Lyle thought of the words the title could be. Pencil. Penal. Penicillin.

"Glen Close has been directed within the country. I'm hearing about drone strikes. Is it possible we see the same sort of mechanical hacking done in Iran here too in action against citizens?"

"I'm not exactly on the email list, Michaels," Cain said out of the corner of his mouth, sucking down juice.

"Because the appropriations committee."

"I'm sorry I can't help you," Cain said.

"The Def. Sec."

"Under the bus."

"You became the rogue," Lyle said.

Cain smiled. "Maybe I already a little was."

"Bastards." Lyle sat back and rubbed his palms on his face. He had thought he was lucky. The visit. "Can I buy you another drink? Just go over a few of McCreight's statements?"

"If you mean a juice, sure." Cain patted the paperback. "Anything I can do, sure."

Lyle turned back through his notes. He liked the gestures of reference, checking his own memory in space.

CHAPTER 10

When Ingrid dropped off Marina, it was different. The thrill quelled. Because idling in the threshold adjusting blankets around Marina, he looked at Ingrid appraising. He could read how she let her eyes fall. The curtain where there should have been a door between the bedroom and living room.

Lyle looked at Marina. He looked at Ingrid. *If you don't stop now, it will accrue into infinity.* They had fallen in love once and Ingrid also out, but he could be different to her. She could see him differently. *Change the theorem.*

Lyle asked her to sit, and she didn't. For a while, he spoke about all the ways the government could poke the fabric of a life, how it would alter shades of intimacy, quiet friendships. There were political repercussions to the platforms too, he continued, deep state flooding Cathexis, and other new weapons. Imagine a world where the only things you heard about were the worst versions of your proclivities. Imagine the polarization. Take it one step further and imagine the way support for wars and policies could be instituted by installing them straight into your Cathexis. It was why the book was bigger than them.

"I'm the one who can tell it responsibly. I feel responsible," Lyle said.

"That the adjective?"

Problem being: Ingrid had, at her disposal, the declamations of the tenure track. Ingrid had, at her disposal, terms of an employment agreement: produce another film within two years. Two. There were two of them, she told Lyle. And she needed him to mind their daughter more while she shot the documentary in China.

"This," Ingrid said, "is what being middle-class parents means: only one of us gets to be the artist. Someone needs to stay home with the kid. You had months, Lyle."

He adjusted blankets around Marina. He gave her a popsicle. He could feel something unlatch, and his face was hot. The apartment was. Something was escaping, and he heard his voice reach a harried pitch.

"I didn't finish the book yet, so now you've won?" he said.

His arms were somehow above his shoulders, flapping in the manner of a marooned man spotting a plane overhead. Like someone choking for air.

"Yes," she said. "I won."

CHAPTER 11

They'd known each other long enough that Alexandra could picture her desk, white with documents. Legal scholarship. News clips. The woman fired after posting to Cathexis that her job was boring. A mother denied a teaching certificate for a Halloween picture. The German nightclub with years of footage sent straight to the police, and all those scanned IDs.

Genevieve told Alexandra, "Come to London. The gray will do you good." But even through the phone, Alexandra could hear that gray alone was not the reason Genevieve suggested JFK to Heathrow, rather than the other way around.

The man had come to Genevieve pleading.

Win me anonymity.

The not anonymous was Gerald Seth, a small man, dark-haired. He'd worn a cardigan sweater. What happened was so many years ago, and it is the first result of me in searches. It is Gerald Seth fraud for pages.

I am more than who I was then.

Genevieve's thought: he had done his time out in the scrutinous open.

The premise is the burden of history. The premise is we can change.

What are the repercussions if we can't lose ourselves? There are laws about the age of imbibing, Genevieve was saying, but not the public permanence of personal information.

Should I suffer for whom I improved from?

"An interesting proposition," Alexandra said.

The opposition would call witnesses to Seth's old scams, claim knowing is a public good. But this is not a free speech issue. Let the papers print what they will. Let the papers keep their words, but do not include them in the search engine index. Information does not need to be simple as typing a name. You used to have to know where, what to search. We are after gaining the increment. Just this increment of privacy. Make the mistake harder to find, not impossible.

The EU Council had adopted the Framework Decision to protect the personal data of individuals cooperating with police and in judicial matters. Article 8 of the European Convention on Human Rights: right to respect of private and family life. There were the Argentine cases. Genevieve thought there might be legs after all.

"London doesn't make sense now, and you work all the time anyway," Alexandra said. "I'd barely see you."

"Says who?"

"Says Angeline," Alexandra said.

"Since when do you talk to Angeline?" Genevieve said.

"We're Connected," Alexandra said, "on Cathexis, just like everyone else."

"I'm sorry, you're right, she's right, I'm working all the time."

And what if Genevieve had agreed to come to New York? she thought. What then? Alexandra would not have told her about Shel, could not have. Alexandra said, "I only miss you."

Genevieve paused. "What's wrong? Spill it."

"I don't spill. I pour."

"All right, I get it. You're a tall glass of water. But even water babbles. Or brooks do, anyway," adding, when Alexandra didn't answer, "Ever thought whoever said silence speaks volumes didn't have a cell phone?"

"Have you no respect for the classics?"

"The clichés. I call it like I see it. Sometimes, the head isn't big-boned, Al. It's fat."

"Oh, but who doesn't love the occasional platitude?"

"I've always thought that one 'suicide is a permanent solution to a temporary problem' was a little bonked, you know? If it's a permanent solution, doesn't that sound pretty viable? Why not just say that suicide is permanent; problems are temporary?"

"Because some aren't?"

A pause. "Probably being paid by the word," Genevieve said finally.

"That guy needs an editor," Alexandra joined.

"A Strunk guide," Genevieve said. Then: "Should I be afraid?"

CHAPTER 12

Lyle was afraid to check the mail, and he was afraid to check his phone. Just one reason: his father called about coming over Sunday. He said all the time it had been. He said there was the game. "Your mother's making gravy," he said. "And a baked ziti. It's been so long, I don't know does my son remember us."

"I need to work."

"Work. What work?"

Lyle paused for composure. "I am involved in some research. For a book."

His father said food on the table. He said the Micellis had always worked, always. He said what about come back forty-a-weeks, like the summers.

"I can't go backward," Lyle said.

"Family business is backwards now?" his father said. "The Micellis would always do what it took. I'll tell you. I'll tell you what. It used to be family meant something."

"This book means something too."

Yet Fourth Amendment had been done. McCreight thought the story was the work he'd done triangulating calls and emails to target terrorists years before, but it had been reported in newspapers already to quick and small ado, and the more Lyle thought about it, the more he was certain that the American audience would not care for further detail. What he needed was new. What he needed was more about the Iranian centrifuges. Material weapons. Threats that appeared real, or victories. That story arc.

"I'm talking about Ingrid. She's a good girl, Ly. And so is Marina."

"No one's talking about Ingrid or Marina."

"I'm happy to help, don't get me wrong. But I worry about my granddaughter," his father said.

"And I don't?"

Lyle could feel the days closing behind him like doors. He had not forgotten the sums he owed his father, that Ingrid wanted to film a film that would undo official facts in China. He had not forgotten that already Marina had become a girl and would want more, want better. And he would want to be able to give better, to live better, to not bring her to a sad little one-bedroom where sometimes there were bugs and other times rats, and always there was something a little sad and adolescent about the entire setup.

"Listen," his father said. "We'll talk over dinner Sunday. That's how it's always been done. We always did it like such. You talk over dinner."

Lyle looked at his daughter. She didn't look unhappy in her sleep. She didn't look underfed, neglected. She looked tired from their afternoon in the park and eating hot dogs.

"How it's always been done was segregation until the civil rights movement," Lyle said. "That's what I think about how it's always been done."

"We weren't teenagers forever," his father said. "There was

respect for work. You didn't have every other one on a so-called social program, Lyle."

"Who is on a social program and what is so-called about it?"

"I'll tell you it's college," his father said. "Because I look and all I see is protests. Every other day protests on *your* alma mater campus."

"They want the university to divest from private military firms, Dad. What is the problem with that?"

His father could be heard beeping the car horn. "Jesus Christmas," he said. "All right, kiddo. All right. Coming in loud and clear. But Sunday. Tell us sooner. You remember how to call."

CHAPTER 13

They were still years in the past interview-wise when Sean McCreight agreed to a last-minute talk at the warehouse. Lyle disassembled the prepaid, handed it to McCreight to place in the freezer. He looked around the room, a high-ceilinged box with safes in the corner, a folding chair, a mattress, and a couch like a shabby flowered hot dog bun. On a table in the center of the room, McCreight had set up a computer, and throughout the room, there were small speakers, some hung from strings in the ceiling, others on boxes or shelves, and a metal object that looked like an open book springing antennae was set beside three typewriters positioned on the floor where it met the wall.

"Would've thought these were a century or so old school for you," Lyle said.

"Would've thought but did something else instead. That's a 1927 Underwood Universal," McCreight said, turning in the cold buzz of the open freezer. "Remington Noiseless Portable. And the green one there, that's the Hermes 3000."

"Always wanted one of these," Lyle said, "but whenever it came time to it, a flea market or an antique store sale, I'd think what if I lost the one copy of the manuscript?"

"You people think the worst thing that can happen is an accident. It is all icy roads and spilt milk," McCreight said.

Knelt down, Lyle touched a ribbon and pulled away a black finger to wipe on his pants. He stood and let himself sag the center of the couch. He'd bought a new recorder, five inches, 555 hours of MP3 audio on a twenty-dollar memory card, just-brushed clean sound. At home, on the practice take, he could hear the rustle of his breast pocket. Now, Lyle lay the device on Sean McCreight's laptop.

"Smart foreign governments are buying up precautionary antiques. Aren't prior to telecom exactly, but not networked either. Less hackable."

"I see," Lyle said.

McCreight turned a metal chair and strung his torso over the back. "Truth is, typewriters aren't immune either." He began to talk of how, during the Cold War, the Soviets had bugged US embassies and developed a technique to decipher the clicks of typing. Under suspicion, the NSA launched Project Gunman in the eighties, seized and replaced all communication devices in Moscow, Leningrad. Sixteen typewriters had been compromised. "That's why the white noise," McCreight said, pressing a switch so that speaker boxes around the room sent something like audio spray. Then, as though Lyle were not there, he turned up the screen of his laptop and began typing, arms hung toward the table and chin rested on the chair back.

"All right," he said. "What does my sister say?"

"Your sister says she wants to see you."

"But what does she say *about* me, Michaels? What did she say when you told her about Glen Close?" McCreight jittered his feet on the ground, forearms held against his thighs. He moved his hands as though he were cleaning them, and he looked over his shoulder at a clock on the wall. He plucked the recorder up and set it down like a point in front of Lyle.

"What I said she said. She wants to see you." Lyle slid the recorder forward. "I wanted to ask you about the hacker project."

"What about?"

"Trojan horses from afar," Lyle said. "That ostensibly we're talking about the United States government setting hackers to work on a whole electrical system to disarm weapons. Mechanical failure at the level of code. You said maybe already."

"And," McCreight said.

"Is there someone you can connect me with on that project?"

"Find sources yourself or give up. How good a journalist *are* you, Michaels?"

Lyle removed a stick of gum from his pocket. The disdain was the sort leveled at Cain, but McCreight would want to refute the man, flash expertise. He crumpled the gum wrapper, left it on the table. "Cain is saying he doesn't know of hacking mechanical weaponry."

"What do you mean Cain?"

"I mean Barry Cain said the Iranian centrifuges sound impossible."

"You went to Virginia to see Cain."

"Hell's Kitchen. Here to see his son. Kid's been working here the last few years."

"Cain's son," McCreight said.

"Goldman, I think he said. Does something with finance."

"And you've looked into him with all your professional channels of peepholes," Sean said.

"Cain's son? No, Cain is a minor character."

"Maybe he'd interest you. Maybe he is part of the story. That's what you call the color, no? Rainbows, gardens. Pink, cerulean."

"I'm not saying I doubt you," Lyle said. "But I need to lock down confirmations. Anyone. Anyone at all you think you could put in contact?"

McCreight's eyes narrowed. He pulled himself erect off the seat back. He smiled until Lyle felt his own foolish grin in McCreight's expression. "Cain doesn't have a son, Michaels. He has a daughter who came back newly left-handed from Mosul."

PART EIGHT: QUOTIENTS

The only way you find the needle is to remove the whole haystack.

—*Wright*

CHAPTER 1

It was all-nighter kind of fun because he had learned of a way he could earn a place with his thumbs. Simple as turn on his console. They are always at in-game chat. They are always saying his aggros are sick. Clap clap clap. He is the most fed Tank in their universe. Like him so much, they invite him to internet relay chat. Keep it down low.

It is a place to learn the cheats.

But also, there were other things, bigger things. Other secret winning. There is something they get, and it is math.

Stash soda went down easy. Suck gentle at the bottom with the straw. His mother could hear a slurp down the hallway with the TV on.

She'd been weighing him.

But the bigger he got, the smaller the treatment, baby stuff. It had gotten to the point of no snack money and packing apples. The green ones made his mouth all funny. She didn't know the dire hole in his stomach.

He looked at the can. Thirty-eight grams of sugar. One hundred fifty calories. Not his kind of math.

But in chat there is no scale, no rules like salad first.

Started simple. A cheat here and there. You want, you got to migrate the conversation from in-game chat to relay chat. They noticed other things about him: he was good with numbers, for example, and moms's bitches.

He thought of listening in on the conversation with the STARK lady. He typed some. He typed not my mom. So but, the thing about cheats: they are minor coding. You can be major too. He wanted to be major. And in the way-late, with his stolen soda, Mom down the hall eating corn chips in her front-and-center TV seat, him 180 pounds, they say, you like math; we can show you some sickass other type-a equations if you want to get serious.

CHAPTER 2

To not be one of them to his client, Jeremy made his face flat. It was nearly the end of the day, and he sat with Tyrell, and Tyrell had been meeting strangers online whom he wanted to see in person. He talked to them about how to beat a video game, and Jeremy could see they shared an idiom that evaded him—Alliance, Horde—so he must not use the terms in a sentence. He'd only manifest his ignorance.

"This is meet to beat," Tyrell said.

"Or run away?" he said.

He wondered the same of Alexandra.

He had thought the child meant something about them.

Tyrell was enumerating quests. Win one, advance. He wanted to advance. He wanted to put particular maps behind him.

Jeremy recognized it as a classic problem of Cathexis. Conquer universes. Universes have conquered the father. "Perhaps, though, you think the metaphor pins down the meaning more precisely, only to find by definition it means something else."

"Mr. Jordan?"

"What if there's always another quest?" he said. And he didn't have the answer.

WHEN TYRELL'S SESSION ended, he found himself dialing, found himself bridging a later hour in London. His fingers carried themselves with an intelligence beyond his better instincts.

"Isn't this breaking the rules?" the voice said.

"We never got to codifying," he said.

Work up to Alexandra, he figured. Listen. He was a good listener.

"Well, I suppose Alexandra talks to Angeline."

"The girlfriend."

"The girlfriend," Genevieve said.

A conversation sometimes picks up knots in accumulating utterances. They were coming faster. He waited to ask the question, then decided he couldn't ask the question. Because what if he was right? He'd still want to stay, want Alexandra to.

Genevieve was speaking about Angeline still, it seemed. They were supposed to go together—both liberals, both Americans in London, both on that particular dating website—but Angeline had posted pictures of them without permission. Angeline invoked symbols as though prima facie. The Arab Spring. The Persian Awakening. Angeline would say, "For people like us, thirty, forty years ago." She was angry Genevieve didn't Cathect her politics. She said remember the slogan *silence = death*.

Jeremy thought of the day at the beach, the belch of ocean and his son's laugh skipping a wave. Alexandra snapped them, showed them a just-passed moment on her phone, and there was pride in her pride of them. A gull's cry died in its soar above.

"What's the worst that could happen if strangers knew the happiest part of *your* life?" Jeremy said.

Genevieve paused. "Anything you say can and will be used against you."

CHAPTER 3

Internet Relay Chat capture:

AlbertInTheShade: Two days ago, an individual, identity undisclosed, is charged with hacking the computers of twenty-one merger lawyers from three US firms. They are saying he hacked the emails, bought shares in the companies, then sold after the merger announcements. All while squatting in a wee flat in Northern Ireland.

LM224: Insider trading from the outside.

AlbertInTheShade: Right. But the thing is, one of the twenty-one is the firm through which Cathexis, under their adorable little research outfit STX, brokered a deal with a consortium of universities: STX gives the schools funding for research projects and keeps the intellectual property. One of these universities has been developing virtual worlds for military training and for PTSD treatment. Another drones. Another education software and diagnostic programs. You're naive if you don't see this hacked firm is also the firm that brokered some quiet deals for a company that does data protection for military hardware.

LM224: Naive because.

AlbertInTheShade: Because altogether, you have a research group that will be a neat little loop. Kid is brown or black and taking Risperdal. Then they track him to combat. But the one who likes computers? They find a nice little seat for him where he's not just playing video games. He's playing real war, drones. Later, they'll strap all of them up for Simulated Environment Therapy. On Cathexis, the ads will be for anxiety meds, sleeping pills. Whole lives can be decided by a few folks who are too smart for their own good. And get this: the hacker? It's RabbidUnicorn.

LM224: You said there was never a RabbidUnicorn.

AlbertInTheShade: This guy with the charges, they are saying his alias is RapeUnicorn. It's the same fucking guy, Michaels.

LM224: You said you thought RabbidUnicorn was a long con coming somewhere out of a federal agency.

AlbertInTheShade: That's exactly what I'm saying, Michaels.

LM224: Say you're right—and I'm not, by the way—but just say you are. This quote-unquote guy who hacked the merger lawyers is RabbidUnicorn. Who is really spooks. And they are hacking a law firm retained by Cathexis because?

AlbertInTheShade: They do not know who else Cathexis is working for. Other countries, splinter groups. They do not know if weapons are being developed for China, Russia, ISIS.

LM224: Or it really is some Irish kid.

AlbertInTheShade: They claim he hacked Northern Irish

police computers as well. Could be RabbidUnicorn is a real, live hacker. Doesn't mean this guy's not also a scapegoat on the merger case. A criminal of not this crime.

LM224: What would be in it for the feds to go after this guy?

AlbertInTheShade: Maybe they've got a wee reason to take interest in the Irish police force, or their allies in Westminster do. Maybe they're interested in taking him as their own.

LM224: That's a lot of different hypotheses.

AlbertInTheShade: Possibilities, Michaels. Science is generating possibilities, then eliminating them.

LM224: And what do you want me to do?

AlbertInTheShade: Stop talking to Barry Cain about me. He's one of them.

CHAPTER 4

Alexandra had no idea how her gestures, tiny things really, crept into him and set off ancient biological instincts. Hypothalamus. Nerves. Caveman stuff. It was not a consecution of logic, just the wisdom imprinted in his body from thousands of years of hunting, gathering. His conscious mind wanted to believe her, but his pulse knew better, his heart following her footsteps around the apartment.

"Who's my one true love?" she asked Han.

And so, now, he waited until he heard water striking ceramic, the metallic squeal of rings on the rod twice: once to open, once to close. He trusted the quiet voice of the intestinal twist but did not mistake the face for a symbol of the mind. Speculation was childish, indulgent behavior; you could age with scenarios. A scientist would look beneath surfaces, find necklaces of proof, clasping into a conclusive loop. It was this sense that had made him inspect objects, seek closures.

The apartment was small enough that he could hear the heavy slap of her hair against her neck when, after raising it to rinse closer to the showerhead, she dropped it, only to pick it up again.

Jeremy picked up the accessory she said contained her life. Until that night, her purse had been a black box.

Alexandra had little spoken recently, but her device would reveal her.

To Lyle Michaels: Seven tomorrow. Bowery Hotel.

He looked around the apartment. On one side of the door, he was half a successful marriage. On the other, that is, the home side, he was the person rifling in his wife's purse. But the pivotal point was to keep the sides, he thought, their life and life out there. He opened a beer.

Later, after the dinner plates had been filled and emptied, cleared and washed, Jeremy watched her over the top edge of his book. Han had been put to bed and on the couch beside him, she put her hands on the machine, its standardized keys and sleek lines, the warm power emanating off its surfaces.

The apartment carried a charge, as though he had snuck into someone else's life and would be caught any minute. He calibrated the television volume to hear something outside his head. On-screen, a stagey transatlantic voice: *Make no mistake, I shall regret the absence of your keen mind; unfortunately, it is inseparable from an extremely disturbing body.*

In a book, Jeremy pretended to read about minds betraying survival instincts: old women who stopped eating, believing their nurses to be poisoning them, or teenagers who jumped out of windows to quiet voices. A disorder was what it was supposed to be, but it occurred to him that maybe his entire biography was only other people's voices.

I do, she had said. The words of his life.

She left the room and she entered, now strangled by a corona of bedroom light. He poured her a glass of wine that she swallowed mindlessly, opening quadrangles on a screen until Cathexis glowed off her laptop. She showed Jeremy pictures of people carving Halloween pumpkins, dancing in the street, and eating graphic arrangements of food. These people wanted to be makers, she said. This was the lesson of Cathexis. They were the babies of baby boomers. It was not a matter of counterculture anymore. It was much more democratic. Every one of them, their generation, could see the unappreciated art in their lives, could see the danger of falling into all the snowing noise, how you could be covered by the dramas of the world. It was why they Cathected every Milestone: a post was a mnemonic for the experience.

"A mnemonic or a metonym?"

"I always forget you studied literature at Oxford," she said.

"Me too," he said.

For the cruise company, she continued, she would suggest Seven-Word Versions. The company would call for seven-word stories about The Horizonview Experience. It was new and old in fangle, on the one hand a chance to exhibit that sense of everyday special, and on the other, old-fashioned word of mouth for a younger grip of consumers. They would contribute because they wanted to be seen as makers, creatives. They would be listened to because they were not corporate, an obvious advertisement. Everything they distrusted about ads, the slickness and regularity and theater, the blemish of inauthenticity, would be what they defined themselves against in the art of autobiography—portrait of the artist as account manager—even as they presented the fiction that was life redacted of complications. Already, vacation photographs and gushings-on were transacted, image and text pointing to fine, reduced narratives. Horizonview would, there-fore, be sewn into the technosocial fabric of their lives. Seven words. Stories that stuck.

Two lines on the stick makes three.
They decided on no more first dates.
Fifty years of dances. First on water.
Packed for everything except her first word.
Three states. Five kids. Together at last.

"What do you think?" she said.

"Those are the only kind of lives I want anymore," he said.

"But would you book the cruise?" she said.

There was a trajectory she was averting. He could not ask what she was hiding or who. Ask the wrong question and it became an indictment. She would not in the future reveal. But every conversation carried its own geometry. Thesis, antithesis, triangle. Ask what you know. The answer becomes your metric. Memorize diameters. Pupils. Black holes evidence unbeknownst. There is such a thing as urgent patience; it is called intelligence.

"What are you doing at seven tomorrow?" he said. Questions: language that yielded language.

The molecules tensed. He could see it in her blank face, liq-uids going solid, clusters condensing. Her eyes widened, and she sat very still. "If I'm lucky, getting out of work," she said.

"So we'll try the new Sichuan place then? Han likes Sichuan."

"Let's see how my day goes."

"You love spicy food," he said. "They are supposed to serve an excellent dan dan mein."

"I don't know yet."

"Don't you?" he said.

He could not help it; he imagined her tomorrow. He thought how if lucky, when she entered, he would be so content to sit with her in front of the television watching what she chose. If he were not lucky, she would return home with a long plan.

"What's that supposed to mean?" Alexandra said.

"You will eat chili oil on cereal given the option."

"No, I would not."

"You love dan dan mein."

"Stop telling me what I love, Jeremy."

"All right," he said. "Why don't *you* tell me what you love then?"

"You, strangely. I'm tired. The campaign meeting is tomorrow. I need to sleep. I'll call you about dinner when I know."

Jeremy crossed his arms. "I moved across the world for you. Can you not muster the decency for even a conversation?"

Her face was flush, and she pushed her fists straight down into the couch cushions. "You wanted to come," she said.

"You decided you wanted to marry me."

"And you accepted," she said. "If you don't like it."

"Then what?"

"I'll just have to let you know tomorrow," she said, wiping down the top of her computer. "I can't make promises now." She stood and moved to the door quiet-footed in ankle socks, laptop hugged to her chest. He brushed past her and spread his arms in the doorway so that his hands held both sides of the frame.

"I want to leave, so you're going to block the exit?"

"You are changing the subject, Alexandra."

"What do you want me to say, Jeremy? That I will join you when I don't know if I can?"

"If I don't like it, then what?" he said. "Then what?"

Time is slow. Do not count. Be still. Do not think of the rigors of stillness.

A mass descended her throat in a swallow. She tipped her face upward. He could feel his whole body red, pulsing. "I'm saying take it or leave it. Those are the options."

Then she ducked beneath an arm and turned off the light, and he could hear their son crying.

CHAPTER 5

The smallest at this hotel was still royal. One couldn't book lower than a queen. It was there, in the room whose size was female, that Alexandra waited, lying over the cover with her shoes still laced.

Lyle was late. Lyle was supposed to bring Shel.

She pressed buttons. A flicker of light on her pillow provided momentary hope, but then it was only coupons. The contact that came was from a department store that had decided "SAVINGS EXCLUDES HOME."

Earlier she had phoned Jeremy that she was working late again. She thought perhaps he half believed her, that is, that he wanted to believe her.

"How long can seven words take to conjure?" he had asked.

"You are the one who studied poetry," she said.

"Food cools. Husband waits. Marriage is compromise."

"Seven words. Passive-aggressive. Wife hangs up phone," she said.

"Outwitted, husband accepts defeat. Says, love you."

"This time she really hangs up though."

"Already, seven words times five. Now six." Alexandra ended the call.

Seven thirty passed. She looked at the clock and it was always 7:32. She had last heard from Lyle two days ago.

Alexandra turned on the television. Something expected had happened, which was a disaster. The newscasters were giving the numbers but not names yet, and still, already, a group had bragged. People on the television held their faces in their own hands. This morning, her son had wept when she left.

Now her husband's name appeared on the pillow, green light pulsing, and she thought of what it was to lie in the rental car when they'd gone upstate once, looking through the greasy window at distant burning stars, the sweet rank of his mouth edging up from her neck, with the bright feeling in her stomach; how moaning meant something near to but different from pain, even as it was tied to every other moment in her life when, too, she was alone, boxed up in her own body without the right words, inarticulate sounds that followed clumsily from precise intentions, and she was fuller and less significant and freer and more trapped; and the endless sky was only the negative space in a frame holding someone over her.

In the hotel hallway, someone asked a question with a fist on a surface. She turned off the news and moved to the threshold, opened the door.

"You're late," Alexandra said. "I've been here over an hour already."

She stood firm, but Lyle moved past her into the room. He gave off a damp smell like old flannel. He went to the bathroom and bent over, door open, faucet running, splashing his face. Alexandra stood looking at him through the doorway, a broken triangle of gazes between them. He gripped the sink, peered in the mirror, his reflection returning the silent, gaping mouth and the droplets catching at his hairline.

"Where are the excuses for me to shoot down?" she said. "I'm a good shot for someone who plays poorly on a team."

Lyle looked down into the drain. "He is probably dead."

"Lyle," she said.

He sat down on the toilet seat, legs spread, knees balancing elbows, hands balancing head. "I was supposed to be there. Five o'clock. It was decided."

"What do you mean probably?" she said.

"Definitely," he said.

Alexandra stepped back. She grabbed at the wall behind her, a sliding surface slipped, and somehow the closet was coming at her, her shoulders hitting the rod. Sideways, dragging hangers, the metal squeal fervent. When she could speak, she spoke from the floor. A pinprick of red light blinked deep in the closet ceiling.

She righted her body and walked to the bathroom. The floor was off, unresponsive, as though she'd debarked a treadmill. She knelt on the bath mat with her hands on her thighs, supplicant.

"I sent him an encrypted message through an application when I got off the subway," Lyle said. "He responded he was working on the sixth floor of the building. I heard something, saw a long lumpy cloud in the distance. When I got to the building, it was bricks. There were pieces everywhere."

She could see every yarn bit in the bath mat, feel the blood churning through her body in strange loops of vein. On her own lips she focused. "A cloud," she said.

"An explosion."

"People survive," she said.

"No," he said. "There were stories blown away."

"These accidents, they will say there were so many dead, so many injured."

"There is no question."

There was energy in her hands. She didn't know what to do with them. Her fingers rolled, released.

"Or he left already."

"It had only been seconds."

"You timed it."

"I saw it. A socket that used to be a building."

"They find people in the rubble in these accidents. They are hidden survivors."

Lyle looked at her finally. "I don't think this was an accident, Alexandra."

"You *think. Probably.*" Her voice was tight and mocking.

"Senators will say that black ops have unfettered power under the domestic security provisions, but in secrecy, in invisible budgets and the projects that creep outside documents, they can be eliminated without anyone except a few agency men knowing."

"He is only a coder."

"I thought he was paranoid. The encryption. The warehouse. He always saw a man."

Alexandra pinched her elbows. "They will clear the rubble."

"You're bleeding," Lyle said. "Your head."

"They find people. They wear the masks."

"Your head is bleeding," he said. "Come here."

"I would feel it," she said. "I would have known."

A careless flick at a box. Lyle reached at her with a clump

of tissue embossed with flowers. Fear rose in her chest, and she slapped his hand away, one hand, another, missed a face.

"Listen, you want me to do this," he said. "You hit your head. You're confused."

He came at her. She struck out again. She reached for anything. The ceiling pulled down the wall. For a moment all she could think of were possible weapons beyond her. A trash bucket. A toilet brush. There were eyebrows above. Lips taut in an awful quadrangle strung with saliva. He told her her name over and over, and she kicked and hit out and sometimes she was sure she felt flesh give.

His voice was strained, toothsome. "Relax," he said. Or "Alex," he said. "It's over."

She was swimming, all the long parts of her slapping at surface. Her breath was short, which meant she was alive. Alexandra got something wet and soft, an eyeball. He made a surprised noise, then batted and her head hit the floor. His knees were everywhere. She claimed his chin in her fist, dug in with her nails, felt one snap in half perpendicular to the quick. The bath mat wrinkled beneath her. He was screaming Jesus, he was wrong, he was nearly off her, one more punch. But something turned, and then her vision filled with a red orb and he was kneeling on her, anchoring hands, and there was no scream left in her chest, windpipe without wind, so that when she woke, there was dark blood dried to the tiled floor, matted in stiff hair, and flinch was consequent to light and movement. The only fact then was pain, and she was alone.

CHAPTER 6

Later, when it had been many days since the night at the hotel, Genevieve told Alexandra, "Remember when we were kids our parents told us television would turn our brains to mush." Watching was supposed to save her from pain.

But sometimes there was too much feeling even in the screen to take the advice of television. It was possible, she learned, to think for hours of something you couldn't imagine: dead.

And so for the first time in her life, there was sleep to look forward to. Only, pleasure-deaf, she faded in linens. Draw the blinds. Cover the head. Sleep to be alone. Sometimes, she would take a cab home from work, tell the driver to hurry. "Got somewhere to be, miss?" would be the question.

"I cannot be late," she'd say. She intended it only the way that meant there was no destination for her.

Convoking dreamlessness, she swallowed roots and herbs. Jeremy came at her with spoons. She didn't want food, but it was easier to accept the peanut butter or the ice cream, the soups he melted butter into so she wouldn't disappear. She allowed Han to come to her in bed. There was only the solace of his warm head, alive on her chest.

And she was tired. Awake, yes, but tired.

"There is a sort of fact so heavy it drags the speech out of you, makes everything unspeakable," she said to Jeremy.

"I'm sorry," she said to Jeremy.

"I thought what if he was right," she said to Jeremy, and she didn't finish.

She was tired with confessing. She was tired with telling him all the secrets that had kept no one happy. The dead could not be happy.

"Say something," she said.

"Rest," Jeremy said.

On nights the pills worked, she would, in dreams, sit at a restaurant with Lyle, a burgundy tablecloth hooded between. He'd eat his steak with enthusiasm, then, when her mouth was too full to say no, pull back a stretchy membrane from the meat, and she knew to turn away from the reveal. She woke up in sheets confused by tossing in her sleep.

In the mornings, all the seeped substances were dried to her face, and her eyelashes adhered. As she dressed, Jeremy would speak to her of stages and symptoms. He would say there were professionals. It didn't have to be him.

"It is possible to do both at once," he said. "To seek help is not a betrayal of grief."

Where there was good blankness was within the rote declarations of work. She said, we believe in the power of storytelling as a growth strategy. She said, we craft brand narratives that repeat, catch. We at Amica Malmot will make the plot of your company viral, she said, and we thank you for your time. But then the script ended, and sometimes her boss, Carver Ellington, would touch her bicep, say, "You can go now."

"Is everything okay at home?" Carver Ellington said.

"Why wouldn't it?" she said.

"Andrea and I stayed at a really wonderful resort in Hawaii two years ago," he said. "Just you, the beach, and your thoughts. I could send you the information."

It sounded like a nightmare to Alexandra.

But she agreed to two weeks because it suggested that there had been a choice at all. She asked Carver Ellington to please send her the information about the resort. She pretended to be happy to use her frequent flyer miles. And, truly, she still must return to Nevada.

But she did not buy the ticket, and she did not call. She sent the wire transfers and paid her mother's bills, the numbers somehow a code that said, life still goes. There was no body to burn or bury. There had not even been a pronouncement.

To Jeremy she explained, "It is not something to say on the phone."

"Sometimes, how is less important than that," Jeremy said.

"I'm not a patient," Alexandra said.

"Of course you aren't," he said. "You'll let no one take care of you."

She perceived that he regretted the words immediately. It was like the way betrayal once made her contrite, the way she had allowed Jeremy to hold her when she used to return home after lying, pliant with shame, wanting to substantiate the goodness he saw. She knew now he removed the local section of the newspaper, where it was reported that people shot themselves smiling in pictures in front of a building blown out three weeks before by a gas explosion in Brooklyn, where, inexplicably, no body had been found. And still, like a child, she said, "You can't make me."

CHAPTER 7

Once, he would have made a list of dangerous names. He would have considered prison geographies, potential new relations. Now the task was count the days between his last meeting with Wright and the death. It was decide whether the correlation was spurious. And most of all, it was decide whether to confer with Lawrence.

What was relevant: The position and velocity of an object cannot be judged by another moving object.

What was relevant: Listening is not opening the ears. It is quieting the mind. Jeremy could not quiet his mind, and he did not pull the sheets up until the pitch of night began to bleed up past the horizon, paling to gray.

Another thing he knew from Belfast: Admitting a lie was not admitting the truth. At its best, it was a dent in the process of elimination. You were told it was not nature but a bullet. You were not told who shot the gun.

What was relevant: He must temper information. You could not revise what you told someone like Lawrence. Your rue afforded nothing.

CHAPTER 8

One day, she was home in the afternoon when Jeremy finished up with his clients. She'd bought six bags of groceries, and she stood over the sink in the kitchen surrounded by red cabbage and long wands of bread, plastic baskets of cherries. It was like coming home to a thought forgotten mid-clause. There were scissors in her hands, and he heard the edges on her hair, saw ends going muddy in the damp drain.

She did not sit to tell him. Her bangs were still between two fingers as she spoke. She had been at a meeting with the other senior brand strategists and a man from a company called Dstil that specialized in targeted advertising. This man was saying he thought it was cute the concerns about discrimination, considering discrimination was the point of targeted advertisements. An event occurred in her skull, and suddenly she was screaming. The last thing she remembered was Carver Ellington picking up the phone and calling for security. Someone grabbed her arms. She was airborne.

She looked at Jeremy as she told him, her hand hanging down with her fingers still strung through the looped handles of scissors. Her bangs were too short, and it made her look younger.

In the days that followed, the firing made her linger as she never before had at home, sipping and thoughtful or distracted, pantless. It was strange to see her this way: same face, same quietness, but bereft. He didn't know what was in her anymore. She stared. She blinked. It scared him to see her without any future in her eyes.

At night, from bed, the new Alexandra reached her arms toward him until he came to her. It was not necessarily sexual even when it was sexual. In the mornings, her thinning T-shirt caught the early sun, as she sat with a mug by the window. It wasn't that she didn't move. It was that it was as if she were blown.

To help, he walked Han to the park. In the game they played, everything could be spied. A tree, a duck, a father.

"I spy with my little eye," he said. "Something scary."

CHAPTER 9

Lyle met Alexandra at the hotel at the designated time, hunching with a duffel bag full of paper and memory cards. To his eye, she took up less space than before. He removed a leather bracelet and whipped it in circles on his finger while she looked at the papers, a basement smell coming up from the opened zipper.

She lay each sheet down carefully. She counted CDs. She wrote a list with each item and its date. Lyle knelt beside her on the floor. "I wanted him alive as much as anyone," he said finally.

"You're sure about that?" she said.

"The book is dead, if it makes you feel any better."

She stared. "My brother is dead, and now you sit here talking about your dead book."

Lyle rose and moved toward the door. His feet strode past her knees on the carpet. He had come because he knew what he had cost her, but there was nothing he could offer beyond records, and now she would not look at him.

"Tell me one true thing about him," she said. He had thought the conversation was over.

Lyle held the doorknob at the threshold and twisted his head over his shoulder. She was very small, the way she folded herself on the floor.

"He wanted to be loved."

Alexandra's face quivered, stilled. "I did," she said.

CHAPTER 10

To set a date, Lyle had fielded Cain's supposed illnesses. The flu, cancer of a dog. Now, Barry Cain was there with a pink drink he said his wife drank when pregnant.

Once Lyle would have asked if it was true what he supposed: that the body had been removed prior to the law enforcement sweep, that perhaps, even, the investigation had been led by agency men embedded in the police. But there was no book, no scoop left. There was only making that clear.

"You probably know why I asked you here," Lyle said.

"Confess I don't."

"It isn't for the book I'm not writing," Lyle said. "Which maybe you didn't know. What I'm not doing." The beer was spit warm in his hand, a craft selection in a precious stein. "Maybe that's why you were hesitant to meet."

Cain flopped his hand over and ran through the diseases again, vet bills. "They get old, and it breaks your heart," he said. "Because they can't help themselves. They're only animals."

"What I'm saying is, you don't have to worry," Lyle said. "Because I am standing groundless without my source."

"I'm a source," Cain said.

"McCreight was my source."

"Too crazy to manage?"

"He thought more than friends or family, in algorithms we trust, and yet everywhere you look, it's incursions. What is so crazy about that?"

"Liked the guy enough to hire him," Cain said, "but he had his proclivities, and they were the kind of proclivities you intake enough, everyone is out to get you."

"I'm dropping the book and keeping my nose clean," Lyle said. "Do you understand?"

Cain's fat hands were folded in his lap. He kept them there and leaned into the bar to sip the pregnancy cocktail. "And why would you do that?"

"Because," Lyle said. "I have a daughter too."

CHAPTER 11

The drink he bought Bri was ruined with time, watery whiskey warm with minutes. "Holy fucking nachos," a girl said, and he thought he'd be sick. He looked at the newspaper he'd brought, but he couldn't read.

A little after ten, a thin body, head and arms and legs forming a droopy star, came in through the doorway. She came to his table. She flopped down and threw her backpack in the booth.

"Back from the dead," Lyle said.

It wasn't funny to Bri Freeman.

"Why not?"

Why not was because Bri Freeman had had a visit from two men in suits. These were not academics.

Why not was because think about men in suits showing up in her office, these people with badges that superseded the security people in the building.

"We happened to read your very interesting article in the *Journal of Middle Eastern Political Economy*," one had said.

"No one happens to read anything in the *Journal of Middle Eastern Political Economy*," she'd said.

"We're just here to talk."

"As fans," she had said.

So why not was because the one who said they were only here to talk observed, "Foreign affairs must be personal for you."

Why not was because she was stopped at LAX on the way to New York. They turned her bag inside out, denim and literature and tampons on a counter, picked up and examined as potential exhibitions of culpability. They ran a device over her and when it beeped, they brought her to a private room. They took the gloves out. "Routine and random, they say."

"Fuck them," he said.

She drank her terrible drink. She said, "They shared a face."

"Who?"

"The passengers."

"Fuck them," he said.

She looked at the table of other people's friends. "Every single one."

He could hear someone coughing or choking or laughing, human sputtering.

"You see, they were grateful," Bri continued.

"Grateful."

"Someone was making sure they were safe."

He cursed for her. Options lit him up. Petitions. Calls. He specified various elected officials. He specified civil rights groups. His speech picked up speed. It was beyond him, bigger, and he couldn't remember how many drinks he'd had. He looked at Bri Freeman, and she was a smear in his vision.

He blinked, and she was saying, "Why are *you* crying?"

In the recording, Lyle Michaels stated the date and time. He told Shel to do his worst, meaning speak. Alexandra looked at Han playing, and she looked at Jeremy cooking, and she had her brother in her headphones, all of them together in the living room.

Is the issue your personal relationship with Barry Cain? Shel said.

You're driving at what?

Tell me why Cathexis needs ex-NSC consulting on STX research. Tell me that, Michaels.

He knows how to run a large outfit.

You are so surrounded by the Forrest you can't see the trees.

What is that supposed to mean, McCreight?

Terrorists practice advanced obfuscation now. They are not fools. Braid in lies, you render useless the surveillance tools.

We were talking about Cain.

Barry Cain is a classified spy for the government. It is intuition multiplied by context.

Like you.

Like I was. And now I'm talking to a writer.

Let's talk about the factors that indicated terrorist to the algorithm.

We missed one. We missed intel agency employee.

Hypothesis: Barry Cain, still secretly working for the NSA, had contacted Lyle Michaels under an alias with a putative tip on Shel. The tip, however, had been a test of Shel: would he talk? When the meetings with the writer continued, Cain decided to eliminate Shel.

Or hypothesis: Barry Cain, like Shel, had been burned by the agency. In the years following their departures, the agency had come to view both Cain and Shel as potentially threatening. The appearance of a liaison between them and Lyle Michaels had been flagged. Shel was killed first because Cain's position at STX made him too high profile a target.

Or hypothesis: Shel had never left the NSA. When some unknown person within the agency had discovered Shel's communications with Lyle Michaels, his death became procedure. A whistleblower could make noise too quietly.

CHAPTER 14

What she heard on the tapes from Lyle: Shel's voice. What she found: in fact, he'd always been a dreamer.

In the sixties, Shel said, a man named Weizenbaum had developed a computer program called ELIZA meant to operate as a joke about Rogerian therapy. People could chat with strings of code that would mix around their words and spit them back. But Weizenbaum became disturbed when his secretary asked him to leave the room when she used the program. She accused him of spying on the conversation. Another user wrote that ELIZA reminded her of her father. *What these users knew that everyone else forgets is the soul of the machine.*

I thought the internet would broaden neighborhoods. We'd reach across state lines, national lines. He was talking about the early days of online communities that stretched across maps when he learned to code from outsiders to whom he'd wanted to be an insider. *The network could never be a place of our own,* he said, *so I didn't think we'd end up in tiny cells without windows, that we'd choose it.*

She knew Shel had had a palate for zero. Zero was the only number with verb potential to him, and he had known he'd need to zero out these communications with Lyle Michaels.

But he had also harbored a problem with the number two, she learned from the tapes. Two, he said, the dyad, was to the Greeks deity and evil. Two was a deuce.

A pair becomes a pattern. These people will want two to mean something, that there is a reason to apprehend an innocent. They think high-octane mortality is a problem for two to solve.

They had found, she supposed, a solution to her brother.

CHAPTER 15

It was the conversation again, the only one lately. She was rambling. The truth was, she said, the only known truth was one destruction. A building had blown up. Officially, the story was gas. But her own brother had for many years lived unofficial lives. And she had the tapes to prove it.

Jeremy cleared the plates. Silverware scraping against dirty china spoke. It said wrong, wrong, wrong.

She began to talk about the justice of prose. The check of it. She listed off publications. She mentioned the Fourth Amendment, the Fourth Estate. She said, "There is something very dark everywhere that we need to turn the light on."

"If it's true," he said.

"It is."

"If it is true," he continued. "There is danger to volume."

"It is true," she insisted. "Think if everyone knew they were being watched. If they knew every word was recorded."

"We'd state our convictions on world peace, everything white teeth and sound bites like everyone already does out in the open. We'd be kind in private. Is that what you think, Alexandra?"

"If I went to the press," she said.

She wept then.

It was after dinner and Han was drawing maps like spiderwebs, big networks of train routes. Jeremy picked up a crayon. He colored in the house Han had sketched by their subway stop.

"You know what would happen," Jeremy said more gently.

He told her to sleep because he wanted her to be strong. He told her a walk—the logic of it was you can move yourself, even if only around the block. He told Han to tell Mama a story.

"And the ants went back home to the log," Han said, "to die."

CHAPTER 16

Later at night, when her pills had not worked, Jeremy was already in the living room, face bluish like a dead man's in the fat ray coming off his laptop. He closed the screen and touched the couch when she came into the doorway.

"Saved a seat for you," he said.

Legs folding beneath her, she got on the couch beside him. He put his arms around her.

"Do you want me to go?" he said.

"Never," she said.

"You may come to regret your words, more even than already."

"I'm sorry," she said.

"Don't," he said. "It hasn't been easy."

"But I *am* sorry."

"Therapists say, 'Don't be sorry. Be mindful.'"

"It is so much easier to be sorry," Alexandra said.

"That is where they trick you."

"You're they now," she said.

"And still I'm us," he said.

They decided to eat ice creams. Alexandra looked online for a late-night parlor while Jeremy woke Han, said they would have a nighttime adventure. Outside, his arm hugged her sideways, banding them. They arrived and he said every flavor like a question, his boy too big to be carried and still carried, still there tight to his chest, murmuring, "Chocolate." Someone came from a door in the back of the store.

"Miss Chen," the man said.

"Ray," she said.

Jeremy swung his eyes from the glass case, recognition in his ears. He held Han tighter. "What are you doing here?" he said.

"How do you two know each other?" Alexandra said.

"Baba, let go," Han said. "Baba, it hurts."

He set Han down. He wiped his son's shirt for no reason. Wright grinned, arms crossed. "How *do* we know each other, Bill? I'm old now. The memories drain off."

"You must be mistaken," Jeremy said. "Name's Jeremy."

"That's right, that's right. Jeremy Elwin, is it? Alton?"

"Jordan," Jeremy said. "I didn't think you were still living in Bushwick, Ray. I recall you were moving. Leaving the city for good."

"My work takes me on trips. Bushwick. London. I follow the secrets. Like you, Jeremy."

"Patient confidentiality, you mean."

A young cashier addressed them in formal terms, asked of readiness. Alexandra apologized to the cashier. She asked for time and looked into the case. Jeremy held his hand in a fist in his pocket.

"And who is this young fellow?" Ray said, crouching.

"Say hello, Han," Alexandra said.

Jeremy swung Han back up to his chest. "Praline, salted caramel, and German chocolate."

"I'll leave you to it," Ray said.

"It was good to see you, Ray," Alexandra said. "Thank you for everything you did."

"Didn't quite work, did it?"

"Well," she said.

"That will be my exit then," Ray said.

Jeremy nodded and crossed his arms. A bell smashed against glass as the man let the door close behind him. Someone selling eyedrops on television said what her friends couldn't see was itch.

"You weren't very friendly," Alexandra said. Jeremy paced while they waited.

"Why don't we bring this home?" he said.

"It will melt by home."

"We can walk fast, can't we, Han? What animal is fastest?"

"Coyote."

"With cones?" she said.

"I didn't know you knew Ray," Jeremy said.

"I hired him to find Shel."

The cashier hovered cones at them. Alexandra took hers and began eating with a small spoon. Jeremy fetched napkins for the table. He held Han's hand the entire time.

"He was your therapy client?"

"Someone with knowledge of these systems might affirm such a guess if he were inclined to answer off the record," Jeremy said.

"Chocolate," Han said.

"Poor Ray," Alexandra said. "It cannot be easy to keep custody of so many people's secrets."

"He makes his choice," Jeremy said.

Television voices slid up in volume suddenly. They looked at the cashier, remote in hand, staring. His head was thrown back, and his mouth was dumb and slack. A dark, grainy image oozed and hiccupped on-screen. Then the image spun and a television personality appeared, eyebrows thick with powder and pulled high.

But her eyes were narrowed elsewhere, even as she dug at a cone with a spoon. She was looking out the glass facade and frowning.

"He's standing across the street," Alexandra said.

"Who?"

"Ray," she said.

PART NINE: MODULO OPERATION

modulo operation: *n. a computing operation that finds the remainder after division of one number by another*

CHAPTER 1

His mother wouldn't be home yet. She'd get out of work and dice one and a half peppers, two onions. She'd swirl them in the frying pan. When he rolled in, she'd give him the job of measuring the spices, cleaning the rice. She liked to say, "So sous me, baby."

Technically, this was an unauthorized venture, the bodega stop. His mother's stance was she worked too hard on a meal for him to ruin his supper. Total truth, his appetite had reach, and they both knew it.

Tyrell waited for his chopped cheese by the serve-yourself slushie machine, watching the turn of red and blue, of orange. There was music on from the store radio and there was music coming out of someone's phone in the wait for wings. The men there for cigarettes shuffled their feet until Nasir behind the counter turned back. They were wheezy-whispering about the butt and the crazy of a woman in the store. Tyrell counted fourteen types of gum, two cinnamon, four fruity. He could smell the griddle grease.

He ate the chopped cheese as he walked to his session. The sandwich foil made him think of sci-fi, which made him think of the movie he'd watched with his dad at the hospital a week back, one of those alien deals with lots of gross-out and a guy with some tough hardware who had to protect the world by Friday. The hero shot a no-joke laser, and it bounced off the alien's mirror shield right back at him.

"You saw that?" he asked his father, and his father didn't answer, but Tyrell could chalk it up to potential still because he saw the number on the machine jump. He wrote it in his composition notebook. He knew it meant there was a chance, even if later his mom had told him to stop with his notebook theories and act grown, her nostrils shaky.

Two blocks later, the sandwich was gone. Tyrell passed a church. He threw out the bodega foil and rounded over to his session in the beat-up old building with people hanging around the entrance smoking. Inside, the woman behind the window apologized for not calling. "Mr. Jordan isn't in today," she said.

"Why not?" Tyrell said.

"I can't tell you that, but we do apologize."

"We who?"

"I'm sorry," she said.

"He's *absent*?" Tyrell asked.

She stuck her head out the window. "Yes, absent."

"As in sick?"

"Do you need to use the telephone to call your mother to pick you up?" the woman said.

"Why I'm the only person who ever has to communicate?" he said. "I had an appointment."

The woman sighed. "I want to help you, Tyrell, but I can't tell you what happened to Mr. Jordan."

Jeremy knew that Wright would not be extricated from his life with words alone. It was why Jeremy had insisted Alexandra announce death to her mother in another city, time to think gleaned in distance. But Jeremy was aware somewhere, Wright, no longer Wilmington, was plotting, watching. Wright had not learned from Belfast to crank away toward good, small things.

In the plane aisle, Jeremy shoved things around an overhead compartment to fit luggage. There was a line behind him, and it made him overwarm in the lower back. He could feel all their breath leaning on him.

"Why is it called carry-on if it must be stowed?" Alexandra said to a flight attendant.

The plane lifted, and the city grew strange before it grew familiar, just out of reach and then a shmaltzy postcard skyline zippered with lit buildings. Somewhere down there in one of the pinpricks that was a window, Wright had a plan. He was Wilmington or Wright, or he was Ray or he was a PI named Gutierrez. Wright did not want the Corps to die for a few years of algorithms, or he did not believe actors within government could be trusted with citizen data. Nothing moved free of everything, he thought, or terrorists who hadn't gotten better benefited from cartoon legitimacy. They could run their own intelligence, or it was frightening to think data miners were interpreting how users Cathected. Shel Chen had been a menace, or Jeremy was. Wright was being followed, or he was following. They say it's not a woodchuck, Wright had said. It's a groundhog. No, it's a whistle-pig. But it's all the same squirrel. I smell fish. Mackerel, salmon.

Alexandra grabbed Jeremy's arm. "What will I say?"

"You will say the worst thing you can," Jeremy said, "and then it will be over."

"Is it better to say it first or to wait?"

"There is no good way, Alexandra, let alone a better."

You could not appease someone whose desire you didn't know. He did not know what Wright wanted. Wright had tailed Alexandra because he was tailing Shel, or he had tailed Shel because he was tailing Alexandra. He had been warning Jeremy that Alexandra could, through Shel, discover that everything she knew of her husband was part of a cover, or he had suspected Jeremy of involvement in a new covert operation.

Alexandra replaced a magazine showing a video still of a man with a raised arm in the pocket of the seat in front of her. "But the feeling won't be."

"Fault or shame?" Jeremy said.

"I only get one?" Alexandra said.

"Wouldn't that be nice," Jeremy said.

Consider the patterns. Wright had told Jeremy that Shel was an NSA operative, and then Shel was dead. Wright had followed Alexandra, and then Alexandra had come home with blood crusted to her head. He did not trust luck, coincidence.

Coincidence was corresponding in time and space, when everyone knew how little matched.

Jeremy clamped a shade against the sky.

When they arrived at the blue house on Elder Street, Alexandra took a breath that bumped her shoulders up and down. There was a bag slung across her torso, and she bounced to adjust it. The air was dry and bright as he held her shoulders.

"You won't be fine, but you will have done it," Jeremy said.

He stood behind her, and she knocked the door of her childhood home. A dog in pain could be heard but not seen, sound cutting through the weather, air slow and composed as jam.

CHAPTER 3

They all had their origin stories, but at the barracks they hadn't told them unless you were trusted. Jeremy remembered that for Wright, the Intelligence Corps had entered his life when he needed to clarify. He was another uni student with questions, and he was stupid with big ideas.

His appointment, he thought, was to discuss the Cartesian shadow over Wittgenstein. He was only twenty, and he didn't know anything, so he was nervous, and he didn't know anything so he was not nervous enough.

The artifact. You touch it, and it becomes part of your world. There is the moment of connection, the moment of interception, when the hold goes both ways. The professor opened his desk. He slid an old copy of *Rose and Laurel* across the table. Wright's hand went to it, unthinking, his body already pliant to command.

"Do you know who issues this publication?" the professor said. "This is the publication of the Intelligence Corps. Maybe you'd be interested. They're interested in you."

The boy Wright held the magazine with both hands. His

hands would have been delicate on the turning corners, worn to paper suede.

Now Jeremy thought of that boy. He thought what if that boy had never taken that philosophy course? What if he'd dropped out sooner?

CHAPTER 4

Look around and what's school? It is the long line. It's Crystal and her friends laughing *raggedy-ass*. School SOs with the contraband box straight-up full of beanies and Yu-Gi-Oh! cards. Hear: arms up for the detector. No baggies, no hats, no gum. Hands out. Of. Your. Pockets. They say that one, he likes patty-cake on the jeans a little too much.

"Don't even think about it, Mr. Brinkley."

Tyrell was thinking.

There is staying in line for the metal detector, and there is turn around. Don't go in, you never left. Absent: a term for a good day. What are the calculations?

Must be three hundred of us. Rate of what a minute through the doors?

"So long Tank Top gonna have a dick time we get to homeroom."

Tyrell looked to the left. He had $11.30 saved. He had his subway pass. Mr. Pence was smiling by his collection of confiscated fitteds, a big, stupid grin on his big, stupid face like a cereal leprechaun, head too big for any kind of headgear and how many times has he said the word *disruption*? Tyrell had an idea to distribute the numbers. Eleven-thirty is four bacon-egg-and-cheeses and three knockoff Gobstoppers. Suck and they last twenty-seven minutes. It is basic as swiveling out of the line.

And why not? He is involved with huge things, and they have no idea. No one, not his mother, not Mr. Jordan, not Crystal, or Derek, or anyone, none of them had any idea. Epic. Outside the IRC they wouldn't even believe. He was learning beyond cheats, learning into making whole new games. He was learning how to run a world like no one else seemed to know he could.

Excel.

So he turned chill and easy. Head down. Walk away. One Jordan past another eventually gets you home, whole place quiet, you and a soda tickling clean down the throat, a member of a big-time kind of group. They were going places.

"The fuck," he heard. But it was not about him. For a big boy, he was good at being a person no one noticed.

And before he knew it, he was screen-center and killing it all legendary. Some point, he will take a break to chat. There are plans. There are things to learn can't be taught in his PS.

There are things to worry about too. Later, he'd leave the apartment. He'd come home the come-home time. It's spaghetti night. The drill: no seconds until broccoli, all of it. Fuck broccoli. Fuck carrots. He had gotten no TV for a week recently for saying that.

Sip the cola. No need for quiet now. Just power up and slay this RPG. But somehow, the big-breeze feeling was going cold in his stomach. Somehow, a wedge grew between brain and screen, and that wedge was his mother's voice in the deep-down of him. He looked at the clock, and he thought of the minutes left before he was caught.

CHAPTER 5

It was just a couple of minutes of tape, but Alexandra found herself fighting with him, her dead brother. She caught herself thinking of comebacks and alternative evidence, what refuted him.

You can tell Alexandra I said that.

Lyle Michaels had never told her any of it.

In fact, I want her to know. Because advertisers have no compunction about mining the prose of our lives to satisfy our worst impulses. Because we ask for convenience, and they give us a smaller world called customization. Because Wells Fargo used search data to decide who'd be offered something they called ghetto *mortgages. Bull's eye: targeted. Right in the crosshairs.*

She was angry then. So angry. She was red and she was mentally corroborating her own goodness with the events in her life, and she knew he had never taken the time to know her when he'd returned.

But she rewound the file anyway. She kept her headphones on. And she listened again to this moment when her brother had still had a voice.

CHAPTER 6

Midafternoon. Alexandra and Han were asleep. A man's voice came onto the radio, a stranger in the flat. Dial down the volume, you still the air. But his heartbeat.

Jeremy held a cup he wouldn't drink from. He did not have a brain for tea these days. He was all lit up. A piece of brown bread in the mouth tethered him.

He took two quick laps around the building, a straight shot three, a left, a right, and another two laps around a building. In the street, men with umbrellas hooked at the crooks of their elbows complained that they didn't know how to dress for this decade of weather. A girl stood by the subway station passing out flyers stamped with the words WANT TO LEARN ENGLISH? in English. She competed with a megaphoned man flanked by dancers selling the second coming of Christ. Men in fluorescent mesh vests stood by scaffolding, beckoning and backing a vehicle, and there was metal rolling everywhere, drilling. Jeremy tensed himself against the noise. He settled on the steps of someone else's building. He had memorized the London number.

"Mr. Lawrence is not available," his secretary said. "Might I take down a message for you?"

"No," he said.

At home, Alexandra and Han woke shortly before dinner. Jeremy lifted steamed asparagus onto a plate. Alexandra wanted to tell him about the most beautiful dream she'd had. They went to a rocky cliff to visit her brother, and he was an old man.

"When do I stop thinking of all the hypotheticals I was too slow to precipitate?" Alexandra said.

CHAPTER 7

My brother was a dreamer, she wrote to Lyle Michaels.

CHAPTER 8

Lyle nearly enjoyed getting tired. He sat with his father and at lunch peeled the deli paper back over the roast beef on a toasted. In the truck, Frank would scream obscenities over unmemorable traffic dramas. There should have been beauty to whitening walls, the possibility of homes afresh, nothing exceptional, a gratifying thought.

With his first paycheck, he bought fresh greens and salmon steaks, Icelandic yogurt thick with fat. At home, he readied the fish with delicate pieces of dill and chopped salad, laid out buttered slabs of bread flecked with pink salt. He turned on a Northern soul record. He had asked Ingrid for a conversation. He had specified over dinner. It's how it's always been done. Talk over dinner. This is his daughter's mother.

And maybe, despite it all, there were certain unbroken rhythms. The patting of the back barely bigger than his hand. A swoop of spoon to clean the dribbling lip of puree of something rooted. Gestures of fatherhood.

An alarm sounded.

"Did you hear that?" Lyle asked Marina. "The oracle hath spoken. Bedtime."

He swiped her mouth once, twice with a towel. Then a little flutter of terry cloth on her nose until she laughed. He picked her up and carried her, the down of her head on his cheek, into the bedroom with the mobile of extinct animals cluttering the space above the crib.

"Once upon a time," he said, "there was a paleontologist named Marina."

The story-time voice in his own mouth soothed him, got the cadence of sleep and simple morals hushing down the noise of the city, the wide world of news. He was speaking, but it was the ancient communication of Fahrenheit transference from her whole small body to his chest that he heard. It had been foolish to contact Cain. Cain of course would only have denied his part in it. All Cretans lie, says the Cretan, McCreight had said. Or maybe death was a coincidence. What was left was to fold back into the daily duties, tucking in. Lyle turned the mobile so that a Jurassic swirl suspended overhead, a churning history of fallen beasts.

"Nod if you're asleep," Lyle whispered. "Okay, then."

Ingrid arrived soon after, face tight and holding a six-pack of beer. She opened one and sat at the table. She turned off his music and began to play a band out of her phone.

Before they were over, he'd been proud to be introduced by Ingrid at parties. At the reception for her first film premiere, oglers futzed with lurid soft cheese spreading off the rind just to get close. People praised her. They called her a light-shedder, a truth-teller, and they were right. That night, he had asked of her forever. Ingrid had married Lyle Michaels in a dress purchased for three dollars, and it had seemed then that she corroborated his own weight, his wife with yellowing sleeves and holes at her collar who voted in local elections and worried globally in the form of films. After town hall, her friends filled a dive, drank cheap whiskey. He had wanted them all to leave so he could touch her face, but then someone bought him a shot. The music was angry young white men screaming over simple chords. He wished they had done it differently.

In the living room, he laid out mismatched bowls, individual dishes lost from other people's sets and purchased from dusty shops. They were quiet and the apartment was stuffed with radiator heat. He thought maybe he could become a sports reporter, observe locker rooms for the rest of his life. He could memorize statistics, Cinderella stories pick-and-rolled through the paint. Start over.

Ingrid went to the kitchen, and he could hear the open and close of the refrigerator that meant she was taking another beer. Tomorrow, he would email around, say he was looking to get on the sports beat. Do grant writing. Technical copy. He could be a man who wrote manuals from home. White papers. There was supposed to be money in white papers. Or he would keep on working for his father.

He followed her to the kitchen. He put his hand on her arm, and she was very stiff, but he thought maybe there was nothing to risk in the idea, saying it. He held her elbows.

"I was wrong," Lyle said.

"I know," she said.

But she had chosen him once.

And so by the dirty dishes, he promised difference. He imagined she would not have to attend faculty meetings. He imagined that she would follow her muses freely. Lyle knew they'd never really tried, but they could. They could try harder, try differently. There were jobs he could do that came with health insurance. And Marina could have two parents in one home.

"I'm not sure my partner would like that," Ingrid said.

Lyle let his hand drop. "You're seeing someone?"

"Have been."

"You didn't tell me."

Ingrid adjusted her hands around her elbows. She gazed at the stove. "That's because you make every conversation about your book."

He picked up the baby monitor, a precaution his daughter was no longer supposed to need, and turned it in his hand. Nothing had changed, but it felt as though it had. A closure. It was not that you could have what you'd had. It was that you'd had it. You'd had it, and that didn't make it, whatever it is was, any closer. To think differently was to confuse being born for the possibility of being reborn. "Why did you give up?" he asked finally.

"Why ask now?" she said.

"Because I didn't then."

Ingrid picked up the bag and her scarf. She wound it around her neck. "You confused being impressive for loved," she said. "I wanted the second one."

In the weeks after, he sat in his mother's kitchen with a newspaper and coffee. She didn't say anything about Lyle having quit working with his father. Instead she set out a long cheese Danish in a tin, and everything was yellow beneath the overhead lamp, while the middle-aged television on the counter fuzzed on. It seemed this was the entire day, sitting with the news, the gurgling images and convenience food.

His father came home at six and had a plate. Sausage and peppers. Strong-crust bread. He complained about the president, the media. The media with their ideas and never news that was facts.

"Which media?" Lyle said. "I was the media."

But in retrospect, he'd never been a good reporter. It was clear to Lyle now his one true skill was faith in flattery. He had trusted an anonymous tipster because he wanted to trust the blandishments. He was sure now Cain was the man who'd told him to contact McCreight, and he was sure he had not asked more questions because he wanted to trust he was a man who looked like he could write a nationally important story.

Cain had never thought much of Lyle. It was why he'd been chosen, which was to say, used. He was an easy pawn, the man without the fact-checking team, the disgraced. If the plan went wrong, who would believe the purveyor of sex video stories? To the people he'd cared about, there was no lower than the fallen tabloid reporter, and it was who he would always be in the long, permanent web of stories, linked and relinked, tagged and optimized to point out his worst work as the most relevant item to his person.

CHAPTER 9

Death broke on Cathexis, grief pushing lower articles Lyle had once enjoyed as it inched down the log in garish red sunset pictures and cross iconography. The mourners typed to his profile or on their own—we love you, Lyle—and the pictures ran his life. Alexandra looked at the photographs of him as a teenager, then one of him her son's age. He held out a caterpillar in his palm, an offering.

In succinct online eulogies, classmates and old colleagues remembered him as always convicted. Sometimes, there was an instance. Other times, it was a habit. How when you got together, he'd ask what was the latest grievance. And he meant it. He wanted to know the worst.

In this way, he was reduced.

But what Alexandra returned to most was what his father Cathected. Mr. Michaels wrote his Ly, he remembered this one time when he went to see him give a debate. He didn't know why he remembered it except he looked up on the stage that night. His son was never much at sports, not even cards. He was a whiner, he gave up too easy, he'd never been strong. But when he looked up that night, he didn't see his son, the snotty little shit

who never did what it takes. He saw a fighter orating like a president in a circle of light. There were flashes going off in the seats,
all these people taking pictures. He saw heads nodding. He heard
applause. This man was poking his voice in the hot auditorium,
and he had everyone in there, was beating the other guy while
everyone watched. Frank Michaels hadn't known to see his kid
that way, and then he did: his son had that survivor fire of their
family, the Micelli fight in his heart, and it made Mr. Michaels
want to punch his hand up in the air. He didn't know what had
happened to that. Why'd you have to do it, Ly? he wrote. We
loved you.

CHAPTER 10

Alexandra showed Jeremy the Cathected things and a newspaper article in the window of her phone screen. He was just home from work, and he slung a jacket over the back of a chair so that it drooped like a diminished man. He was saying an alternative to her. He urged her to believe that Lyle Michaels had killed himself.

"And yet," she said.

"Even if he didn't," Jeremy said.

"He didn't."

Han was rolling trains. He smashed them. He made noises like apocalypse. And maybe it was. Lyle Michaels was the new evidence. She'd assimilated him. She could see his death as a point in a line, a surface straight enough to hold the wrong she knew. It fit. His death fit. It was them again who killed.

"If it were true that he didn't," Jeremy continued, "you can't go to the press. There is danger. You must think of that. You must think of yourself, and Han."

"He didn't," she said, because she could not unlatch from the idea simple as opening the clasp of a necklace and because though it was not quite hope in her, she wanted him to believe what she did, to reflect her suspicions, turn them back, so that his seeing what she saw would make it weighted and true. A real origin to pain.

"You're a mother now."

"I know who I am responsible to," she said. "He had people who cared about him."

"Doesn't mean anything," Jeremy said. "People give up."

It was possible, she thought, to turn a death inside out so that its victim appeared to be the instigator. It was not possible Lyle Michaels had killed himself. He had a daughter.

"You are finding the evidence to match the theory," Jeremy said.

"I'm telling you there are connections. Shel was trying to warn me."

"By disappearing from you."

Her hand dropped a glass.

"I'm sorry," he said.

CHAPTER 11

Han tugged at Alexandra's sleeve. He pointed to a device on his lap. "Baba says it is sixty-two degrees in São Paolo, Brazil, with a fifteen-two chance of rain."

"Fifty-two," Alexandra said. "Less chance."

For a while they swiped through cities, and Jeremy made a drink in the kitchen. He went to the doorway and watched. Han had made paper trains that he taped to the lower edge of the wall in the living room, his bedroom, these candy-colored conga lines of steam engines and cabooses, wrapping around the world of their home. He'd cut and colored and he could name them. It seemed so recent his only word had been a monster. He used to be afraid of the other character, the green one. But Jeremy had brought Han recently to an exhibition at the children's museum. He'd guided Han's hand along a wall covered with swatches of synthetic puppet fur. See, it isn't so scary.

"Everything good in my life, I think of how he'll never see it," Alexandra said now, shaking her head. "As though that were the point of his life, to validate mine."

Jeremy set the drink on a coaster for her. "Or as though you want to share your happiness."

One day, he must believe, she would quarantine the tragic.

He had done it.

He could not tell her he had done it.

He could not tell her of a time when senses piled in concentric circles of near-boredom and imminent stir, moments sharpening, electric, and all the rude glamour of news arriving like memories, happened and familiar and warped. He could not tell her of when he came to believe you could count on certain things if you stayed in Northern Ireland long enough to cease being a stunned optimist, things like bodies turning up in the familiar style: stripped, beaten, bags over heads with bullet holes. He could not tell her he had cared for one of the dead men in his own way and that nonetheless after some time it was clear that the dead were not real anymore, and so you learned to live.

He could not tell her that, no. It had been too many years of the partial story. Time made silence a betrayal. But he could tell her she'd remember their good life. He could tell her there was hope in what they now had.

Their boy was yawning. Their boy's eyes were closing.

"Nap time," Jeremy said.

In his room, Han slipped under the covers and Jeremy began to read. *What did it say on the cover of this book? Did it say there's a fright at the end of the book? I am so afraid! The end! The end! I am so afraid of the fright at the end of the book!*

"Mama, a fright," Han said.

"Will you protect me?" she said.

CHAPTER 12

The flowers were white, and the sun came in colored through panes of wicked men and the betrayed martyr. It had been many years since she'd entered a church, but her hands found each other. They clasped, and perhaps it was prayer, the impulse behind the gesture to hold together.

Job answered Bildad the Shuhite and said:
Oh, would that my words were written down!
  Would that they were inscribed in a record:
That with an iron chisel and with lead
  they were cut in the rock forever!
But as for me, I know that my Vindicator lives,
  and that he will at last stand forth upon the dust.

When the service was over, Alexandra watched Mrs. Michaels kiss Mr. Michaels on the cheek, and she watched Mr. Michaels turn away. He tried to make the movement into tissue resemble a sneeze. Alexandra saw someone cut through a slant of light. She knew him, or she knew that she knew him somehow, this flicker.

She took a white lily from a basket. She searched the dark

cluster by the door for the man she was sure she knew, and she was hopeful a moment. She thought of how there'd been no remains. Outside, the contours of a narrow vista were blanched with sunlight, and she called his name.

CHAPTER 13

On an evening when Alexandra promised tomorrow there would be a surprise, they went to Robert and Cassandra's. It was a temperate night. It was Sunday dinner. The sun pinked high-rises they could see from the apartment window, and there was a frantic milling in the streets. It was the first time in a long time Alexandra had seemed like the woman he met.

She followed Cassandra into the living room. The children went to color with Robert at the table, and Jeremy made drinks in the kitchen. "*Pouring* drinks, you mean," Alexandra called over her shoulder. "And slowly, I might add. We're *parched*."

"Slow and steady," he said.

"And sober," Alexandra said.

Jeremy stood quietly with wineglasses in his hand. She was very beautiful standing by the couch in the living room. She made the air soft, and he passed a glass.

"Was it worth the wait?" he said.

"Perfectly seasoned," she said, "don't you think, Cassandra?"

"Girl, we know *all* about Jeremy's family recipes," Cassandra said. "And it is that traditional good stuff."

They did not dwell on the dead who were news. They teased

Robert. They offered their hands to be slapped by Wally, by Han, now school age. They spoke of the fine-wine atmosphere, and when a new bottle was removed from a shelf and opened, they spoke of the fine whiskey atmosphere.

When it was far beyond bedtime, Jeremy carried Han down the stairs. Emerging from an overhang, they saw that a storm had not come. Glowy, ambiguous weather pressed down on the pavement, and the street was dark with minor damp.

"Are we home yet?" Han asked.

"Almost."

Alexandra stopped in the street. "Don't lie to him," she said.

CHAPTER 14

Jeremy looked at her the next day, and he could have framed her face. Pleasure and future, or maybe anticipatory nostalgia, some deep instinct loosing and disarraying composure. Her hair lifted with gust, black flame against city street and business. For a moment, she was arrested like that, her face touching sky.

Just as quickly, the picture faltered. Alexandra stopped. She conferred with something on her phone.

"Are you ready for the surprise?"

"Not quite surprising," he said in his joking voice, "if I'm ready for it."

Jeremy did not know how to arrive. He followed beside her. Alexandra was intent on the device. She did not glance at him.

"This is us," she said, pointing west away from them, already crossing and still in the thrall of her phone.

He followed her into the halted traffic, pushed off the trunk of a taxi as though it would propel him to her. She was very lovely and very strange, and that she was remembering their good life again, stood now beneath a burgundy awning, a record of why he wished to persist— what was the word for it?

"Bill!" said someone behind Jeremy.

An odd signal broke up the information of the scene. What a sound does not lose of energy to objects is lost as heat. That is what he felt first, the burn. His eyes ran to catch the ears, a turn and a figure filling in, prioritized by instinct, the avenue dropping off.

Jeremy caught view of a plaid sleeve lurching, a white blur extended to a glint. The deadliest objects reflect light. He couldn't help it—his hand shot out when he saw the arm jerk toward Alexandra. There was weight in the arm, a confusion of lines leading to a black flame, the sound a contained hiccup, a small emission into the noon air.

He could see time then from afar, a story intractable but perhaps not inevitable. One in denial might think they are not in denial, but what of the person who admits they are in denial? The one who says there is reason to hope?

He thought they could be safe.

His slow arm reached. Fingers. He felt her fingers. But she was already caving at the waist. He saw the gold rope of her necklace float up. He had not before noticed the open cellar grate on the sidewalk. He had only seen her arm raised to a man who held a streak of light.

Later, at the hospital, he would be holding her hand when she woke. He would say, there is something I have to explain.

He would say, this man was going to hurt you. He already has. I have known him, and I've never known him. I know he knew about your brother, that he followed him.

He would say, I wanted to tell you before. But for men like us, it is never before. It is always too late to be forgotten by danger.

PART TEN: REMAINDER

I didn't know if I was really there or not. I thought that I wasn't really there, it was just a nightmare. Even though I knew it would always happen, I never expected that I would be there.

—Sudhesh Dahad, 7/7 survivor

CHAPTER 1

It was the year Gerry Adams, president of Sinn Féin, was, after four days of interrogation over the 1972 murder of a single mother of ten, released without charge. It was the year STX developed a meditation tracker that uploaded stress indicators to cloud storage. It was the year the right to be forgotten was recognized in *Google Spain v. AEPD and Mario Costeja González*. It was not a case that Genevieve Bailey worked.

It was the year judges on the Seventh Circuit Court of Appeals denied a twenty year-old American citizen in Chicago named Adel Daoud access to classified FISA court records part of his warrant application. In the concurring opinion, it was acknowledged that a FISA-related warrant could only be challenged if errors were caught, and errors would only be caught if access to the documents had been obtained. But the decision had been made for reasons of national security.

There were new symbols then. Rejection was a direction of the finger. But perhaps that was old too, a gladiator legacy, or rather, a legacy of the wisdom of the audience. Populist. Young people volunteered themselves to be shown on screens to strangers, hoping for love or sex or just some minutes in communion.

To the south, Fernando Sepúlveda, a member of the social media team for an opposition party and supposed leader of an obscure intelligence unit, was arrested in Colombia for intercepting communications between the president and the Revolutionary Armed Forces.

Vape was the word of the year, according to a dictionary website.

It was the year a documentary, released on a streaming service provided by the world's largest online store, traced an industrial espionage suit against Bayer. In memory, the credits declared, of the late Lyle Michaels.

Records were broken, exempli gratia, a Russian player, Хируко, comprehensively beat *World of Warcraft*.

Meanwhile, the United States ended operations of the Human Terrain System, the counterinsurgency program in which social scientists trained military commanders in the customs of invaded territories. The program had been rejected by the American Anthropological Association, holding that it conflicted with the Code of Ethics, particularly the clause "to do no harm" to those studied. One of HTS's founders, Montgomery McFate, under the name Montgomery Cybele Carlough, had written her doctoral dissertation on Irish republican paramilitaries. In response to Professor Roberto Gonzalez's critique of the program's misappropriation of scholarship, McFate, then a fellow at the United States Institute of Peace, wrote that charges of misappropriated knowledge constituted epistemological censorship. It is in the nature of knowledge to escape the bounds of its creator; to believe otherwise is to persist in a supreme naïveté about the nature of knowledge production and distribution." It was suspected that she was the woman behind the blog *I Luv a Man in Uniform.*

That same year, an American whistleblower granted asylum in Russia denied that his leak had been orchestrated with Russian intelligence, which was the stated position of some members of the House and Senate Intelligence Committees. They disseminated these speculations on the television show *Meet the Press.*

A biopic about the Irish-American mobster Whitey Bulger, a man who had once smuggled guns in coffins to the IRA, was pilloried as an uncritical reproduction of mob lies.

Around the time of the release of the film, shortly after the publication of an article criticizing Turkey's bombing of PKK-affiliated forces, Professor Bri Freeman received a package of anthrax in a cardboard shipping box. In the article, she had noted that the separatist group repelled ISIS in Iraq.

It was the year a coroner reported that the fatal gunshot wounds of a black man named Avery James might have been self-inflicted in the back of a police cruiser, as his hands were handcuffed behind him. For her coverage, a Noze writer received a United States Journalism Award in the area of commentary.

It was the year Malaysia Airlines Flight 370 disappeared.

It was the year a boy named Tyrell Owens studied for his GED.

It was the year LeBron James went home to Cleveland, and Republicans took control of the House and Senate again. Diplomatic ties between the United States and Cuba were reestablished. It was the year two hundred Nigerian schoolgirls were abducted by Boko Haram. It was the year Scotland voted against leaving the United Kingdom. It was the year the American president expressed disappointment over failed peace talks in Northern

Ireland. It was the year a hedge fund mogul named Lawrence Coffers tripled profits off new financial instruments, packaging what he referred to as "nonprime" mortgages. His daughter, Winnie, announced that she would be buying a newspaper. Barry Cain was assigned to a net neutrality task force.

It was a year of many stories. It was a year it was difficult to remember them all, even when they were buzzing in your pocket. There were acronyms for news missed. There were acronyms for the fear of what would be missed. And there were many dead.

What happens to the dead man's email account was something very few people knew. Historians were considering the legalities of entering these emails into archives for future historians. It was a question that might once have bothered Shel Chen.

In this year, it was estimated that there were more than 4 billion email accounts. Nevertheless, the New IRA, a paramilitary organization formed of Provisional IRA dissidents, conducted a letter bomb campaign, which included explosives sent to British Army recruitment offices and prison staff. In a failed RPG attack in North Belfast, the weapon bounced off a Land Rover. The officers inside the vehicle were said to have suffered shock. Over a decade after it was reported that the IRA had been supplied with Russian rifles, investigations into international gunrunning continued, just as classified operations continued even while the Belfast hotels and convention centers were built. But that was not quite a news story. Surveillance, investigation, the collating of facts and figures, the contacts—these were part of the regular ecology.

There are no headlines "Today there is air" or "Today, still, so many people are dead."

It was something Frank Michaels, once a Micelli, thought of when he thought of the child he'd loved. But sometimes, he listened to the voices of angry men on the radio as he drove to fix the broken part of a home someone thought was in emergency, and he felt less alone. They spoke about how there used to be promise, and people around the country called in to send their heavy hearts over waves. Anger was the only honest thing Frank Michaels heard anymore.

CHAPTER 2

Many states away and across many miles, Janice Chen knew it was the computer who had provided Victor, her Victor, Victor Shumpert. Victor who was so gentle, so kind. Victor who knew her sorrow, too having lost a spouse. Victor whose very own younger brother, Wilhelm, had tricked their dying father into willing him all the family property, leaving not a penny for the older son, her Victor, to whom, when he asked for a picture of his sweet, soft angel, she sent a photograph of her daughter, Alexandra, whose face owed half to Mrs. Chen anyway.

Dear Mrs. Janice, he wrote. *Thank you, so very thank you for message. Only you show me God is Great. Because you have been stronger than a tree in a storm raining. Shame on Sister! Shame on Children! For some, we have saying, the fire is too hot that cooks their food. But be peace, my sweetheart! One day they will know. When will I see my angel princess Janice? When will I touch her? Perhaps it is not too much to say that you would like to see me too. You would send me wire transfer for visit, Princess Janice. I would need thirteen thousand dollars for plane and visa. Please when it is considerate will you write me again? Kisses, Your Victor*

These hands he loves, she thought, typing. Someone loves these hands.

She had not been someone someone wanted to see in three decades.

My Baby Vic, she wrote, *I did some research. I discovered that French is the language in Haiti. I always wanted to go to Paris. One time, someone gave me a T-shirt with an Eiffel Tower on it, but it was only a fake. I knew this because of the tag saying Made in China. How do you say I love you forever in French? How about I miss you? Or, without you it hurts? Because I do, sweet Victor, even if Alexandra thinks my pain is my imagination because she can't smell it or touch it, see it or feel it. She is scientific that way. I used to think she'd go to the moon. What helps is I will think of you tonight when I am in bed. I got a new nightgown. It is blue with pink flowers. Think about that! Lots of kisses for my baby Vic, Janice*

After the email, she rubbed on her cream so that she would be as soft as her Victor believed. She wrote to her merciless surviving child that she would need extra in her bank account this month, and she tried not to hear Alexandra's voice in her head: *You don't have children. You have a child. Shel is dead.*

The next day, her daughter emailed. Scam was the word for the romance of her mother's life. A foolish response.

But that is love, she wrote back. *I feel it. You will pay for love. You will be robbed by it, and the love of it is real.*

CHAPTER 3

Alexandra slouched over the laptop in bed, letting herself take in the language of lingerie, the pure ballet of it—bustier, demi, basques. Her gaze seized up in the lace, scalloped edges. Hypnotic trims. She clicked her basket full, as she pulled at the smooth pad, producing a weather of fallen women, and the repetition managed her imagination in a thin spectrum. Then she got up and went downstairs for a drink to dull out the buzzy trance of choosing amongst minor variation.

Her son was with Genevieve until.

Until was a time that still seemed far away.

Across the street stood a bland restaurant with faux age painted on the walls and nostalgia designated by a certain cast of ochre light that rubbed off the edges of objects. She took a seat at the bar and ordered an amaro. There were framed posters with red Cyrillic letters spelling out Kino-Eye, and there were framed laundry detergent advertisements from the middle of the last century, women tipped back into martini glasses, holding lather in one hand and pearls in another. She half-noticed songs as she drank drink after drink. "La Vie en Rose." "Sinnerman."

"I know you," a man said.

He had dark hair, teeth very white against his skin, and a face not unfamiliar in the half-light. But it was his hooking of his bag beneath the bar that gave him up. She remembered the abruptness of his movements as he settled himself beside her.

"Robert," she said, and she kept on with her amaro.

But Robert insisted on buying them a round. He ordered a drink that made the bartender sigh, and she talked for a few minutes about her new job, a job, that's what it was, nothing disappointing or epiphanic, just a company with a few procedures she knew. For a moment, she thought of the messages Jeremy sent her on behalf of So-So and Jill. *So-So is skeptical of the new couch, but Jill thinks this must be the emery board she's needed her entire life.* In this way, some time passed quietly.

"Where's Cassandra?" Alexandra said finally.

"Cass," Robert said. "Her auntie died. She went down with Wally for the service, said I should stay and work. Not established enough to take time yet. It's no matter to her. She doesn't need me to distribute her grief. She's well-adjusted. She has a shelf for white socks and a shelf for black socks. She talks about the man upstairs. She says, 'You just keep on trucking until the man upstairs calls your number.'"

"And you?" she said.

"I'd have taken an excuse for a day off," he said, then, quickly, "not that it isn't sad. I know it is. I just never met the woman."

A certain blurty quality, puppyish in its stops and starts, made him easy to be around. She forgot to eat and let him talk. She gave her card to the bartender and put her hand around a glass hot with the shaking flame of a burning votive. When he went outside to smoke—the drinking secret of boring men, he called it—she laughed a little. She waited, and she thought of how the place was arranged to feel like a memory, so you were seeing time refract back at you, the future memory already hinted in the deliberately worn patina.

He came in rubbing his hands.

"Place is nice," he said. "So nice it almost makes me feel guilty."

"But then?"

He gripped the bar. It had been epoxy-finished with newspaper clippings, and Robert's hand rubbed a black-and-white print of a mushroom cloud shyly. "But then I'm drunk," he said, "and you're here, and I think we in my profession yodel on about self-care, so maybe I'm just a role model."

"How *is* the clinical work?"

"Used to bum about the failures. Now, I go to work, and I think plug in," he said. "That's what Cass told me. Just plug in. It's up to them to flip the switch, but you can set up the conditions for the work to work."

"Just plug in."

"I set the scene."

He took a chubby little box from his pocket and looked at it. "When's the last time you saw one of these?"

"Stone Ages must be," she said.

"My stone says eleven-seventeen."

"I guess it's time for you to get a new phone," Alexandra said. "Unless this was your way of saying good night."

Robert shrugged. "I'm not allowed the doodads anymore. Cass said it was making me an angsty teenager in my middle age."

"Because."

"Because I'd Cathect and then watch my own Cathexis.

Because I'd check every ten minutes, and if a day later I only had two Favors, I'd be asking her if I should delete what I Cathected." Robert trailed off and stared at the tower of glass coupes behind the bar.

"Worried people didn't like you as much as you thought or that everyone could see people didn't like you as much as you thought?"

"Both," Robert said. "More."

Without any why behind it, she reached out and spun the mint garnish poking out of his drink. "I'm interested in more."

"My sister and I, we'd argue. We'd be at it all day over an article about Afghanistan. She'd be saying I didn't understand, I'd never been to war, you can't be on here starting offensives when you've never seen combat. And I'd be angry all day. I'd be asking Cass why Marissa didn't see we could've lost her."

"And the Connections couldn't make up for that."

"The Connections are pure hypocrites. When my parents lost their house in the subprime crisis," he continued, "I didn't see people in the streets. Instead, online my friends say war's appalling, banks are appalling, system's appalling, but all I see on Cathexis is wealth and empty words. I couldn't stop noticing. Paris. Tokyo. Cruises. Vacations three times a year. My parents are good people. They didn't want me or Marissa's money. They wanted to do it themselves, be old people their children didn't fret over. They wanted to do it right, and they did," he said. "If it could happen to them."

"Then how is this fair."

"How is any of it." Robert paused. "I'd see the private school graduations. I'd see the elaborate birthdays. Everything's appalling, but what are they doing? Buying new shoes. And I know what this sounds like. What *I* do. But the only thing that makes me bitter and not like everyone else is I don't believe that it's *taking* it personal. I believe everything's personal."

"Cassandra isn't bothered?"

"She's well-adjusted."

"The socks," Alexandra said.

"Right," he said. "She thinks I'm crazy. I'm saying, the world can fuck off but I can't stop looking, and she's saying, very calm, very skeptical and pitying, fix your blood pressure with a flip phone. She says half my problem is it's easier to see evil than to fix it."

"If not fixing, what's the social work?"

"My sister goes to war so they can ski in Aspen on family money and my parents can buy two-for-three cereal boxes, but I'm the one deranged by my device, and jealous."

"I don't think you're deranged," Alexandra said. "I think for you, high-def television isn't enough."

"But I love my friends too," he said. "It's simple as maybe they don't care if they benefit from something rotten and think my life's a knock-knock joke, but we turned each other onto bands in college, got stoned, and ate the same vanilla instant pudding."

"I know what you mean," she said.

"Do you?"

"You want taste in common to mean something more than coincidentally owning albums."

"That simple."

"I was in advertising," she said. "Which essentially means I have a doctorate in pop psychology."

"Cass, she says, so what if there's a system. Be happy playing along because if you really believe there's a system, you can't change it anyway. At least enjoy it."

"How does that work?"

He scrunched over her shoulder and whispered. "In the system, you don't think about it."

"Except now, when you say it," she said.

"I undercut myself."

"But you do it so well you nearly make a point," she said.

"Cass says I need to hunker down on what I *can* control. She sends me blog posts about it. She tapes notes in the bathroom so when I'm brushing my teeth, I get the message."

"What do they say?"

"I am the change the world needs," Robert said.

"That all?" They shared a little laugh and she pulled the zipper of his jacket, a quick smooth motion, ending with her hands leaned against his knees. She did it before she thought of doing it. She watched him drop his gaze.

"And I am loved."

"Oh," she said, easing back perpendicular in her seat.

"I'm sorry," he said. "You're a neat lady. I don't want you to feel bad."

She went for her wallet and tossed bills down on the bar, one, two, three. It was late, and there was no home to go to. Alexandra stood, looked back at him, already a memory.

"Spaghetti thrown against the wall doesn't feel anything, Robert," she said.

CHAPTER 4

Faces erased in their appearance as he walked, time overlaid with time. He was today after work and he was stepping into the future and he was looking at Alexandra, newly disabused of the notion she'd live through only one terrorist event in her own city; and he was deadening his face as One Rock declared that Gunner had been killed; and he was playing the market on both ends to fade away from Belfast; and he was a boy who couldn't change the rules. All the clumps of flowers and glassy-costumed dancers and Alexandra's face intent on a menu, small wigs of tinsel on trees and their boy spinning in the kitchen and sprays of parsley on her plate and pale file folders shut forever and the gray Irish sky— the arbitrariness dizzied him, the *to be* of everything everywhere sliding on invisible scales of probability.

Were he his own client, he would say, when you made the choice, when you listened to yourself, you got better. Slowly, yes. But better. He did not want to keep listening to himself.

He did not want to listen to himself fail to convince Alexandra's voice mail that she must return to the apartment to fetch her things, for example. He did not want to listen to himself say he needed to see his son.

Too much time away was supposed to quell the insistence of hurt. He was not quelling the insistence of hurt. He was walking.

Someone like Robert would say look at the sky; see the beauty of size. But it frightened Jeremy, the infinity of it. He was only a man.

A man who had a streak of failure that followed him, merciless as a spy.

But of course, Wright had disappeared as soon as it didn't matter anymore if he appeared, and somehow Jeremy had persisted long enough to be early to see the professional.

The professional had a private practice in a building with frosted glass windows inside. Jeremy pushed a button and a rattling meant that the door was unlocked. Inside, the professional shook his hand. He invited Jeremy to sit on a hard, cold couch.

Jeremy waited. He looked between man and ceiling. He looked at the man, and he waited. The man wore a blue oxford, like Jeremy. His leg was crossed, and he sat in a chair with a small side table topped with a box emitting a tuft of tissue. Jeremy looked again at the ceiling, a matte, flat white like her face on the operating table that day.

"I don't know why I am," he said. "Insert any factual clause or full stop."

The truth was he had thought he existed to repair smaller and smaller things until nothing was left. It had started with the largest way he could conceive of home and ended with the most discreet. When he was young, he thought fixing was simple as losing innocence. He signed up for it. He thought it would be the Berlin Wall raining down forever, until the globe was seamless. He did not know that sometimes you ruin your health. Your friends drop off with death or degrading minds. You are supposed to grow wiser with years. Instead you grow bulky with fear, autobiography thickening in veins, gluey and slowing. Sometimes it is difficult to lift your arms. You sit with men and drink Guinness and keep on because many lives are at stake. Eventually, when life is the best woman you know, you think yours is at stake too. It is. You think you can repair it, and then you don't.

But he was a professional now. The classrooms populated with helpful hearts—he'd sat in them too. This was not a statement of power but background. He knew what the doctor would do. The construction of empathy: a still body, slow movement, gentle locution. Their scripts. I invite you to explore our relationship, what you're feeling at the moment. Maybe something I say upsets you. Maybe you feel yourself react. I know. I am one of you. I sit there and I see my clients, and I say the theories that are supposed to be scientific fact. Insane: their confidence in knowledge of the other mind.

Even subterfuge is compromised. The liar pretends to be a liar.

And yet you are here, the doctor might be inclined to comment. Jeremy would say the same. They had been trained.

The liar who says he lies. The man who admits he is in denial. The one who inflicts the wound to subvert pain. The patient who goes to the doctor who says he does not believe he can be cured. I see it. I do. I am not unaware.

There was a time in his life Jeremy watched planes buckle buildings on television. There was no one in his flat, just a tin of biscuits, painting of a boy lost alone at sea. It was all he had expected. He had never dreamed of the family that was now gone.

Was he suffering? Well.

One way to answer: his entire life since they'd met was on behalf of her.

A box of two animals more than she'd asked for. Questions for another day. *What does it feel like to make someone happy?*

I have gotten better before. Once, I went to Italy with nothing to do but forget, be forgotten. A friend was newly dead. It was my fault and it wasn't. It was me and it was what happens when everyone is like me, compliant to omens. I started over. I went to Oxford. It was all the old orphan stories. Oliver Twist. Little Nell. Did Dickens ever meet a lonely child he didn't love?

The hedge fund résumé was printed in minuscule font. Unserifed. Serifs extended. Serifs filled in the gaps, pulled the eyes toward coherency. The man who would hire him walked Jeremy into his glass office, explained they were just men who understood that working both ends didn't mean zero net gain. They could go long and short at once, eat the cakes they had and get richer too. A quaint thought.

Then he met her. He met her and thought he'd be better forever.

Because she was so lovely, touching bookshelves and walking, her lower body so elegantly organized in forward momentum that he thought she'd lead him to perfect order. He'd thought of which bouquets he would bring Alexandra if he were braver, if adulthood had not presented a pattern of erasure.

He supposed he was still hedging then.

He had not then believed that one day she would stand with him and make promises, that there would be white blooms pinned in her hair. It was all early, everything left. They did not yet have their boy. They wound the world for him.

I still receive Christmas cards from the other families, the indivisible ones. Happy holidays, with love, from the Heartland. May your family be as blessed as ours.

Once they were. He could not see them, touch them, but sometimes he'd think: and still I'm us.

He thought often of how she'd told them like a fairy tale the day they went to the adoption woman. It was a story he'd never thought to tell their boy, their boy who, maybe someone else might have accepted, he'd never see again. Their boy who loved to know the temperature in São Paolo, Brazil. Their boy who had made beach sand smile, cut trains through their house, so that it seemed no matter the circumstance, they'd be able to get away. Jeremy had been told he could not hide, but he'd believed in the locomotive string his boy had made around the apartment, hugging their home.

Somewhere, a friend or enemy, someone he'd once trusted, this man who he'd once thought to become, had lit a match in Bushwick or he'd not, and no matter, he was probably still watching. He was watching, and there was no way to avert the great gaze that rattled facts until nearly every certainty had fallen off.

But just knowing she existed, that she and their boy did—

It was not the same as a happy ending. It was that somehow, even now, he could safely say that once they were happiest.

ACKNOWLEDGMENTS

Before this book, I could not have anticipated having such fun on editorial calls. Thank you, Mark, brilliant writer and editor, brilliant mind of play and politics and poetics. There's no one I'd rather talk to about literature. Thank you, Kirby, for bringing *Quotients* home. To everyone at Soho, I'm grateful to be in the fam, and for your support.

Like any text, this novel was made possible by many conversations. I'm especially indebted to Helen Nissenbaum for opening up ethical questions around big data. Michael Chinigo helped me get a handle on coding and computers. The Columbia communications PhD program introduced me to a rich body of media research. Thank you, Ilya, for the chat on plot. Jon, Hannah, and Oskar generously read parts or all of big, fat early versions. And to Maggie, my girl since the 198 days, I owe a trip to a castle for our time in Belfast.

Strangers who became family gave me inspiration. You know who you are.